"You're going to die a terrible death, Marshal. It'll take days, maybe even a week, but it'll happen. You've got water around your neck you'll never be able to drink and a bullet in your mouth for a gun you'll never be able to use. Even if you do get free, you'll want to use that bullet to kill yourself, but the gun's too long to make that easy. Game's scarce out there anyway, so you'll starve to death in no time. But I want it to take time, Beck. I want it to break you before you die because if there's one thing in this world I hate more than an Apache, it's a goddamned lawman."

RALPH COMPTON

◇

RIDE THE HAMMER DOWN

A Ralph Compton Western by

TERRENCE McCAULEY

BERKLEY
New York

BERKLEY
An imprint of Penguin Random House LLC
penguinrandomhouse.com

ISBN: 9781984803405

First Edition: December 2020

Printed in the United States of America
1 3 5 7 9 10 8 6 4 2

Cover art © Dennis Lyall
Book design by George Towne

THE IMMORTAL COWBOY

This is respectfully dedicated to the "American Cowboy." His was the saga sparked by the turmoil that followed the Civil War, and the passing of more than a century has by no means diminished the flame.

———◆———

True, the old days and the old ways are but treasured memories, and the old trails have grown dim with the ravages of time, but the spirit of the cowboy lives on.

———◆———

In my travels—to Texas, Oklahoma, Kansas, Nebraska, Colorado, Wyoming, New Mexico, and Arizona—I always find something that reminds me of the Old West. While I am walking these plains and mountains for the first time, there is this feeling that a part of me is eternal, that I have known these old trails before. I believe it is the undying spirit of the frontier calling me, through the mind's eye, to step back into time. What is the appeal of the Old West of the American frontier?

———◆———

It has been epitomized by some as the dark and bloody period in American history. Its heroes—Crockett, Bowie, Hickok, Earp—have been reviled and criticized. Yet the Old West lives on, larger than life.

———◆———

It has become a symbol of freedom, when there was always another mountain to climb and another river to cross; when a dispute between two men was settled not with expensive lawyers, but with fists, knives, or guns. Barbaric? Maybe. But some things never change. When the cowboy rode into the pages of American history, he left behind a legacy that lives within the hearts of us all.

—*Ralph Compton*

CHAPTER ONE

Marshal JOHN BECK knew he had gone insane.

If he had doubted it before, it was confirmed now by the impossible sight he saw just outside the opening of his cave. The same cave he had been forced to call home.

Beck knew he must be hallucinating. There was no other reason what he was seeing could possibly be real.

A lone man atop a horse. All the way out here in the desert.

It was impossible. Why was he out here?

Beck had forgotten how long he had been living in this cave. Long enough to grow an uneven bristly beard. Long enough for his normally short hair to grow well past his ears.

He had not seen his reflection in as long as he could remember, but he imagined Dulce would hit him with her wooden spoon if she saw him now. She would be angry to see how far he had fallen. In his appearance. In other ways, too.

And as he watched the mirage of a rider and horse roam the arid landscape of the Arizona desert, John Beck began to wonder about the exact moment he had gone insane. When had his mind broken its tether to reality and sailed away from him?

Had it been when Beck had decided to drown the demons that haunted him at the bottom of a whiskey bottle instead of enforcing the law?

Or had it been that cursed moment when the Brickhouse Gang had ridden into Mother Lode? Or had it been just after that, when Bram Hogan and his men finally found him in Dulce's Saloon and sought to make an example of the reluctant lawman?

Beck knew he had never been much of a sheriff but had won the office based on his skills as a marksman with the Sharps .50-caliber rifle he had brought with him when he had first come to Mother Lode.

He also knew that he had won the office because no one else in Mother Lode, Arizona, had wanted the thankless job of town marshal. Hell, Beck had only taken the position because it came with free room and board at Dulce's and all the beer he could drink. That was a mighty tempting offer for a man who had come westward to escape the complexities of his own mind.

But being the law in a sleepy desert town like Mother Lode had proven to be far more challenging than he had been led to believe. The drunks were meaner and the teamsters more cantankerous than he had expected. He had only survived because of his ability to know how to throw a punch and take one, too. The skills he had acquired in his previous life in Chicago—how to read a man, his movements, and the shift of his eyes—

had helped him figure out what a man would do before he did it.

The townsfolk of Mother Lode did not like to see a paying customer buffaloed without a good reason, but they hated lawlessness even more and liked the way John Beck carried out his duties.

Mother Lode had proven a challenge, but not enough of a challenge to keep his past where it belonged. He had thought he had left his old life behind in Chicago, but some memories were too stubborn to die. It only took about a year for the old ghosts to track him down and start howling in his mind.

The ghosts gave him an excuse to take Dulce up on that offer of free beer that came with the job. Maybe he had wanted someone to come along and take his badge away, as well as the burden of being a lawman along with it.

But he had never considered anything like the Brickhouse Gang coming to a place like Mother Lode. And he had never dreamed that he would find himself banished to this cave.

As he continued to watch the horse and rider that had to be a mirage, John Beck remembered that he had still been sane when Bram Hogan and his brothers dragged him from Dulce's and into the street. He remembered he had not been able to put up much resistance on account of being fairly drunk at the time.

And he had still been sane when they dumped him in the horse trough and laughed at him. Sane enough to remember Bram Hogan laughing as he told his brothers to "strip this law dog down to his long johns, boys. We wouldn't want the fine marshal here to catch his death of cold."

Beck remembered the names of the men who had

done Bram's bidding. The flea-bitten drover called Lem. The sharp-featured Mexican bandit named Laredo. The miniature version of Bram Hogan they called Steve. And the hawk-nosed craggy-faced giant of a man they called Pearson.

Beck could no sooner forget their names than he could forget his own. He remembered it must have been about ninety degrees that morning as they set to pulling off his clothes and dividing them up among themselves.

He remembered still being sane when the brave men of the Brickhouse Gang set to beating him, too. A seemingly endless torrent of kicks to the ribs and back, punches to the face that quickly shut his eyes, and perhaps a whip or two across the back. The pain blurred into one gory memory and had been dulled just a bit by the beer that had still been in his system.

The pain had come later, and with a vengeance, in the days of hell that had followed.

He remembered being tied by the neck like a dog to the porch post of Dulce's Saloon while the gang argued about which one of them would get his clothes and who would get his fine Sharps rifle.

Beck remembered Dulce and some of the other townsfolk crying at the sight of their lawman beaten and laid low. He remembered wondering if they might be crying for themselves, too, for Beck was the only thing that had stood between them and the ravages of the worst gang in the Arizona Territory.

Beck knew he was not the only man in town who could fight them. Mother Lode had no shortage of miners who were rough enough to oust them and shop owners who could band together to do the job. There were more than a handful of men who worked the few ranches spread about on the outskirts of town who could make quick work of this ragged bunch.

But even in his sorry state, tied to the porch post of a windswept saloon, Beck knew no one would lift a finger to stop these men or even help themselves. The risk was too great and the reward too thin. These people would endure the Brickhouse Gang just as they endured the heat of the unforgiving sun and the thirst and the bitter winters of the Arizona Territory.

These people did not fight. They survived, and if they did not think they could survive the Brickhouse Gang, they would simply pack their things and leave.

So, while John Beck appreciated the tears they shed for their fallen sheriff, he knew none of them would raise a hand in his defense.

And he was not disappointed.

Even from the dark seclusion of the cave he now called home, as he decided if his eyes were playing tricks on him, John Beck could still remember watching through swollen eyes while Bram Hogan made a show of recusing himself from the discussion about which of his men would get the Sharps.

"Always preferred to be an up-close kind of man myself," he proudly declared to the outlaws who followed him. "Pistols and knives are more to my liking. Always thought long guns were akin to women's guns. A coward's gun. Thought so in the war when I watched sharpshooting Rebs take down my friends. And I still hold that opinion today."

Beck remembered the outlaw leader turning his attention to him as he struggled to remain conscious out of fear he might wake up dead. Bram grabbed a handful of Beck's hair and said, "You agree with me, don't you, Marshal?"

Bram even pulled and pushed Beck's head so it looked like he nodded, to the laughter of his gang.

Beck remembered he had still been sane, even through all of that torment.

It was only when the argument among the outlaws had lasted too long and grown too loud for Bram's liking that the leader pulled his pistol and fired once into the air to quiet the yelling.

"Enough!" Beck remembered Bram shouting at them. "Since none of you bastards can decide on your own, I guess I'll have to do your thinking for you, just like I've always done."

Beck remembered crying out when Bram grabbed his hair harder than before and jerked his head back so the lawman had no choice but to look up at his tormentor. He remembered the feeling of the blood from his broken nose running back down his throat but refusing to give Bram the satisfaction of hearing him gag.

He remembered Bram's spittle hitting him in the face as he said, "Today's your lucky day, lawman. Since none of these fools can decide, it looks like I'm gonna have to do it for them. Now, since I firmly believe that the Sharps is a fine coward's rifle, I've decided to put it to a better use here today. You see, while we were fixing to ride in here today, we had ourselves another argument about whether or not we should kill you."

Hogan pulled Beck's head back by the hair and aimed his head at Bram's younger brother, Steve. He was a younger version of Bram who looked like a cheap imitation of his brother. He was shorter and stockier but wore a perpetual scowl in an effort to harden naturally soft features.

Bram said, "Steve here wanted to kill you outright. Put a bullet behind your ear and be done with it. That's my little brother for you, Beck. Straight and to the point."

Bram slowly twisted Beck's hair until he looked at the other three Brickhouse Gang members, who were clustered together. He pointed at Laredo. "Our Mexican friend here wanted to kill you as bad as Steve, but he wanted to do it slowly like the Apache like to do. Make you last for a couple of days as an example to any of the good townspeople who might think about giving us any sass or kicking us out."

Abraham pulled Beck's head closer to him and whispered in his ear. "Gotta say, I kind of liked that notion myself, though I give pause when considering using the ways of those heathens in the hills."

Bram Hogan then pointed to Pearson. "The big fella over there wanted to beat you to death, but I discounted that one out of hand. I thought it sounded too close to what Laredo had talked about, cursed him as a cheater and a scoundrel." Hogan laughed. "Even docked the big man a full day's rations for when we go back out on the trail." The outlaw looked up at the giant. "And don't think I'll forget about that when the time comes, Pearson. I'm a fair man when it comes to punishment and insist on discipline among my men. Discipline is the hallmark of success. Learned that in the army."

Beck remembered losing consciousness as Abraham continued to talk, only to have his head shaken violently by the outlaw until he woke up again. "Pay attention when I'm talking at you, boy. You're missing the best part of my wisdom."

He pointed to the last man in the gang. "Lanky

Lem over there might not be too much to look at. He sure as hell ain't bright, God help him, but he had the best idea of the bunch. He wanted us to do something creative with you. Something we ain't never done before in any of the other towns we've visited. He was thunderstruck to come up with an idea, of course, but I figured the dimwit was onto something."

Abraham pulled Beck's head back slowly and grinned down at him. Beck remembered the outlaw's scarred face and gray-streaked beard and teeth that were whiter than they had any right to be. He remembered wondering how a man like Hogan could have such white teeth as the outlaw told him, "And, as God is my witness, I hadn't thought about how we could do that until this very moment. Fell two trees with the same ax just like my daddy used to do back in Kentucky."

And Beck felt his stomach turn to jelly when Abraham's grin faded and he brought his face to within an inch of Beck's. "We're going to ride you out of town on a rail, boy. Turn you out in the desert and let the coyotes and the scorpions and the snakes and the spiders have all they want of you. And we won't ride you out on just any old rail, mind you. We're going to ride you out of town on the same bone of contention between my boys here on account of how I can't afford what the army calls 'dissension in the ranks.' Learned that in the army, too."

He thudded Beck on the back with a couple of heavy slaps. "I think it's a brilliant idea even if I do say so myself. We're going to tie you up to that long gun of yours and kick you out into the wilderness."

Abraham threw his head back and laughed. The men of the Brickhouse Gang joined in with him. Beck could not swear to it, but he had thought some of the townspeople did, too. Dulce may have cried out in horror, but he had not been sure.

Abraham was still laughing when he said, "Yes, sir. I think it's a fitting way to treat a law dog such as yourself. Using the same damned thing that made your name to be part of your disgraceful demise."

The outlaw must have read something in Beck's swollen eyes, for he said, "Don't take it so hard, Beck. The boys and me are doing you a favor. When you woke up this morning, all hungover and feeling bad, you were just another drunken town marshal in the middle of nowhere. After this, you'll be famous. Your ghost will get the blame for every bit of misfortune that befalls this town from here on in. These yokels will think it's the Black Beck curse and blame you for avenging your death."

Abraham laughed again, this time alone. "I kind of like the sound of that." He looked at his men. "Better than anything you idiots came up with." He looked down at the lawman again. "No need to thank me, Beck. Taking your town from you will be thanks enough."

Beck remembered Abraham had released his head with a shove as he stood and spoke to his gang. "Steve, Lem. Tie him up to that fancy Sharps of his like I told you. Crossways like our Lord and Savior had it done to him. Tie his hands good and tight, too. I don't want him suffering from rope burns on his journey. After all, no reason to be unkind in all of this, now, is there?"

Beck remembered they were all laughing when they untied him from the post and dragged him up to his feet. Every fiber in his being had wanted to collapse.

To let his legs go and give in to the unconsciousness that was tugging at his soul.

But something in him had refused to give in to that. Something that had not been there when he had decided to take up the bottle but had come to him now that all was lost.

CHAPTER TWO

WHILE HE SAT in his cave, trying to determine if the horse and rider he saw were real, Beck remembered back to Mother Lode, back to when he swayed on his feet as Steve Hogan came out of the town jail—Beck's jail—with the leather scabbard where he kept his Sharps. Pearson had a beefy hand on Beck's neck to keep him from falling over.

He vaguely remembered the catcalls from the outlaws as they admired the fancy stitching on the scabbard. He had bought it back in Chicago with the money he had earned from the Pinkertons. They had called him a city slicker when he had first joined up with the detective agency, but by the time he decided to leave their employ, his skill with the long gun and his fists had earned their respect. He had felt himself worthy of a fancy gun and scabbard.

Now, as a final indignity, the Brickhouse boys mocked it.

"Would you look at that, Pearson?" Steve said as he held up the empty scabbard like a dead rabbit carcass. "You ever see anything so pretty before in your life?"

The giant grunted as he held Beck firmly in place.

Beck watched Steve set the scabbard on the boardwalk outside the jail with mock solemnity. "I'm going to put that to better use than you ever did, Beck. Make it a fancy belt or holster or something. Hell, I could get two holsters out of that. You got yourselves a good leather worker in this here town?"

Beck would have spat at him had he had enough water in him.

"Knock it off," Beck heard Abraham say from somewhere behind him. "Let's get this over with."

He remembered Pearson holding him tightly as Steve held out Beck's left arm and tied it tightly to the barrel of his Sharps. Then, with the gun across his shoulders, tied his right hand to the stock. Steve had set it so that the trigger guard dug into Beck's shoulder. One final indignity.

Trussed up like a scarecrow with his own rifle, the outlaws stumbled away from Beck as they laughed at their handiwork and the sad sight of the lawman.

The men were still laughing as Abraham stood in front of him and crouched so he could look into Beck's face, which was pitched forward from the gun stretched across his back.

"Yes, sir. They strung you up fine, Marshal. Very fine indeed. But I don't want you to think we're sending you off into the wilderness without a touch of mercy in our hearts. Wouldn't be the Christian thing to do. No, sir. I believe in giving a man a fighting chance in this world, and that's exactly what I aim to do."

Beck remembered thinking Bram Hogan had actually managed to look noble as he motioned for one of the men to hand him something. Beck remembered how his spirits rose when he realized it was a canteen. He watched Abraham go over to the horse trough and fill it to the brim before popping the cork into it.

But instead of allowing him to drink from it, he had placed the canteen around Beck's neck. "We're sending you out there with a full canteen of water. Not that you'll be able to drink it, of course, but when someone finds your bones, they'll at least be able to say you had a chance."

The laughter from the outlaws had grown into howls.

Abraham ignored them. "They'll ponder themselves silly wondering what happened to you, but that'll only add to that legend we talked about earlier. Might even cause one of them writers from back east to come out here and write about you."

Beck remembered how he had hoped they were done with their torment, but his hopes were quickly dashed when he saw Abraham dig into his pocket and produce a single .50-caliber round for his Sharps. "Now, we all know how dry it can be out there in the desert. And, since we don't want you to die too quickly, I suggest you keep this in your mouth. They say it'll keep the saliva going and, for your sake, I sincerely hope they're right."

Beck remembered he had almost gagged when Bram popped the large slug into his mouth. But Beck had not gagged. He had bitten down on the bullet. Bit it hard.

Abraham took hold of him from Pearson and turned him toward the seemingly endless expanse of desert that surrounded Mother Lode. Beck saw nothing except the parched wilderness that would soon become his home for however long he lived.

"And to make it even easier for you," Bram had said, "I'm going to do one last kindness before you go."

Beck remembered watching Abraham pull a knife from his belt and disappear behind him. He felt a tug at the back of his long underwear and, as the men laughed again, felt the warm air against his bare backside.

"There you go, Marshal," Abraham mocked as he put the knife back in his belt. "Make it easier for you to do your business that way. No need to thank me for that, either. Like I said, it's the Christian thing to do."

Beck's skin still crawled at the memory of how Abraham Hogan had taken him by the neck and walked him away from the others to the edge of town. Now that they were alone, the outlaw's voice had taken a harder edge.

"You're going to die a terrible death, Marshal. It'll take days, maybe even a week, but it'll happen. You've got water around your neck you'll never be able to drink and a bullet in your mouth for a gun you'll never be able to use. Even if you do get free, you'll want to use that bullet to kill yourself but the gun's too long to make that easy. Game's scarce out there anyway, so you'll starve to death in no time. But I want it to take time, Beck. I want it to break you before you die because if there's one thing in this world I hate more than an Apache, it's a goddamned lawman."

He released Beck into the desert with a hard kick to the backside. "And don't think about coming back, now. If you do, I'll have no choice but to gut-shoot you and make you watch us kill Dulce while you're dying."

But John Beck had no intention of coming back to Mother Lode just then. He had no intentions at all except to keep putting one foot in front of the other until the mocking laughter from the Brickhouse Gang faded behind him. He'd had to walk a long way before that happened and it was not even noon yet.

Yes, Beck remembered. *That* had been the precise moment when he had gone insane.

CHAPTER THREE

N OW, IN THE cave that had been his home for so
long, still trying to understand why he was seeing
this horse and rider, John Beck's fractured mind drifted
back to those first horrible days in the desert. Alone.
Trussed up on a poor man's cross. The water sloshing
in a canteen around his neck that he could not reach, as
if to mock him. A bullet in his mouth he could not use.

The unrelenting heat of the Arizona sun had beaten
down on him with a merciless rage. But Beck had kept
moving forward. One foot in front of the other in spite
of all reason. Being carried on a wind blowing from
somewhere deep within him that was strong enough to
keep him upright and moving.

He remembered welcoming the night and the coolness that had come with it. He knew that lying down
would be lethal. His arms stretched out from him as
they were, it would have been impossible for him to get
back up again. Instead, he had found a way to sink to

his knees and force all the muscles in his body to relax as best they could. His arms and shoulders ached, and he feared his hands might turn blue from lack of circulation, so he continued to make fists with them whenever he could. He even found a way to use his tongue to angle the bullet into the corner of his mouth so that it would not fall out when he finally lost consciousness. He had dared not think of it as sleep.

He had lost consciousness for periods of time, but there had been nothing restful about it, for although he welcomed the chill of the desert night, the howls of the coyotes kept him aware. Not that he could do much against them if they came for him, but instinct took over.

When he had felt as though he had rested enough, no matter the hour of day or night, Beck remembered how he had forced himself to stand again and resume his trek into the wilderness. One foot in front of the other. He had resolved to continue on this way for as long as he could. He might not have been able to control his life anymore, but he had been determined to die as well as he could. He had hoped that might count in his favor in whatever might be waiting for him in the beyond. If he found anything at all.

Since the sun only hurt his eyes, he had always kept them closed as he walked, looking around only in the pitch-blackness of night. As he thought back on it now, he remembered hearing something in the distance as he stumbled through the desert. He had ceased to think about how parched he was. He had trained himself to ignore the growling from his empty belly and focus instead on the sounds of the desert around him. Time had seemed to pass a little easier that way as he kept putting one foot in front of the other.

Mostly, he had heard only the dull desert wind in his ears. Sometimes, the cry of a bird from high overhead. At night, he had heard the coyotes close by, a little closer with each passing night. But on that particular day that stood out most in his mind, he had heard something else.

A rattlesnake shaking its tail in warning at him.

Beck still remembered forcing the fog from his brain to recall that snakes always sought shelter from the intense heat of the sun, often beneath a rock. He had decided it was worth the risk to open his eyes this one time to see if he was right.

And before him, half-covered by the blowing sands of the desert, had been a jagged rock not twenty feet away.

Behind it, a rattler had raised its head. Its forked tongue had flicked out as its rattle grew louder to warn the intruder who had dared to enter its territory.

Every instinct in Beck's body had told him to get away from that place. To run before he risked the snake biting him. He had heard such bites were venomous and a terrible way for a man to die.

But for a man who had nowhere else to go, Beck had realized his instincts no longer counted for much. He needed that rock more than the damned snake did.

Beck recalled forcing himself to rise as fully to his height as he could manage with the Sharps across his back, and tried to roar. What came from him instead was a weak rasp that would not have woken a sleeping baby.

Beck had used what he could, staggering toward the snake and back again, kicking sand at it wildly. Realizing he had nothing to lose, Beck even worked the bullet out of the corner of his mouth and spat it at the snake, striking it in the head.

Somewhere during his staggering fury of dust and noise, Beck had realized the rattle had stopped. And when he had finally stopped kicking sand in the snake's direction, he saw the reptile slithering away and disappearing down a hole in the sand several yards away.

Had he had any water left in his body, Beck would have cried, for this was the first victory he had enjoyed since his banishment.

He remembered staggering over to the flat, jagged rock in the sand and dropping to his knees as though it was an altar. He shifted himself as best as he could in the soft sand until his left hand—which was tied to the gun barrel—was nearest the edge of the rock.

Realizing he had measured the space as well as he could manage in his condition, Beck had allowed himself to pitch forward. He had landed flat on his face in the burning sand.

But his bound left hand had landed on the rock.

His head, already pitched forward by the rifle lashed across his back, was at such and angle that he had not only been able to breathe, but had been able to rock himself back and forth so he could use the edges of the rock to saw into the rope that bound his left hand to the rifle barrel.

He remembered how the sweat had poured from him as he rocked to and fro, some of it gladly streaking along his face as he did so. He had gladly swept it up with his tongue and swallowed it.

He remembered having no idea how long he had been sawing at the rope that bound him when he felt the gun barrel raise a bit. Not much, but by more than it had since the moment Steve Hogan had tied it. Keeping his enthusiasm in check to conserve his energy, Beck had continued to saw away until he felt the scrape of the rock on the skin of his wrist and the rifle rose in the air.

His left hand had been freed!

Beck remembered how he had allowed himself to sob. He had no idea where the tears could have possibly come from, but come they had, and had flowed freely. His body shook as he laid his freed left hand on the rock and, for the first time in as long as he could remember, pushed himself upright without the yoke of his rifle across his back. Despite the pain and soreness in his back and shoulders, he had raised his head and closed his eyes as he looked up at the sun, the unrelenting heat of it beating down on his face, drying his tears and baking the sweat into his dry skin.

"I'm alive," he remembered whispering to himself. To the desert. To the world. "I'm alive."

H E REMEMBERED SITTING down, ignoring the burn of the hot sand against his bare bottom and pulling the long Sharps free of the rope around his right hand. Since Steve had tied it around the thick stock of the rifle, the bond was easier to undo.

He had thought about throwing the ropes that had bound him for so long as far from himself as he could manage but decided against it. They might come in handy at some point in his journey.

He found the bullet that he had spat at the rattler next to the rock that had helped him get free. He examined the bullet and was glad to see it was still usable, save for the bite marks around the casing. He quickly slapped the bullet into the chamber of the

Sharps for safekeeping. He would not have to worry about losing his one precious bullet anymore.

He had remembered the canteen around his neck and pawed for it, quickly opening it and glad to see it was still as full as the day Abraham had placed it around his neck. He had allowed himself to drink only a quarter of it, no more. He had wanted to drink the entire thing dry but had known it would have to last him for the foreseeable future. He also knew he had not had anything in his stomach for a long time. He did not want to waste the water by getting sick.

He had put the plug back in the canteen after drinking the prescribed amount and slipped the strap around his shoulder. He remembered making a promise that he would never carry anything around his neck again for as long as he lived. He had slowly eased himself up to his feet and, for the first time since he could remember, stood upright. He ignored the pain in his neck and back and hips and stretched as far as his joints would allow him.

He could still remember that blessed feeling of blood flowing once again in his veins. He had remembered feeling reborn. Perhaps because he was.

It had felt good to be able to stand tall again. He had been six feet tall before his run-in with the Brickhouse Gang and hoped his time in the desert had not given him a permanent slouch. One of the best things Dulce had always admired about him had been his posture. She would not be happy if he returned to her as a stooped-over thing. And he had intended on returning to her. Someday. If she was still alive.

He remembered the other thing Dulce had admired about him was his looks. She had often told him he had a handsome face and a thick head of black hair. He

had heard such compliments from other women before. He had run his newly freed hands over that face
and was glad the swelling from his beatings was almost
gone. His cracked lip almost healed. His broken nose
had also healed, though it felt more crooked than he
had remembered. Since it had not been set, that was to
be expected.

He had normally preferred to be clean shaven, but
he had felt a thick beard then that had only grown thicker
still during his time in the cave. Given the growth of it,
he knew he had been in the desert for five days or so.
But time did not matter to him just then. Shelter did.
He had known he was running on excitement and little
else. He had needed a place to rest and heal for a while.
A place where he was sheltered from the blazing heat
of the day and the cold of the desert nights. From the
predators that had stalked him, too.

He could still remember how he had brought his
shaking hands up to shield his eyes from the sun, grateful for being able to do that much again, and looked
around in all directions. The horizon had shimmered
and shook as it still did, making it difficult to tell if
something was real or only present in his imagination.

He had found a large outcropping of rocks in the far
distance and focused on it long enough to determine
that it was actually there, not just a shimmer of heat.

Beck had picked up his rifle and begun walking toward what he had seen. One foot in front of the other,
just as he had begun that forced journey all those days
before.

CHAPTER FOUR

T HAT WAS WHY it had taken Beck so long to determine the horse and rider he was witnessing now
outside his cave were real.

He was satisfied it really was a man. On horseback.
Ambling through the desert without a care in the world.

It was the first man Beck had seen in all his days in
the wilderness; days he had tracked by scratching lines
on the cave wall.

The tarantulas had called this cave home long before he had, but he had quickly dispatched them with
a slam of his rifle butt. They had made for poor meals,
especially since he did not have a fire, but what sparse
meat they provided had helped keep him alive in those
first days. Snakes provided more meat and were easy
enough to kill with rocks.

Eventually he had learned to generate a small spark
by slamming two rocks together and used the rope he

had salvaged from his bonds to make small fires that made the meat a bit easier to keep down.

A small stream of water that trickled down from the rocks at the back of the cave had provided a steady if slow source of water. The smell of their own dead in the cave kept the spiders away from him, even when he slept.

His sleep had been deep those first days in the cave and plagued with nightmares, in which he relived the beatings he received from the Brickhouse Gang every time he dared to close his eyes. The pain never had failed to follow him into wakefulness, just as it had only moments before when the sound of the approaching horse and rider woke him.

The sound of a jangle of a bit in a horse's mouth.

Everything John Beck had suffered in the weeks since he had been driven from Mother Lode had caused him to doubt his own senses, which was why it had taken him so long to realize the horse and rider were real.

The rider was a short, broad man with a forced scowl. He wore a familiar black flat-brimmed hat and a fancy black leather vest now dusty from time riding the desert. He wore fine leather boots that had once sported a classy shine. He knew they had once shone because Beck had kept them that way.

Those clothes had once been his.

And the man wearing them was Steve Hogan and he was following a trail of prints in the sand. A trail that would lead him to the cave.

This was not a dream. This was real.

John Beck did not think. He reacted.

In one movement, he rose to a knee, grabbed up his Sharps rifle from against the cave wall, and brought it to his shoulder. He took careful aim at the man and squeezed the trigger.

The .50-caliber bullet slammed into Hogan's chest, a bit lower than where Beck had been aiming, and knocked the outlaw from his horse. The animal skittered a few steps forward but did not run away.

Beck took the rifle with him as he walked out of the cave and clambered down the rocks, careful of his footing. He was barefoot now, forced to eat his shoe leather the week before, and did not want to risk getting a cut. It would not do to have survived all he had endured only to die from an infected cut.

Beck took his time in approaching Hogan. The sand was hot on his feet and the man was not going anywhere. Even from a good distance away, Beck could see the size of the hole in Hogan's chest was bigger than his fist. He was going to die. No doubt about that. Beck only hoped he lasted long enough for him to offer a proper farewell.

When he hobbled over to Hogan, Beck found he was still lying as he had fallen from his horse, on his left side. The right side of his chest was mostly gone.

But he was still gurgling when Beck moved around in front of him, blocking the sun so he could see his target and, more importantly, his target could see him.

It was Steve Hogan, all right. Beck took comfort in the knowledge that his time in the desert might have robbed him of his sanity, but it had not dulled all his senses.

But his aim had been off and that concerned him. He had been aiming for Hogan's head. A clean hit there with the .50-caliber round would have saved most of the clothes. And he would be needing clothes now, especially those the Brickhouse Gang had stolen from him.

He looked down at Hogan, twitching in the bloody sand like a dying bug half stepped on. The shirt was bloody enough to be a complete loss, unfortunately, but his fancy leather vest was still in good condition. Bloody, of course, but something could always be done about that. The boots were in fine condition, as was his hat. The pants might be salvageable if he got them off Hogan before he died. He decided to set about doing that right away.

But a voice stopped him. Hogan's voice.

"No. It can't be."

Beck stopped unbuckling the belt. He had no idea what Hogan was talking about. "Can't be what?"

"You," Steve rasped. "You're alive. You can't be."

"Kind of gotta be, don't I? After all, I'm the one who shot you."

"But you're dead. You have to be. No one could live that long out here. No one."

Beck undid Steve's buckle and realized he should probably pull off the boots first. But he knew he would have to hurry. The pants would be ruined if he didn't have them off before Hogan died.

"Well, here I am," Beck said as he pulled off one of Hogan's boots, then the other, before pulling the pants off. "Can't be a ghost on account of me shooting you and stripping your corpse like I am. Though I guess you're not really a corpse since you're not dead yet." He glanced at the chunk missing from Hogan's side. "But I guess you'll be dead soon enough, so the distinction hardly matters."

Hogan let his head drop into the dust. "I can't believe this. I come out here to fetch that Sharps of yours and here you are, waiting to shoot me."

Beck held the pants to his waist and realized these were his, too. They were a bit big around the middle, of course, given all the weight he had lost, but that was what belts were for. Beck took a closer look at the gun belt and saw it was not his but would do nicely. So would the Colt .38 in the holster.

He was about to look over Hogan's horse and saddlebags when something the dying man had said came back to him. "I wasn't exactly waiting for you, you know. You just kind of ambled along while I happened to be looking. What'd you say you were looking for again?"

"Your rifle, you damned idiot!" the dying man rasped.

Beck grabbed up the rifle and held it out for Hogan to see. "You mean this one?"

"Yeah," Hogan confirmed. "That's it, you stupid son of a—"

Beck brought down the stock hard on Hogan's face. He never gave him the chance to finish his sentence. He was pretty sure what he was going to say. And it had been so long since he had heard anyone speak that all the talking was giving him a headache.

He approached the horse and began searching the dead man's saddlebags. By the time he was done, he had found a reasonably new bedroll, a decent blanket, a new shirt, and a fair amount of jerky. A quick search of the other saddlebag came up with a box of cartridges for Hogan's Winchester, a handful of rounds for the Colt, and a small bag filled with ten dollars in gold coins.

Beck felt a rush of excitement wash over him and he gripped the saddle horn to keep from falling over. He had endured so much for so long. Finding all of this good fortune at once seemed too good to be true. He shut his eyes and thought hard, praying this was not just another illusion. Another trick his broken mind had decided to play on him. He hoped not. He did not think he could take it after all he had endured.

But when he dared open his eyes again, he felt his hand still gripping the saddle horn. He smelled the salty sweat of the horse and knew this was not a dream. This was now. This was real. And it would only get better from here on out.

Until the day he took back Mother Lode and put Abraham Hogan down once and for all.

CHAPTER FIVE

BACK AT THE saloon, Dulce Ramos remained in the kitchen, too afraid to go out into the very saloon that bore her name. It might have belonged to her legally, but the law had not meant much in Mother Lode since John Beck had gotten himself ridden out of town on a rail days before. She had not bothered to count the days. It would only prolong her agony.

Come to think of it, John Beck had not been much of a lawman since he had decided to crawl into a bottle and pull the cork in after him. He had been good with a gun and better with his fists when he had to be. He was handsome, too. Handsome in the way the dime novels from back east liked to draw town marshals of small towns like Mother Lode.

Dulce supposed that's what had made Beck a good marshal. He was not tough, but resourceful instead. He was eloquent, too, and tender. Perhaps that eloquence was what had haunted him so and driven him to drink. He was too eloquent to tell her what had been bothering him and too proud to let her help.

She found herself wishing he had been a tougher man. At least tougher in his battle against the bottle. Then maybe she would still be sharing her bed with him instead of that bastard Abraham Hogan.

Hogan was everything Beck was not, except for the failing of being a drunk. She had never gotten around to finding out what had caused Beck to try to drink himself to death. He'd always either just change the topic or distract her in one of the many ways she liked.

Bram Hogan, on the other hand, was the worst kind of drunk there was. The petulant kind. The kind who drank to forget all of the rotten things he had done in his life, only to remember them the drunker he grew. And meaner because of it.

When he didn't cry, which he did a fair amount of the time, he got nasty and took it out on her. Fortunately, she could usually see it coming when he got a certain look in his eye, and managed to get out of the way in time.

Usually.

And when she did not, she usually spent a good portion of the night figuring out a way to wriggle out from under him so she could finally get some sleep. When she did manage to get away from him entirely, she either slept on the floor or in one of the empty rooms down the hall. It was the only refuge from the hell she now endured.

There were more and more empty rooms in the saloon since the Brickhouse Gang had come to Mother Lode. While she had not come to town expecting a bustling metropolis like Chicago or Denver, business had never been this bad. She used to be able to rely on a steady trade of mining engineers or speculators to come through town looking for a nice place to stay. Unfortunately, the Brickhouse Gang had succeeded in draining the town dry and driving off regular business. She imagined people went down to Amenia now, or parts elsewhere.

No one stayed at her place any longer because no one came to Mother Lode anymore. Not unless they had a suicide wish. The Brickhouse Gang had practically killed the town just as sure as they had killed poor John Beck.

In many ways Mother Lode and Beck were the same in that neither was meant to stand up to the likes of Bram Hogan and his men. It had always been a wide-open, easygoing town, where a man's word was his bond and his work spoke more about the type of man he was than any boasting could. People there tended to give one another the benefit of the doubt and preferred to settle their rare disagreements over a bottle of whiskey or a glass of beer.

But the men in the Brickhouse Gang were not easygoing men. They would rather take whatever another man earned rather than work for it themselves. They cheated at cards and at the other table games. And when they lost, they just waited for the winner to get drunk and take the winnings from him. The few who had dared to fight back were never heard from again.

Dulce did her best not to be around the gang when they boasted about what they had done to troublemakers. The less she heard, the better off she would be. If none of the other people of Mother Lode had the guts to fight them, why in the world should she?

How could she?

Abraham Hogan was nothing more than a brute

and a bully, but he was more than Dulce could handle on her own. He was a large man, bigger than Beck had been, though nowhere near as big as the giant Pearson. She was ashamed to admit, even to herself, that she knew the leader had scars of different sorts over all of his body, particularly on his hands and wrists.

He had tried to tell her the story behind each scar after he was done with her, but she refused to hear it. She might not have been able to stop him from using her body, but she would not allow him into her mind. When he spoke, she only listened for the gradual snoring to begin so she could find another part of the saloon to sleep that night.

She knew how all of this would end. She was already seeing the edges where the Brickhouse Gang was beginning to fray. Running roughshod over a town was hard work. Once the shopkeepers and townspeople were cowed, there was not much for the gang to do except sit back and let the money roll in. They killed time playing cards and bothering the few strangers that did not know enough to stay away from Mother Lode these days.

Boredom eventually set in and, as Dulce knew all too well, bored men tended to drink. The Brickhouse Gang had proven they were no exception. When they had first come to town, they only did their drinking after sunset. Gradually, that rule slipped until they were at it morning, noon, and night. They were forgetting to collect from the few shopkeepers still open. Those who were left laughed at the gang behind their backs. The outlaws slept too long and ate too much. They were getting fat, slow, and stupid.

All of them except for Steve Hogan.

There was something about Abraham's younger

brother that had frightened Dulce from the moment she had laid eyes on him. She had often caught him looking out the saloon window in the same direction Hogan and the others had sent poor Beck into the wilderness. Trussed up to his long rifle like a pig on a spit.

Part of her wished they had simply killed him and been done with it. She had never spent much time in the desert. The size of the place and the danger that lurked in it had always terrified her. At least if they had shot Beck, his suffering would have been over quickly. Days lashed to his own gun in the sweltering heat and burning sands of the desert was just about the worst fate Dulce could contemplate for any man. Especially a flawed, gentle man like John Beck.

She tried not to think about how long he might have lived before he had ultimately succumbed to thirst and pain. She hoped his death had been as quick and as painless as possible. She had never allowed herself to fall completely in love with him, for she had always sensed a dreamy restlessness about him, but she had come as close to loving him as she had loved any man since her husband had died.

She was grateful to her late husband, Philippe, for so much, especially in how he had taught her how to live with a brutal man like Abraham Hogan. He had taught her how to weather the tirades, how to absorb the abuse, and how to hold on to patience until the right time came to kill him.

And Dulce knew she would kill Abraham Hogan one day. For what he had done to her and this town. For what he had done to John Beck.

Before he killed her, too.

She opened a drawer in the kitchen and found the long carving knife she had chosen for that purpose. She kept it wrapped in a towel and shoved in the back of the drawer lest any of the Brickhouse Gang find it in their rummaging and take it for their own purpose. She took the knife out of the towel and held it up so that it glinted in the dull sunlight that came through the filthy kitchen window. Yes, she would have her revenge, and soon. But for now, the knife would have to wait for another time. The right time.

Dulce placed the knife back in the towel and folded it over before placing it in the back of the drawer. The blade's time would come. And soon.

Just as it had come for Philippe.

CHAPTER SIX

OUTSIDE IN THE saloon, Bram Hogan reached for the bottle of whiskey but changed his mind. He decided he'd had enough whiskey for now. He feared it was beginning to make his brain soft and he could not afford that. Not now, not with an entire town set against him and restrained only by fear. No one was afraid of a drunk. Not for very long anyway and not in the way he needed them to be afraid of him and his gang.

But the real reason he had not taken another drink was Steve. He tried to wade through the whiskey-colored bits of random images in his mind to remember the last time he had seen his younger brother. But he could not remember and that was why he set the bottle back down on the bar.

He looked around the table and was disgusted by what he saw. Lem's head was on the table and he was snoring loud enough to wake the dead. Pearson's head was back, his mouth as open and as slack as it had been since he had passed out an hour before.

But across the table from where Bram sat, Laredo was the most sober member of the gang. The Mexican had always preferred tequila to the whiskey that the white man drank. And since the saloons of Mother Lode had chosen never to stock tequila, Laredo had chosen to remain mostly sober since the day the Brickhouse Gang had ridden into town. And on the rare evening he did drink, Hogan noted, he only drank enough to kill the boredom that had descended over the gang.

"When did you see Steve last?" Bram asked Laredo suddenly.

"I don't know." The old bandit shrugged. "He's not my brother. Why ask me?"

Bram realized that had been another element that had raised its ugly head since the gang had come to Mother Lode. Insolence. Indifference. Sass.

Out on the trail, Bram Hogan ruled the gang with an iron fist. Not even his own brother dared to talk back to him. But since reaping the rewards of the Arizona town, the gang had grown more familiar with him the more they drank. The fear was gone, and respect for his position would soon follow unless he did something about it right away.

"I'm asking you because I damned well feel like it, that's why!" Bram slammed his hand on the table, jolting Pearson and Lem out of their respective stupors. "Don't you dare sass me again, you son of a bitch, or I'll blow you out of that chair right now."

But Laredo did not jump or flinch. He did not look scared, either. He only looked at his leader. His face was as blank as the side of a cliff.

Hogan figured that was as close to a reaction as he

was likely to get from the old Mexican bandit. "The next words out of your mouth better be an answer to my question." He was conscious that the others were watching him now. And since he did not want to have to shoot Laredo, he repeated his question. "When was the last time you saw Steve?"

"Three days ago," Laredo told him. "He rode out into the desert looking for John Beck's rifle, remember? You and he had a big argument about it before he went, *jefe*. Many harsh words were spoken between you. I think it was the liquor talking."

Bram felt Laredo had added the Spanish word for "chief" like it was a slap in the face, but he let it go. The bandit did have a point. He should have done a better job of keeping track of his own brother.

The dull memory of the argument with his brother slowly emerged from the sea of whiskey sopping his brain. He remembered the anger and he remembered the cursing. "He wanted that Sharps I strapped Beck to. What is it with Steve and that damned rifle? He doesn't even like rifles."

"Perhaps it is more than a rifle to him," Laredo suggested. "Perhaps he believes that owning such a gun that once belonged to a man like John Beck is a point of pride. It is like the way an Indian chief likes to boast about the number of scalps he has hanging from his lodgepole. Though I don't know why a gun from a drunken town marshal from the middle of nowhere should be of value to anyone. There is no honor to be had from taking a gun from the bones of a dead man."

"Hell," Pearson croaked, now fully awake. "There ain't no honor to be found in this whole outfit, if you ask me."

Hogan would have backhanded the big man if he

had thought he could have knocked him off the chair. But even as drunk as he might be, Pearson weighed well over two hundred pounds and most of it was solid muscle. It would take a shovel to knock him off-balance and Hogan dared not risk appearing weak in front of his men. He had too few of them left and Steve was no longer around to back his play.

"Honor doesn't pay much," Hogan told them. "Learned that in the army. Learned it the hard way, too." He looked back at Laredo. "Three days is a long time for a man like Steve to spend fetching Beck's gun, ain't it? You don't think he could've gotten lost, do you?"

"The desert is a very strange place, my friend," the bandit told him. "Better men than your brother have been known to get lost out there. Entire armies since the days of the conquistadors have been swallowed up within it, never to be heard from again."

Lem used the back of his sleeve to wipe his mouth. "We ain't talking about no Mexican armies here. We're talking about one man. We're talking about Steve."

"Thank you for reminding me." Laredo appeared amused by his drunken friend's declaration, and it annoyed Hogan. "I can't imagine Beck got that far on foot without food or water, especially strung up the way he was when we sent him from here. But, as I said before, the desert can be a strange place, *jefe*. It is like a good woman in many ways. It can be as forgiving as it can be cruel, depending on its mood."

Bram waved off that sort of high-minded nonsense. Laredo was always talking about the land as if it was some kind of a living thing with a mind of its own. He did not have time for any of that pagan nonsense now. The desert was nothing but sand and rock with a few watering holes sprinkled in for good measure. It was a dead and deadly place where all of the things that lived there did so on a knife's edge, especially men.

The idea that Beck had lasted more than a day out there was hard for Bram to accept.

But Steve had not come back. He was days overdue and that was troubling.

"You boys don't think Steve might have gotten hurt, do you?" Hogan asked aloud to no one in particular.

The question brought another shrug from Laredo. *"Todo es posible en el desierto, jefe."* He quickly translated, though Hogan had understood it. "Anything is possible in the wilderness, boss. A snake could have scared Steve's horse and thrown him. Something could have bitten him, or he could have drunk bad water he found someplace."

"Steve's more careful than that," Bram said.

"He brought more than enough water with him for three days," Lem said. "I remember him asking to borrow my canteen."

The more he thought about it, the more Bram began to worry about his brother. He looked out the batwing doors of the saloon and saw weak daylight bathing the thoroughfare. He was ashamed to admit he had been too drunk to know if it was still morning or going on dusk. He should have kept better track of the passage of time, but he had not. He was no better than the common drunks he rode with.

Bram pulled out the gold pocket watch he had taken from the shopkeeper's store across the street. The old man had told him he was welcome to it, as a gift, but Bram knew that was the old man's way of saving some of his dignity. Bram had decided to allow him to keep his dignity until such time as he had to take it from him. It was a tactic that had served the Brickhouse Gang well in the past.

He looked at the pocket watch, but the hands were pointed at fifteen minutes past three. In the midst of all his drinking, he had forgotten to wind it. He remembered something his father had told him back on the farm in Kentucky. "T'ain't nothing sorrier in this world than a man with the means to own a fancy watch who don't keep it wound."

Reluctantly, Hogan asked Laredo, "What time is it?" The bandit always had a knack for knowing what time it was without having to look at a watch.

"Just after sunup," Laredo told him. "About six or so. Maybe seven, but no later than that. Why?"

That settled it for him. There was not a moment to lose.

Bram kicked Lem's chair and snapped the lanky man awake once again. "Get some coffee into yourselves, boys. We're riding out to see what happened to Steve."

Lem and Pearson looked at him through bleary eyes, but only the big man dared to speak. "You mean we're going right now?"

Bram's hands balled into fists on the table. "Steve's missing, you big idiot. When do you expect me to want to go looking for him? Tomorrow? Next week? Why, it might already be too late. And I've spent too much time drinking in here with you three fools while my brother might be out there busted up or worse."

Laredo surprised him by holding up a hand to stop him. "Excuse me, *jefe*, but will you allow me to make a suggestion?"

Bram glared at the bandit. He had never liked debate, not even in the best of times, but the Mexican was the best tracker in the gang. Bram would be a fool not to listen to what he had to say, and Abraham Hogan did not consider himself to be a fool. "Might as well."

"You and Lem and Pearson should stay here in town and clear your heads," Laredo told him. "The desert is no place for men who are already dry and sick from too much whiskey. Besides, someone needs to stay behind and keep the townspeople under our heel. You have won a hard victory here, *jefe*, and it would be a shame to have to fight to reclaim what you have already won. Let me go find Steve instead."

Bram's eyes narrowed. In his experience, when an offer sounded too good to be true, it usually was. And not for the right reasons.

"I know the wilderness like the back of my own hand, and I will make much better time if I am traveling alone. I can find your brother quicker than you can and my horse is used to the desert."

Bram did not like to admit that he played second fiddle to anyone, but he could not argue with Laredo when it came to tracking. The Mexican's instincts had gotten the Brickhouse Gang out of more fixes than he could count. If anyone could track down Steve, it was Laredo.

"How long do you think it will take?" Bram asked. "I can't be down two men for three days or longer."

"I will be back by tomorrow night no matter what I find or don't find," Laredo told him. "Steve was tracking a dead man. That can take time. But I will find Steve's trail much quicker if I leave right now."

Bram did not like being down to three men to hold the town, especially when they were all suffering from hangovers. But Laredo made sense, as he usually did, and he decided to follow his instincts.

"You just make sure you're back here tomorrow night at the latest," Bram told him. "Even if you don't find anything, you'd better be here."

Laredo stood with a flourish and took his hat from the back of the chair. "I'll get some provisions from the store. Medicine, too, in case Steve is hurt."

"You do that," Bram said, then another thought came to him. "And if you happen to come across Beck's carcass, bring it back here if you can manage it without too much difficulty. I think the leavings of him would look awfully nice propped up outside for all the town to see. Remind them who's really in charge around here."

The bandit bowed slightly before he took his leave of the saloon.

Pearson grabbed the bottle of whiskey in the middle of the table. "Might as well have another one to help me sleep. Anyone want to join me?"

Bram drew his pistol and brought the barrel down on the bottle, shattering it in Pearson's big hand.

The sudden speed of it made Lem and Pearson shake off their drunk for a moment.

Bram enjoyed the look of fear in their eyes. At least he was still fast on the draw. His time on the bottle had not taken that away from him. "No more drinking. You two have had enough. We all have. You boys get up to your rooms and sleep it off for the rest of the day. We're on coffee and water until Laredo gets back tomorrow night. If he has Steve with him, then we'll see about drinking. If not, we'll need our wits about us for whatever comes next."

Lem looked at him blankly. "Not even beer?"

Bram brought his pistol back as if to belt him with it, causing Lem to flinch and cover his face.

"No beer," Hogan told him. "No exceptions. I catch either of you nipping, I'll tan your hide. Now, get out of my sight, both of you."

The two men reluctantly pushed themselves away from the table and trudged upstairs to their rooms like a couple of pouting brats. They clearly did not like Bram's order, but they had no choice but to follow it. The price would have been too dear otherwise.

Bram knew that he would have to keep a closer eye on those two men until Laredo and Steve got back to town. It was only him against an ornery giant and the sly Lem and the entire town of Mother Lode, too. Sure, Pearson and Lem had been loyal to him for years since they had met up, but they had never lived as easy as they had in Mother Lode. They were all getting soft, including him. That would not do. Abraham Hogan knew that he was only in charge of the Brickhouse Gang for as long as they let him be and he did not want them getting ideas.

Bram had been guilty as any of them for getting soft. But now it was time for a change.

"Dulce!" he called out. "Get in here, girl."

He was glad to see the pretty Mexican girl come out from the back immediately. He could have simply barked out an order for coffee and knew she would have brought him some. But he liked to watch her move, even if it was at a shuffle.

He looked at her rumpled clothes and uncombed hair and knew she was doing everything she could think of to make herself look as unappealing to him as possible. She no longer bathed, either, but she had a rugged beauty about her that no amount of grime could hide from him. The young woman would have excited him had she been bald and wearing a burlap sack. He thought she should consider herself lucky that he let her wear anything at all.

She stood in front of the table, silent. The vacant, sullen look in her eyes stirred something deep within him again, but there would be time to feed his hunger later. "Bring me some coffee. A whole pot of it, and make sure it's good and strong. I've got some thinking to do and need my wits about me."

She did not acknowledge him before she trudged back to the kitchen. He watched her the entire way until she rounded the corner. He had not yet decided if he would kill her when they finally left Mother Lode, whenever that might be. He thought about bringing her with him. She would not fetch much of a price on the border. Mexico had no shortage of beauties of its own, but she might fetch a good price in one of the towns to the north. He knew a few places that would pay top dollar for a woman of such beauty.

Or he might decide to keep her with him on the trail as they hit one town after another. A man was known to get awful lonely in the cold desert at night and Dulce had already proven useful to him many times since he'd come to Mother Lode.

Bram felt himself grinning as the thick fog of whiskey began to lift from his brain. He was beginning to plan once again and it felt mighty good.

He rubbed his hand across the stubble on his chin and decided he needed a shave. After all, a leader should look the part.

But his grin faded as he remembered Steve and where he might be. "Where are you, boy?" he said aloud. "Just where the hell are you?"

CHAPTER SEVEN

JOHN BECK PULLED the horse to a stop when he saw the shimmering outline of a town in the distance.

But he did not trust it. The desert horizon had played cruel tricks on his eyes before, which tamped down his excitement now.

He drew the Sharps rifle from the saddle scabbard—he was glad that Steve Hogan had not made good on his threat to cut it into a belt—and looked at the town through the rifle's scope. The glass was cracked and dusty, but usually cut down on the glare enough for him to see what was real and what was illusion. He looked at what he believed was, in fact, a town.

"By God, Pokey," he said to his horse. "Would you look at that? It looks like we've finally found a real live town for ourselves."

The horse responded by hanging its head low, nosing at the dust in the hopes it might find something to eat there.

"I know, boy," Beck said as he slid the rifle back into the scabbard. "You're as hungry and tired as I am."

He had fed the animal some of the snake he had killed since leaving the cave. Some lizards and even some of a mangy coyote he had shot, too, with Steve's Winchester. He knew Pokey would be better if he had grain to eat but Steve had not packed much when he had set out from Mother Lode. The grain went quickly after Beck acquired the animal.

He liked to think of obtaining Pokey as being by way of an acquisition. Murdering Steve Hogan had been a necessity in Beck's mind, which made it easier to bear, just as he always thought of the men he had killed as a Pinkerton were criminals. He knew it was a lie but sometimes a lie could help a man sleep better at night.

But he had been lucky to find water here and there since leaving the cave and decided it was time to give Pokey a hatful. He climbed down from the saddle, took off his hat, and poured half of a canteen into it. The smell of water brought the horse alive and Beck held the hat to the animal's snout to let it drink.

"I'm sorry it's not better," Beck told the horse, "but I'll see to it you're taken care of when we hit that town. I can promise you that much."

The horse snorted as it drank, which Beck—in his current mental state—took as some kind of response. "You'll like that town over there, won't you, Pokey? Get you groomed and fed properly. Maybe a nice big bag of oats. All you can eat. Maybe put you in a stall with a pretty mare. You'd like that, wouldn't you, boy?"

The horse responded by urinating in the sand.

Beck laughed and stroked the horse's head. "Yeah, I figured you'd like that. I might take some time to get myself groomed while I'm at it. A bath, a good meal wouldn't hurt. And I mean a real meal this time. No more snakes and spiders and coyotes for us anymore, old son. We'll get ourselves a proper rest and get fixed up right again. Then we'll figure out what we're going to do next. You and me, my friend."

The horse continued to drink and Beck laid his head flat against Pokey's muzzle. Beck fought hard against the feelings of being weak and scared all over again. Fear that what had happened to him in Mother Lode might happen to him again in this new town on the horizon. His legs began to shake and his hold on the hat from which Pokey was drinking began to falter, but he stayed strong for Pokey's sake. The horse deserved a good drink after all he had done for Beck and Beck would not let him down.

Tears quickly came to his eyes. "I don't know what I would have done without you, Pokey. I was at my end before you came along. Hell, I was at my end in Mother Lode, too, before your owner and his friends came to town. Drinking too much. Not eating enough. Not sleeping at all. And all of it on account of what happened all that time ago in Chicago and all of those strikers I helped bust over the head. Maybe it was about more than that? Maybe I was even a little bit scared on account of me finally finding a home after all I've done. I guess Mother Lode's not much of a home, but it was the closest thing I've ever gotten to one."

The horse lifted its muzzle from Beck's hat, having drunk its fill, but Beck kept his head pressed to the animal's. "You're lucky, you know. You don't remember things like humans do. All of the horrible things we do. You get to carry someone around all day and eat grass and get fed. You just have to lug a rider around to wherever he wants to go. Why, you don't even have to decide where to go. But us humans have to carry around things, too. Things like a past. Guilt over what we've done and haven't done. That's heavier than any rider or cart could be. Problem is, sometimes you don't even know you're lugging it until you stop and, one day, it all comes crashing into you and knocks you flat."

John Beck flinched as he heard the screams from the past echo in his mind once again. The rifle cracks and that sick, unmistakable sound of a .50-caliber bullet striking home. Not the way his bullet had knocked Steve Hogan off Pokey. No, that had been a joyous sound, like a church choir on Easter morning.

It was the other times that had always plagued his dreams, even out here in the desert. The sound of a man's body hitting the ground simply for running away from a railroad track bed. Running knowing it would mean the end of his life but deciding to run anyway because this was no way to live.

The sounds of a wife and her little boy crying over the body of the dead man. The same man John Beck had brought down. Three lives ruined with a single squeeze of the trigger.

He had not realized he was gripping Pokey tightly until the horse fussed and tried to back away from him. Beck immediately let go and stroked the horse's muzzle. "I'm sorry, boy. I wasn't thinking. I didn't mean to hurt you like that. Not you. Never you."

Beck wished he knew of a way that he could make it up to the animal, but he had nothing to give him except more water.

And as much as he loved the animal, he did not dare give Pokey any more than he'd already had. He knew he needed some for himself before they pushed on to whatever town lay before them in the distance.

When Pokey had lapped up the last of the water, Beck shook his hat as dry as he could manage before he plopped it back on his head and finished the rest of the canteen. The warm water he drank served to dull at least some of the echoes in his mind and brought him back to his senses.

He shook the two other canteens to make sure they were full. They were. Beck figured they should be more than enough to get him into town.

Refreshed, he climbed back into the saddle and urged Pokey forward. "Come on, boy. Let's see what that town has in store for us."

B ECK IGNORED THE looks that he and Pokey drew as they rode down the town's main thoroughfare.

He did not dare let on that all of the attention made him nervous. People along the boardwalk and men on wagons stopped whatever they were doing and watched the stranger and his horse pass by.

John Beck had never been fond of receiving much attention and he liked it even less now. Although he had not seen his own reflection since however long he had spent in the desert, he imagined he looked like quite a sight. His beard had grown in full and felt uneven to the touch. He had never grown one and he had no idea if it was one color or smattered with gray or even white. His clothes were caked with dry dust and he bet the passersby could still see some of Steve Hogan's blood on him.

But this was a desert town and he could not imagine

that dusty men were all that uncommon, so he decided to ignore all of the attention. He swallowed the fear that rose in his gullet and looked for a livery where he could see to it that Pokey was tended to properly. He had survived alone in the desert for weeks now. He could certainly handle some curious glances from suspicious townsfolk.

Once he arranged for Pokey to receive proper treatment, he would set about finding a bath and shave for himself. Maybe a nice steak dinner and all of the trimmings. Pokey deserved a little pampering first.

John Beck realized he had ridden the length of the town before he spotted a wooden sign that simply read LIVERY hanging from an eave at the end of the street. That was where he decided to head first.

He had not seen anything to tell him what the name of the town might be, but he still liked what he saw. There were plenty of hotels and shops and even a couple of banks. He had even spotted a town marshal's office and a jail, too. Both buildings looked like they were kept in good order, which told him the town took law and order seriously. That made him feel better. They had not taken it too seriously back in Mother Lode and allowed the buildings to fall into disrepair. He could not help but wonder if that had been the reason why the likes of the Brickhouse Gang had decided to hit the town. He doubted they would come anywhere near a place like this.

Beck rode Pokey over to the livery and climbed down from the saddle. A fat old Black man came out to greet him, wiping his hands on his leather apron as he looked over the strange man and his horse that had stopped outside his business.

"Good Lord," the liveryman said to the stranger. "You look like Death himself."

Beck tried to summon some of the charm for which he had once been known. "I feel even worse." He was surprised by how brittle and raspy his voice sounded.

He handed the liveryman Pokey's reins and the man frowned as he looked over the animal. "This old boy looks like he has been through the wars. A man who treats a horse this poorly deserves himself a good beating and I don't mind telling you so."

"Since I'm not the man who put him in this condition, I agree with you, mister." Beck patted Pokey's flanks. "This horse means the world to me and I'd appreciate it if you could give him the best treatment you can. Spare no expense." He dug one of the gold pieces he had taken from Steve Hogan out of his vest and handed it to him. "Will that be enough to get the job done?"

The Black man looked at the coin in his hand as if he was holding a miracle. "Lord Almighty," he proclaimed before he bit into it. "That's a ten-dollar gold piece you just gave me, boy. Where'd you get it?"

"From a man who shouldn't have had it in the first place," Beck told him. "I know you don't believe me given the shape he's in, but this horse is special to me, mister. He saved my life from the man who hurt him like this, and I want him treated well. He goes by the name of Pokey, or at least he does now that I've got him."

The man watched Beck cautiously as he slid the gold piece into the pocket of his apron. "Does he, now?"

"Well, Pokey is the name I gave him when he saved me. He seems to like it, so I think we'll keep it." Beck decided he felt sort of silly talking so much about a horse's name. "Think you can take care of him, mister? The way I asked you to, I mean."

"Ain't a horse been born yet that I can't fix," the liveryman said. "What's your name, anyway?"

"John Beck." He held out his hand. "Pleased to meet you."

The liveryman looked at Beck's filthy hand before reluctantly shaking it. "Name's Abraham. How'd you . . . ?"

But Beck dropped the man's hand when he heard the name.

Abraham. That was the name of one of the men that had ridden him out of Mother Lode. Abraham Hogan. Bram. He would never forget that name for as long as he lived.

The liveryman grabbed Beck's arm. "You all right, Mr. Beck? You damned near fell over."

"Abraham," Beck whispered to himself. Yes, the name meant something to him. Abraham Hogan. Bram. The name was no longer just a name. It meant something horrible. It meant blood and pain and fear. It meant anger and rage and humiliation. It meant eating things raw that were never meant to be eaten by a man.

It meant having feelings no living man was fit to have.

But deep down, John Beck knew it did not have to mean that. It did not need to mean that now, especially with this man who had been nothing but kind to him and Pokey since they had ridden into town.

"It's just a name," Beck said as he willed himself to be calm. "It's a common name. A biblical name. An Old Testament name. Nothing wrong with it by itself."

He looked at the kindly liveryman as if he was seeing him for the first time. The look of concern in the man's eyes brought him back from the depths of his own mind. "You're a good man, aren't you, Abraham?"

"A good man?" The liveryman slowly let go of Beck's arm. "I try to be, I guess."

"Good Abraham," Beck decided. "That's what I'll call you. Good Abraham it is, if you don't mind. It'll make me feel better."

"Sure, Mr. Beck," Abraham said as he took a step back from the strange man. "Good Abraham is fine by me."

Beck smiled. He felt better now that he had made the separation in his mind. It allowed him to remember that he had other business to tend to. "Do you know a place around here where I could get a room, maybe a bath and a shave. Clean up a bit. I think I gave people a good fright when I rode in here looking like this and I don't want to do that." He patted the shirt pocket where he had the rest of the coins he had taken from Steve Hogan. "I have money, Good Abraham. I promise I can pay my way."

Good Abraham pointed to a place up the thoroughfare. "The Amenia Hotel is a good place. It's right over there on Main Street. They've got a barber, some hot towels, and everything. If that gold coin you gave me has any brothers in your pocket, you'll be able set yourself up there for a decent spell."

Beck looked at where the man was pointing and saw a gray building with a sign that read THE AMENIA HOTEL swinging on a wooden arm out front. "That the name of this town? Amenia?"

"Sure is," Good Abraham told him. "Means 'friendly' in Latin or some such language. At least, that's what they tell me. Don't have much use for Latin myself."

"I do," Beck said, "and they told you right." He

smiled at the liveryman. "Thanks, Good Abraham. You have more than lived up to your name."

But the liveryman grabbed Beck's arm before he walked away. "What about your tack? Your bedroll and your guns? What do you want me to do with them?"

Beck had not thought about that. Then he saw Good Abraham looking at the pistol on his hip. He realized it might not be a good idea for him to walk around a strange town looking like he did, lugging two rifles and a pistol. "Could I keep the rifles here with you until I find a place to stay? Like I said, I think I've given the town enough of a fright as it is. Going around armed to the teeth won't win me any friends."

Good Abraham looked relieved. "You're not as crazy as you look, Mr. Beck. You go on ahead and, if anyone at the hotel gives you any trouble on account of how you look, tell them I sent you. That ought to smooth down some of the rough edges on whoever's working the front desk. They've got plenty of rooms to let in that old place. Don't let them tell you any different on account of your appearance."

Beck waved his thanks and minded his step as he crossed the busy thoroughfare and wandered up toward the Amenia Hotel.

N OT A CHANCE, mister," boasted the old woman perched behind the hotel desk. The fleshy waddle under her chin jiggled as she voiced her indignation. "We don't cater to saddle tramps around here. Nor to drunks nor drovers, neither. I run a reputable establishment here, mister, and don't take in your kind. Never had and I pray to the good Lord above that I'll never have to."

"But I'm none of those things, ma'am." Beck was glad his voice sounded a little stronger now that he was back among people again. He had always thought of himself as a solitary person, perhaps a bit too standoffish. But his time alone in the desert had made him appreciate the value of the company of others.

"I'm just a traveler who wants a bath and a shave and a good meal," he explained. "I need a place to sleep for a while. I don't want to bother anyone. Good Abraham at the livery told me I could come here."

"Good Abraham?" The old woman bleated a curt laugh. "I've heard him called lots of things in my time, but never that."

Beck felt a spike of anger rise in him in defense of his new friend. "He's a good man, miss. He's been good to me when he had no earthly reason to be."

"Then you can go sleep in his loft. Probably just about all you can afford anyway and be grateful that's open to you."

Beck dug a gold coin out of his pocket and placed it on the cracked wood of the front desk. He watched the old woman's eyes flash with greed before they turned soft. He had seen that look many times before. Greed.

But she did not touch the coin right away. "Where did a man like you come by money like that?"

Since riding into town, Beck had felt some of his old senses return. He decided he probably should not be so free with his answers. Honesty was not always the best policy for a man in his situation.

He tried a smile. "It came from my pocket. Now you have it. In exchange, I'd like a room and a bath. And a shave. And something to eat." He looked down at the coin on the front desk. "Will that do?"

The old woman's hand shot out with surprising

speed as she covered the coin before swiping it. "Yes, sir. I believe it will. Ma Stanton is the name and I welcome you to the Amenia Hotel." She quickly opened the hotel ledger and turned it around for him to sign. "I'll just need your name and where you're from right here and we'll set you up in one of our best rooms. I'll have Lilly draw a bath for you, good and hot, with plenty of soap. I'll tell Henry, our barber, to be ready for you. Come down whenever you're ready. He's there till five, then works the front desk for me. He's my brother and owns a piece of the place along with me."

Beck had never ceased to be amazed by the effect a gold coin could have on some people. "You're very kind, Mrs. Stanton."

"I'm not married, son," she said, handing him a pen. "Been a bride of the Lord my whole life and don't aim to change that anytime soon."

Beck doubted anyone had ever been in competition with the Lord for her affections. He took the pen from her and was about to sign his name when something stopped him before the tip touched the paper. Should he sign his own name, or use an alias? Steve had come looking for him and, when he did not return, Bram and the rest of the Brickhouse Gang were likely to follow. They might be able to track him here to Amenia. Just because Bram Hogan had not been aware of the town before now did not mean he could not find it. If Beck signed his real name, they would know where he was for certain and maybe before he was ready for them to know.

He winced when he realized it was too late for such concerns. He had already told Good Abraham his name and, small towns being the rumor mills they were, everyone would want to know the name of the ragged stranger they had watched ride into town. If that name did not match the one in the book, it would raise even more suspicion—and more trouble—for him.

He should have given Good Abraham another name but had not been thinking clearly at the time. He knew he would have to be more guarded from here on in.

He put pen to paper and signed: *John Beck, Mother Lode, Arizona.*

Miss Stanton looked at the name and cheerfully handed him the key to his room. "Lilly will be up in a moment with plenty of water for your bath, Mr. Beck. You just make yourself right at home with us. We always aim to please here at the Amenia Hotel. You know, Amenia is Latin for 'friendly.'"

Beck took the key and forced a smile, hoping his charm could shine through his condition. "It certainly lives up to its name, Miss Stanton."

CHAPTER EIGHT

IT WAS THE best bath John Beck had ever had in his life. The hot water, just shy of scalding, felt good on his dry skin. He allowed himself to soak in the tub for a good long while before he even thought of reaching for the soap. The heat felt good to his bones and the dozens of tiny aches that had crept into his body began to slowly disappear.

When he finally began to use the soap, he found he had to scrub a good deal before getting truly clean. His skin, anyway. Some of the dirt and grime remained where no soap or water could ever reach.

The water in the tub was black when he finally decided to stand up and towel himself off.

He knew the towel was soft, but it was still abrasive against his tender skin. But the air that hit him as he patted himself dry made him feel like a new man. He had forgotten how a good bath and a soak could be so invigorating.

Back when he had lived in Chicago, he had made it a point to bathe every day. Mr. Pinkerton had insisted his operatives always looked clean and professional, even when they were in the field. "The men of this firm must uphold its reputation with as much zeal as they uphold the law," he remembered the Scotsman saying. "A clean body and clean mind is the least anyone can expect of us to do their bidding."

Beck had not thought of Allan Pinkerton in a long time and did not know why he thought of him now. He decided he would work hard not to think of him again. The past was where it belonged and there was too much trouble lying before him in the present to entertain memories of days gone by. He had been careless when first riding into town. He would not make that same mistake again. He had made a spectacle of himself. He had given his true name. He would do his best to keep to himself and heal during his stay in Amenia. The less people saw of him, the better for all concerned.

He cast the towel aside and set about putting on the same clothes he had worn into town. They were the only clothes he owned, so they would have to do for the time being. Lilly, the young Chinese maid, had offered to wash them while he took his bath, but he knew they would not be dry before his shave. And he desperately wanted that shave. A glance of himself in the long mirror in his room made him realize why the townspeople had looked at him so strangely.

Part of his success as a Pinkerton man had been his good looks, which had faded since his time in the desert. His face was tanned, almost blackened by the sun. His thick black hair was shaggy and his beard even more so. His brown eyes, normally attractive to the ladies, looked sunken into his skull and dark circles ringed them. His lips were wrinkled and chapped. His body had always been naturally well toned, but his weeks in the desert had given him an almost skeletal appearance.

Good Abraham had been right. He looked like Death himself. No wonder people looked at him with fear in their eyes. He hoped some time spent with the barber would help soften his look.

Beck did his best to pound the dust and dirt off his trousers and shirt into the tub before putting them back on. The bathwater had a thick layer of dirt floating on the surface. He hoped he would have enough money left over at the end of his stay in Amenia to tip Lilly nicely for her kindness to him. Taking care of a man who had spent so much time in the desert was no easy task and deserved a proper reward. He doubted Miss Stanton showed her much kindness.

Deciding it was probably best if he left his pistol in his room, he was about to put on his leather vest but stopped when he saw the ragged hole in the side of it. The exact spot where his bullet had struck Steve Hogan's chest. He had not taken the time to look over the garment properly back in the desert, but he looked at it closely now. The inside was caked with dried blood that had grown to a dull brown. He looked at his shirt in the mirror and saw dry patches of blood had formed there as well. But since he had no other clothes to wear, there was not much he could do about it. If the store was still open after his shave, he would buy himself some new clothes. Nothing as fancy as the vest, unfortunately, but there was nothing he could do about that now.

Beck shut the door behind him and locked it carefully. He stopped at the top of the stairs as he felt a bout of dizziness come over him. The lines of stairs sped away from him and he would have thrown up if he'd had anything in his stomach.

He gripped the banister tightly before he fell over, then pushed himself away until he stood flat against the door of his room.

A cold band of sweat broke out on his brow and he felt himself begin to pant. He shut his eyes tightly and tried to get ahold of himself.

"What's wrong with you?" he whispered to himself. "They're just stairs, for God's sake."

Then he heard a tiny female voice ask, "Mr. Beck? Are you all right?"

He forced his eyes open and saw Lilly, the Chinese maid who had drawn his bath for him. She was standing in the hall, holding folded towels against her chest. He judged her to be a girl, perhaps eighteen or so, and barely five feet tall, if that. She might have weighed ninety pounds had she been soaking wet, but the warm smile she offered him was powerful enough to bring him back to his senses.

"Yes, Lilly," he told her. "I'm fine. Just got a little dizzy for a moment. Guess it serves me right for not having eaten yet."

"You must eat, Mr. Beck," Lilly told him. "You cannot get better if you don't eat."

"It's as obvious as all that, is it?" Her words struck him. "I guess I look pretty awful, don't I?"

"Not awful. Just tired and ill." Her smile brightened and it made him feel a little better. "Some food and some sleep will make you feel much better in the morning."

Her smile was infectious and he felt himself smiling,

too. "Your English is remarkable. You learned very well."

She bowed slightly and said, "I was born here. So were my parents. They work for the railroad as cooks. They sent me here for a better life."

The memories of his days guarding those railroads flooded back to him and he braced himself against the wall once again.

She set the towels on the floor and came to his side. "Perhaps you should go back in your room and lie down, Mr. Beck. I can get a doctor to come see you if you wish."

His embarrassment outweighed his illness and he forced himself to rally. How ridiculous he felt, swooning like an old maid over a flight of stairs. "Thank you, Lilly, but I'll be fine after a shave and some food." He dared a glance at the stairs again and his stomach turned. "But would you be kind enough to help me down the stairs? I don't want to risk falling."

The fear that came into her eyes saddened him. "Miss Stanton would not like me to use the guest stairs, Mr. Beck. I am only allowed to use the back stairs to service the rooms."

He was relieved that was all that troubled her. "Then could you take me down that way?" Beck asked, his voice sounding more desperate than he would have liked. "I won't mind and I promise I won't say anything to Miss Stanton."

Lilly thought about it and reluctantly nodded. "But I won't be able to pick you up if you fall. You're too big."

Beck laughed. "I'm too big for any of this nonsense, but I have a feeling I won't fall if you're with me. You're strong enough for both of us."

She smiled and picked up her towels and beckoned

him to follow her. The narrow staircase was much easier to manage and did not make him feel nearly as dizzy. He followed her downstairs and, as he had predicted, he did not fall.

B ECK WALKED THROUGH the lobby toward the sign that pointed to the barbershop just past the front desk. He felt better being on the ground floor now and hoped his dizziness would soon pass.

He had half opened the door to the barbershop when he froze.

The place was no different than any other barbershop he had visited in his time. From Chicago to Mother Lode, they were all pretty much the same. The clean smell of liniment filled the air along with the smell of stale cigar smoke. Crisp white linens were stacked neatly on the counter along with an array of scissors and straight blades. The tools of the barber's trade.

At first glance, there was no reason why Beck should be alarmed, but the time he had spent in the desert had changed him. It had caused him to become aware of things, subtle things he had never noticed before. Things he could not necessarily see or hear but rather could feel. Like the approach of a coyote stalking him in the pitch-darkness. Or the sound of something scurrying among the rocks that might serve as food. Nothing he could really identify by sight or even sound, but more like a feeling before it fully presented itself to the rest of his senses.

He got that feeling now from the man who sat in the barbershop.

He was an unassuming man sitting alone next to the door. That was when Beck noticed the sign on the door had been flipped around so that the side that read OPEN was facing him.

That meant the CLOSED side was facing the street.

The stranger sitting by the door wore a slouch brown hat and tan vest. His boots were caked with mud—town mud—and were well worn. Beck's instincts might have caused him to bolt right then and there, but the gun on the man's right hip and the tin star pinned to the shirt beneath his vest kept him from doing so.

Beck swallowed deeply. "You're not Henry the barber, are you?"

"Can't say that I am," said the stranger, "but I've put in my time with a straight edge from time to time." He had hard blue eyes and deep wrinkles in his face that made him look older than he probably was. Beck judged him to be about forty, but he looked closer to fifty.

"Yes, sir," the stranger went on. "I reckon I've done just about everything a man could do to make a living in this world at one time or another. Mining. Ranching. Even drove steers clear up to Montana a time or two."

"And now you're a lawman," Beck added.

The stranger nodded. "For the time being. But out of all the things I've done in my life, I still miss barbering most of all. Some think it's boring, but it's honest, steady work. A man gets familiar with his customers being a barber. Gets to chatting with them. Lots of things a man can learn about a town by being a barber. Kind of like being a bartender in a way, except you don't have to put up with the drunks and the whores to earn a living." The stranger's eyes hardened as they looked Beck up and down. "You understand what I'm talking about, don't you, mister?"

Beck kept his hand on the doorknob. "Guess I do."

"Figured so." The man nodded toward the barber chair. "Old Henry is kind enough to let me keep my hand in with my barbering from time to time so as I don't lose the knack of it. A man never knows when he might need to take up another trade, does he?" He looked at Beck again. "Guess you know all about that, too."

Beck felt himself frowning. "Better than I'd like to."

"That's good." The man gestured toward Beck's face. "Seeing as how you're obviously in the market for a haircut and a shave and I'm sorely in need of some practice, what do you say we get to work on cleaning you up some?"

The stranger held out his right hand flat. It did not shake. Beck had not expected it would. "Still got the steadiest hands in town, I promise. Better than old Henry, even."

Not wanting to test how far he could push the lawman, Beck quietly closed the door behind him and took a seat in the barber chair.

The stranger took off his hat and set it on the coat hook on the wall above him. He went over to where the barber aprons were kept, snapped one open, and laid it across Beck's chest. He tied it behind Beck's neck and went to grab a comb and scissors. "Yes, sir. Some of the happiest times of my life were spent in barbershops just like this one. It feels good to help spiffy a man up. See him feel good about himself afterward. And, if you don't mind my saying so, mister, you look like a man in sore need of feeling better."

"I don't mind you saying it at all," Beck said, "though you don't have to call me mister. You already know my name."

The stranger looked at him in the mirror without

turning around. "You're certainly right about that, Mr. Beck. Mind if I call you John?"

"Don't mind at all, so long as I know your name," Beck said. "I always like to know the name of a man who puts a blade to my throat."

"George Hauser," the man told him. "And when I'm not keeping up with my barbering, I enforce the law in this town."

"Figured that by the star you've got pinned to your shirt," Beck said.

Hauser pulled the comb from the liniment and began combing Beck's knotted hair. "Not by the gun on my hip?"

"Lots of men carry guns," Beck said. "I've got one, too. Doesn't make me a lawman."

"But you kept it up in your room."

"Figured it was safer that way," Beck told him, "me being a stranger in town like I am. And I didn't like some of the strange looks I got from your people as I rode in here, not that I blame them any. I figured walking around unarmed might put them better at ease."

After a few attempts, Hauser finally got the comb to run through Beck's hair and set to doing the same to his beard. "Sorry about the cold reception you received, Mr. Beck. Amenia calls itself a friendly town, but I guess we're a might suspicious of strangers."

"Especially when they look like death warmed over," Beck said. "Like me."

"Oh, I wouldn't say you're as bad as all that," Hauser said as he began cutting tufts of hair from Beck's beard. "People can't always help what they look like. Even folks around here understand that."

"Then why the sudden interest in me? And what did I do to deserve getting a haircut from a sheriff?"

"Strangers always raise their attention, I guess. Especially when they ride into town caked in dust on a half-dead roan and have a gaping hole in the side of their vest," Hauser said as he snipped away. "And when they pay for livery and hotel in gold, well, that'll just flat-out arouse the suspicion of some folks."

Beck had wondered how long it would take for word about him to spread about town. Now he had his answer. "That explains it."

"Even that might be shrugged off, but old Abraham down at the livery said he was flat-out spooked by you. He told me you were acting mighty peculiar. Said you insisted on calling him 'Good Abraham' for some reason."

Beck drew in a deep breath. That damnable name again. "It's a good reason, Hauser. Believe me."

"I'm sure it is. But, with all of that in mind, you can't hold it against people if it sets their tongues to wagging, can you?"

"No, I suppose I can't."

"And you can't blame me for having to look into it."

Beck closed his eyes and let out the breath he had been holding. It was clear that Hauser was only doing what they paid him to do. "Yeah. I guess I can't."

Hauser seemed to be content with the silence that had settled over them as he went about cutting away the thickest parts of Beck's beard.

"You're not in trouble, Mr. Beck," the sheriff said, "at least not as far as I'm concerned. I've got a wall full of wanted posters in my office and more in my desk. You don't match the description on any of them. Believe me, I checked before I came over here. So, you can ignore my questions if you want to, but you'll be doing us both a favor if you tell me your story."

Beck doubted he had the energy to sit up straight, much less tell anyone his story. "And if I don't?"

Hauser stopped cutting for a moment and looked at him in the mirror. "Let's just say I'd be obliged if you did. Because if you don't, it'll be tougher going for both of us. I'm not threatening you, son. I'm just telling you the way it is." He pointed the comb at his reflection. "And something tells me you understand what it feels like to be a man in my position."

Beck studied Hauser's reflection and sensed no malice in him. Not in his tone of voice nor in his demeanor. He decided he already had enough enemies in this world. He saw no reason why he should count Sheriff George Hauser among them.

"You ever hear of me before?" Beck asked. "About me being a lawman, too?"

Hauser went back to cutting. "Can't say as I have, though your name does sound familiar, which is why I wanted to come over here and get a look at you for myself. But when I saw you walk in here, I figured you'd done some law work in your time."

Beck had been afraid of that. "What gave it away?"

"Just a feeling I got, same as the one you got when you saw me sitting in here."

Beck was beginning to like Hauser. "Well, your instincts are right, Sheriff. I'm a lawman, or at least I used to be."

"Glad to see I haven't lost my touch." Hauser grinned. "The ledger at the front desk says you're from Mother Lode. That true?"

"I haven't told a lie since I came to town," Beck said. "Ever hear of it?"

"Some. A mining town about a day's ride from here."

Beck shoved his hands away from him before he realized he had done it. "A day? That's all?"

Hauser did not move. "No more than that. Why?" He studied Beck closely. "You mean you didn't know that already? How'd you get here?"

Beck allowed himself to sink back in the barber's chair. He had not given any thought to how far away he might have been from Mother Lode. Going back there had never factored into his thinking. Not much had. Distance had not counted for much in his wanderings in the desert. Neither had time.

"Sorry for stopping you," Beck said. "Just took me off guard is all."

Hauser shrugged it off and went back to cutting. "Not much to Mother Lode from what I remember. No offense intended."

"None taken," Beck said. "I guess there's not much to it, come to think of it. Maybe that's why I liked it so much."

"Guess they must have liked you, too, seeing as how they went and made you their sheriff."

"Town marshal," Beck said. "And I liked them, too."

"Sounds like a fine, cozy setup for all involved." Hauser finished trimming Beck's beard as close as he could with the scissors and went to get the shaving cream and the brush. "A lawman dreams of having it so easy. Why'd you leave?"

Beck felt his throat close in. He had to swallow hard a couple of times before it opened enough for him to dare to speak. "I didn't have a choice. Or maybe I didn't have the guts to make the choice myself. I guess I let others make it for me."

Hauser glanced at him as he whipped the shaving

cream in a bowl with the brush. "Got voted out, did you?" He sighed. "Had that happen to me a couple of times. It's not a good feeling, is it?"

"Not voted out," Beck admitted. "Ridden out of town on a rail. Used my own rifle to do it, too." The memory of Steve Hogan gasping in the sand kept him from tearing up. "I made them regret it. One of them, anyway."

"Ridden out?" Hauser stopped with the shaving cream and his eyes grew hard as he looked at Beck in the mirror. Beck felt anger rise in the sheriff, but not directed at him. "Who? Who did that to you?"

"Group calling themselves the Brickhouse Gang are the ones who did it," Beck said. He intoned their names like the way the faithful rattle off their evening prayers. "Abraham Hogan. Steve Hogan. A Mexican named Laredo. A giant they call Pearson and a flea-bitten mongrel named Lem. They tied my hands to my Sharps and kicked me out into the desert. I don't remember how long ago it was, but I'll never forget what happened. I won't soon forget the sound of them laughing at me when they did it, either. Sent me off into the desert with nothing but my boots. Even cut the flap off my johns before they sent me on my way."

"Good Christ, Beck." Hauser set the mixing bowl on the counter before he dropped it. "How'd you survive? How'd you get free?"

"I'm not sure I survived," Beck admitted. "Not all of me, anyway. I found a rock while I was wandering, scraped the rope until my hands got free, then holed up in a cave. Lived on just about anything you can find in a cave. Spiders. Snakes. Lizards. Not much, but enough to keep me alive. A trickle of water in the back of the cave gave me the water I needed. I wouldn't call it living, but at least I didn't die."

"But how'd you get the horse?" Hauser wasn't a lawman just then, but a man eager to know what had happened. "How'd you get here?"

Beck had not thought much about it until that moment. It had all been a series of events to him, one leading to another until he had spotted Amenia on the horizon. "Steve Hogan came looking for my remains. He'd been sweet on that Sharps rifle I told you about. He rode out to collect it. Guess he wasn't counting on me still being alive. Can't say as I blame him. He must've tracked me to the cave I was living in. When I saw him, I used the one bullet they left me and I brought him down." He looked at Hauser. "That explains the big hole your people saw in my vest."

Hauser closed his eyes. "Good God."

Beck felt a tear run down his cheek in spite of himself but did not wipe it away. He did not have the strength. "I took his clothes and horse, left him where I found him, and me and Pokey headed away from there. We just kept putting one foot in front of the other until we spotted this place and came here."

"Pokey?" Hauser asked. "Who the hell is Pokey."

"My horse," Beck told him. "My friend. At least I think his name is Pokey. Something told me that was his name, though I don't know for certain. Maybe he told me in his own way." Another tear ran down his face. "He's been a good friend to me, Sheriff. He kept me alive. Brought me here. I hope Good Abraham is good to him. I owe him everything."

Hauser put a hand on Beck's shoulder. "Good God, John. It's a miracle you're alive. After what you've been though. I had no idea. Don't know if I could have survived it myself."

"So that's where I got the horse and the clothes and

the money, too. About a hundred dollars in gold coin. Probably stolen from Mother Lode and half a dozen other places. I know it's stolen and it's wrong to spend it, but it's all I've got."

Hauser cleared his throat and picked up his mixing bowl again. "Think these Brickhouse boys are still in Mother Lode?"

Beck squeezed his eyes shut to clear his remaining tears. "I don't know. Probably. The townspeople won't fight them off. They relied on me to do their fighting for them, as little as it was. I was drunk when the gang rode into town. Guess I made it easier for them to do this to me as a result."

"Five against one ain't likely odds, Beck. Not for anyone, especially against the bunch you've just described."

"Five against none is even worse odds," Beck said. "I might've at least put a dent in them if I hadn't been feeling sorry for myself when they showed up. Maybe I'd be dead, but they would've known they'd been in a fight. I owed the town that much. I owed Dulce that. More than that."

Hauser began to vigorously dab the thick shaving cream on Beck's face. "I'll have none of that kind of talk in my town, Marshal. You saw what feeling sorry for yourself got you once. No need to indulge in that sort of nonsense now."

Beck refused to allow his emotions to come to the surface again. "Dulce's a beautiful, kind woman, Hauser. She's had a tough life. Had a husband who beat her. She doesn't deserve what those animals are probably putting her through right now."

"They're not animals, John. An animal acts because it's scared or hungry or both. This Brickhouse

Gang of yours are men, plain and simple. Only men can do something like they did to you. And there's not a man or woman alive in this part of the world that doesn't know some manner of suffering. I've had my share and the Lord knows you've had plenty, too. If this Dulce gal is tough enough to make a life out here, then she'll be tough enough to outlast anything that bunch of cowards can throw her way."

"Maybe," Beck said. "If she's still alive."

"Whether she is or she ain't is none of your doing." Hauser grabbed the straight blade and sharpened it to and fro on the leather strap on the barber's chair. "But as soon as we're done cleaning you up in here, I'm sending a wire to the U.S. marshal's office. See if we can't get some law up there to clear those bastards out of Mother Lode once and for all time. Hell, I'll call in the army if I have to. Those boys still owe me a couple of favors after all the scouting I've done for them the past couple of years. We'll get you your justice, Beck. That I promise you. Even if you and me have to ride up there ourselves, we'll get it."

Justice. Beck turned the word over in his mind. Justice. It had meant something to him once. When he had first read for the law back in Chicago and again when he had joined up with the Pinkertons. It had meant law and order to him then. It had meant civilization. A right to live as one pleased under the protection of a higher authority.

But justice did not mean breaking strikes at the slaughterhouses or at the mines. It did not mean shooting down fleeing railroad workers desperate to escape the foreman's whip. It did not mean tracking down unhappy wives who had fled from their rich husbands or bringing back heiresses to unhappy homes.

But that was what justice had come to mean for John Beck, which was what had sent him as far away from it as possible, to a little town in the middle of the Arizona Territory called Mother Lode. A town that had given him solace. A town he had not been able to defend when the time had come.

Perhaps that was what burned inside of him hottest of all. The shame of their disappointment. The shame Dulce was enduring now because of his weakness.

He had not realized he had closed his eyes until Hauser shook him. "I'm going to begin shaving you now, John. You ready?"

Beck nodded. He'd had a sharp blade at his throat for weeks now. He figured one more time would not make much of a difference.

CHAPTER NINE

JUAN CARLOS PADRÓN—the man they had taken to calling Laredo—had no trouble following Steve Hogan's trail in the desert. The cocky gringo left a trail even a blind man could follow. The scant desert winds had obscured much of his horse's hoofprints, but not enough to be hidden from Padrón's practiced eye.

An eye the ragged Brickhouse Gang had never fully appreciated.

Padrón had allowed them to call him Laredo only because that was the town where he had first fallen in with the gang of cutthroats and thieves. He had never seen any reason to tell them his real name, for he doubted it would have meant anything to them. Little made much difference to such men.

Besides, he was still a wanted man in his native Mexico. His head would bring a *federale* a fine reward indeed. He decided it best to keep his true identity hidden from Bram Hogan and the others. Bram especially. He was a mean, stupid man, and as long as he thought Padrón just another Mexican bandit, all the better for him.

If Bram had ever seen him as a threat, Padrón would have cut his throat one night as he slept. Instead, he had decided to play it as humble as he could while he bided his time. He sought to gauge the measure of these men before he decided whether or not to take over the gang for his own or ride off one night and leave them.

In the six months or so since he had joined up with Hogan and his men, he'd decided the gang was not worth running. At each town they raided, he hoped other, more reliable men might join their ranks, but none ever did. Hogan killed anyone who might have been an ally, preferring to loot their bodies for whatever was in their pockets and saddlebags instead of adding more mouths to feed.

Bram was a shortsighted, stupid man whose only quality was his capacity for bloodshed. In that—and in that alone—he rivaled even Juan Carlos Padrón.

He had decided he would break away from the gang once they left Mother Lode. Bram Hogan had grown soft with drink and reminiscing about old glory. Padrón knew it was only a matter of time before they bled the tiny town dry. The miners were more judicious with their money and had brought their gold with them when they left the town. It would not be long before word got out about the gang's presence in the mining town and others came to challenge Hogan. If not a rival gang, then a posse of lawmen or perhaps even the army. The Brickhouse Gang deserved the reputation they had earned for cruelty, but they would be no match against a group determined to wipe them out of town. Padrón intended on being long gone before that happened.

But not yet.

He had decided to track down Steve Hogan for reasons of his own. He was curious to see what had happened to Bram's younger brother. Steve had all of Bram's weaknesses, only more so. He was a cheap imitation of his brother, mimicking Bram's every move until they became second nature to him. The young bully would have been killed many times over had it not been for Bram saving his hide.

No, Padrón was not searching for Hogan to ease Bram's mind. He was searching for him because he was bound by a deep curiosity. He wondered if it was possible, even remotely possible, that John Beck might have survived his banishment into the desert and taken revenge.

Padrón had voted to shoot the lawman when they had first gotten to Mother Lode and be done with it. Mercy had nothing to do with his decision. Padrón had wanted to make an example of him by gut-shooting him in the middle of the street and leaving him there to die. His pain would be a stake of fear driven deep into the hearts of all who heard the telling of it. No one would dare stand up to the gang then.

But Bram Hogan's flair for the dramatic had caused them to send Beck out into the wilderness alone. They mocked him, stripped him of his dignity, and left him only a single bullet he could never use.

They had stripped him of his pride in front of the people he loved. They had sent him away as a fool with nothing but his rage to sustain him.

Padrón knew firsthand how rage could keep a man

alive for much longer than nature allowed. He knew a man could live on hate and hate alone well after his body had decided to die. The mind was a powerful weapon. His mother had taught him that. She had taught him that faith had moved mountains. That faith had built his father's ranch out of nothing and had given them the wealth he had enjoyed as a boy.

It had been the rejection of that faith that had caused his father to drive him from the ranch once Juan Carlos had become a man with a mind and appetites of his own. Appetites for women his father found revolting. Padrón, like Beck, had been turned out into the world with nothing except the hate in his heart to keep him warm at night.

Yes, hate was a powerful emotion that could drive a man further than nature and common sense allowed. It had done so for Juan Carlos Padrón. And part of him wanted to know if it had done the same for John Beck.

As he read the tracks, Padrón found that Steve Hogan had taken a wandering trail through the desert in search of Beck's long rifle. He anticipated where the boy would ride next, cutting off more than a day or so of the gringo's wandering. It had taken him longer than it should have to find the outcropping of rocks that sat nestled in the middle of the desert.

But perhaps Steve Hogan had not wandered after all. Perhaps he had been following the confused trail of a man staggering through the desert with his hands lashed to a rifle, dying from thirst. Padrón was not trailing such a man.

He was tracking where such a man could go.

It was then that he discovered John Beck had lived much longer than he should have. For Hogan's track disappeared off into the distance, only to come back again to the rocks.

The buzzards circling high overhead told him something had died out there, just beyond the rocks.

Padrón drew his Winchester from the scabbard and brought his horse to a slow, steady trot toward the spot where the scavengers were circling.

When he reached the spot, he saw a cluster of the birds perched atop the body of a man. A single shot from his rifle sent them scattering, but only a few yards away from their feast. He put the spurs to his horse, knowing they would only stay away from the body for so long.

Padrón reined up just short of the body. The smell of death had made his horse skittish. He climbed down from the saddle and led the horse toward the body. When the horse would walk no farther, he wrapped its reins around one of its legs, hobbling it as best he could in the arid wasteland.

Padrón eyed the rocks as he approached the body. The birds had dined well. Its face already gone. Its swollen belly picked clean down to the reddish bone. It was a sight that would have turned the stomach of another man, but Padrón was no stranger to such things.

There was not enough left of the body to tell him how the man had died, but it was clear to Padrón that this man was not John Beck. Beck had stood almost six feet tall, as near as Padrón could remember. Perhaps a bit more. Despite there being little left to identify this man, the corpse was of a much shorter man by several inches. The few tufts of blond hair that remained on the ravaged skull told him that this man could only have been Steve Hogan.

That meant John Beck was still alive. Or at least he

had been when Steve Hogan had ridden into his path in search of the Sharps rifle.

The body may have been defiled, but it was clear that it had been stripped of all of its clothing. The manure near the body told him Hogan's horse had been here for some time before being led away. The few tracks that were left on the desert floor clearly showed it had moved off under a human's guidance. The depth of the tracks told him it had left this place with a rider on its back.

Padrón looked to the rocks again with a more careful eye. It would have taken a good shot to bring down Steve Hogan from such a distance, but not for a man as skilled with a Sharps rifle as Beck was said to be.

Leaving his horse where it was, Padrón decided to climb up into the rocks to see this sight for himself. He had to know if Beck might still be up there or if he had since moved on. A man left to his own devices in the desert could not always be counted on to act in his own best interests. The desert had a seductive power all its own.

Padrón climbed the rocks and found a cave that might be suitable for a man to live. He crouched among the rocks and fired into the opening, waiting to hear if anyone reacted to the shot. All he heard was the low howl of the desert wind in his ears.

Deciding it was as safe as it could be, Padrón scrambled up the rest of the rocks and entered the cave.

The stench was so strong, it forced him backward and made him retch. He steeled himself for another try, holding his arm across his nose and mouth to filter the smell.

What he found when he got inside was a glimpse of hell.

Countless carcasses of dead tarantulas were piled in one corner of the hovel. The remains of snakes and lizards were piled in another. The foulness that had caused his eyes to water was the same he had smelled in outhouses and latrines. Whoever had lived here had rarely ventured outside. He had grown accustomed to these squalid conditions because they were the only conditions left to him.

This had been the place of a man who had chosen to never give up. He had decided to live at all costs, even if it meant he had to become a beast.

And when that damned fool Hogan had wandered into his path, John Beck did what any beast would do. He struck, undoubtedly bringing down Hogan with the single bullet Bram had been so foolish as to allow him. Beck had used the instruments of his own humiliation to gain his revenge.

No, Padrón decided as he stepped out of the cave. Not just revenge. His survival.

Padrón made his way carefully back down to the rocks where his horse waited for him. The buzzards had returned and had begun to pay attention to his hobbled animal. One had even briefly alighted on his saddle, causing the horse to buck and whinny. Knowing he would be in the same position as Beck had been in if the horse was attacked, Padrón shot the bird, which caused the other birds to scatter. He quickly got to his horse, untied the reins from its leg, and climbed back into the saddle.

Padrón gave the corpse of Steve Hogan one final look before moving his horse away, following the trail of John Beck wherever it led.

He had promised Bram Hogan to return no matter what he had found, but now Padrón had no intention of keeping that promise. And, had he been there, he imagined Hogan would not expect him to. For any man who had the will to live in such a manner for so long and strike out at the first chance afforded him was a most dangerous man indeed.

The kind of man who would first heal his body for as long as he could until the memory of his indignity began to rise. The same spirit that had allowed him to live despite all odds would cause him to come one day to seek his revenge. Under other circumstances, Juan Carlos Padrón would have admired such a man. He might have even been proud to know such a man and seek his friendship.

But as Padrón had played a role in his humiliation, he could not spare sentiment of admiration. For John Beck would kill every member of the Brickhouse Gang, even if he had to spend the rest of his life doing it.

Juan Carlos Padrón had already spent too much of his life looking over his shoulder.

He knew he would have to find John Beck. And he would have to kill him when he did.

CHAPTER TEN

S HERIFF HAUSER STOOD in front of the livery with
Abraham. Good Abraham, as Beck had taken to
calling him.

Both of them were trying not to listen to John Beck's
conversation with the horse he called Pokey. Hauser
did not know the stranger all that well, but he still felt
as if he was intruding.

"They look like they're treating you just fine, Pokey,"
Hauser heard Beck say to the animal. "You're getting
everything you need, aren't you? People are so nice in
this town, aren't they? Nicer than the Hogans ever were,
that's for certain. Nicer than most of the people in
Mother Lode, truth be told. In the store, the nice man
fixed me up with these new clothes. I paid for them, of
course, but he threw in some extras like fresh ammunition for the pistol and rifle. And this good, sharp knife
I've got right here on my belt. Sheriff Hauser says it's
not a good idea for me to walk around with a gun on

my hip, but I can't hardly go around unarmed, either. The knife was his idea. He's a nice man, Pokey. I'll make sure you meet him soon."

The liveryman bit through the hay straw he'd been chewing and spat it out. "Your new friend in there is a might touched in the head, Sheriff."

Hauser was glad there was something, anything else to listen to other than a grown man talking to a horse. "He certainly is, Abraham. But you would be, too, if you'd seen the troubles he has." He ran his boot in a semicircle along the parched ground outside the livery. "Shame. I think he was a top man at one time, at least as far as I can tell."

Abraham looked up at the sheriff. "How do you know?"

Hauser shrugged. "Can't put my finger on it, but a man in my line of work gets to learn how to read people. Like the way he acted when I first met him in the barbershop just now. He didn't get angry or go for his gun. Didn't run out of there like I thought he might, either. He just took it all in, listened to what I told him, and decided to stay anyway."

"I've seen what you do to them when they run," Abraham said. "Him staying put just means he's not a fool."

"Means more than that," Hauser said. He didn't know why he felt so defensive about the younger stranger all of a sudden. "He'd never heard of me before. He acted on what he saw and heard right then and there. That's how I know he must've been a top hand at one point. He's educated, too. I can tell that by the words he uses and the way he speaks. He's got an easy way about him, too. Like how he charmed old Bob in the store before we came over here. Why, he even got that nasty old buzzard to gift him a knife he was admiring in that display case of Bob's."

Abraham would have spat out the straw if he had not already done so. "Old Bob did that? You sure?"

The sheriff laughed. "I wouldn't have believed it, either, if I hadn't seen it with my own two eyes. But it happened just like I told you it did. Gave it to Mr. Beck like it was Christmas morning. And with his compliments, too."

"His compliments?" Abraham repeated. "Mr. Beck must've made quite an impression."

Hauser wished Abraham had been there to see it for himself. Bob Harley was not just a cantankerous old man. He was the nastiest, meanest, most ornery person George Hauser had ever met. He never had a good word to say about anyone or anything in Amenia or anywhere else. Even the local gossips and busybodies kept their mouths shut in his store out of fear that he'd butt into their conversation and ruin their day with his negative comments. People only went to his store because there was no other place in town to get all the goods they needed under one roof.

Old Bob was the kind of man who preferred to keep his mouth shut if given the option but was not afraid to share his opinion on a matter should the opportunity present itself.

That was why Hauser had hesitated to bring Beck over to the general store. He figured the stranger was in too fragile a state to be able to withstand a session with Bob Harley. But the younger man had surprised him by walking in the place as easily as if he had been there a hundred times.

"You Mr. Harley?" he remembered Beck asking.

"It depends on who's asking and why," Harley had

told him before he got a good look at Beck's filthy clothes and hat. They looked even worse now that his hair was shorter and his beard was gone. "My God, son. What happened to you?"

Hauser remembered Beck's smile as he took a good look at himself in the nearest mirror in the store. "Guess I'm a pretty sorry sight at that. But that's why I'm here, Mr. Harley. My name's John Beck and I'm in the market for a new set of clothes."

Hauser remembered cringing when Beck actually extended his hand across the counter toward Old Bob, fearing the storekeeper might just bite it off.

But there must have been a sincerity about this new customer that reached the storekeeper, for Bob Harley actually shook the man's hand. He even smiled. "We'll get you fixed up in no time, Mr. Beck."

What followed was about the most astounding thirty minutes Hauser had spent since he had come to Amenia over a decade before. Old Bob was as gentle as a lamb with Beck as he took him around the store, showing him the full range of clothes and other goods he had to offer.

An hour before, Beck had been a scared, broken man who looked like a scarecrow that'd had all the stuffing knocked out of it. Now he was being given a guided tour of the general store by the meanest man in the territory.

By the time all was said and done, Beck had himself twenty dollars' worth of new clothes, including a new black hat and a knife thrown in.

Hauser laughed at the recent memory of it. "I think Old Bob even smiled once or twice, come to think of it."

"That's a bad omen." Abraham eased the sheriff out of the thoroughfare. "Best get clear of the street, Mr. Hauser, because the Four Horsemen of the end times must be coming this way."

"I think there's more Lazarus than Revelation where our Mr. Beck is concerned," Hauser told him. "That man has got a knack with people, which is another reason why I'd wager he was a pretty fair lawman before he lost his way."

"The way he's talking to that horse in there, I'd say he's lost more than his way," Abraham admitted. "He's lost his damned mind."

"I'm afraid I lost more than that, Good Abraham." Both men jumped when John Beck spoke.

"Best not go sneaking up on people like that," Hauser said. His heart was pounding something awful. "Might get yourself hurt."

"I've been about as hurt as a man can be and I'm still here." Beck gestured toward the bundle wrapped in brown paper he was holding. "But I'm feeling much better now, especially that I have new clothes to wear and good people like you around me. Pokey appreciates it, too. He's thankful for everything you've done for him, Good Abraham."

The liveryman looked at Beck. "He tell you that?"

"Not in so many words, but in his own way." Beck smiled. "Don't worry. I'm not crazy enough to think he really talks. I don't talk to him because I think he understands me. I talk to him because it makes me feel better for some reason. That's all."

Hauser, for one, was glad to hear him say that. He had known plenty of cowboys who had gotten close to their horses. A few had even gone as far as naming them. But he could not think of a man who spoke to one at length the way Beck did. At least, none that were in their right mind, anyway.

Beck surprised him by asking, "Do you think I could take my guns back to the hotel with me, Sheriff? The rifles, I mean. I don't think it's right to ask Good Abraham to keep an eye on them any longer than he already has. And I don't want someone thinking they can steal them when he's not looking."

Hauser caught the uneasy look on Abraham's face at the thought of Beck walking around armed. The sheriff was contemplating a way to talk Beck out of it when Abraham came up with the solution.

The liveryman pointed at the bundle under Beck's arm. "I'd say it looks like you've already got your hands full, Mr. Beck. You don't want to be carrying around those heavy rifles, especially in your weak condition. How about you let me gather them up and bring them over to you at your hotel. They can keep them locked up for you where they'll be safe until you're ready to fetch them tomorrow after you've had a chance to rest some. Get back your strength and all."

Hauser was glad Beck seemed to like the idea. "You're a very thoughtful man, Good Abraham. I think you're right. I probably should get some rest."

Hauser added, "Some food couldn't hurt, either. You can't get your strength back on an empty stomach."

"Food." Hauser watched Beck's eyes get that far-off look again. It was the same expression he'd had back at the barbershop when he was talking about his time in the desert. It wasn't the expression alone that got to him. It was the way Beck's entire being changed, as if his soul had been hollowed out of him, leaving nothing but an empty man before him. There was something haunting about it that made the hairs on Hauser's neck stand up. An almost animal quality no man should ever have.

"It's funny," Beck said. "I've gone so long without thinking about food that I'm not even hungry." He looked at Hauser. The hollow look was still there. "I guess that might sound crazy to you, but it got so I couldn't think about food back in the desert. I didn't dare let myself think I was hungry, even though I was starving. I ate when the chance came along. I'd see it, kill it, and eat it. Simple as that."

Hauser watched something resembling humanity come back to Beck's eyes. "I didn't think I'd ever be in a town again, much less one that had a restaurant. Know any good places to eat around here, Sheriff?"

"The best place in town just happens to be in your hotel." Hauser gently took Beck by the arm and began to guide him in that direction. "What do you say we head over there for an early supper? Then, once you're done, you can head upstairs and take a nice long rest. Sleep as long as you like. I'll see to it that no one bothers you."

"Yes," Beck said. He offered no resistance as Hauser led him back to the hotel. "That sounds awfully nice indeed."

Hauser looked at Abraham and gestured for him to head back to the livery. He did not want to leave Beck alone, as he was not sure what the man might do or where he might go. In his state, he could wander back out into the desert again and that would not do.

The sheriff glanced down at the knife in the scabbard on the back of Beck's belt. Old Bob was a fool for giving Beck a Bowie knife, especially when it was clear to anyone with sense that Beck wasn't in his right mind.

Hauser was thinking about asking Beck for it when the stranger said, "Life sure is funny, Sheriff."

He was glad Beck was talking again. It meant he was not lost in whatever netherworld that was left of his mind. He had seen white captives act this way after time spent with the Comanche. Women, mostly, as the Comanche often killed the men and desecrated their bodies. Women were kept and used until they thought they had used them enough and got rid of them one way or another. Or had them taken away from them by men who rode after them and hunted them down for taking white captives.

Men like George Hauser.

Now Hauser cursed himself for allowing his mind to wander. He wondered if whatever brain sickness Beck had might be catching. "How's life funny, John?"

"On account of, one day, I was in a town full of friends, then kicked out into the desert the next. Yesterday, I was roaming the desert, not knowing where my next meal would come slithering by, and today I'm back in a town full of friends. With you and Good Abraham and Mr. Harley, I mean."

Beck struggled with his footing on the first step up to the boardwalk, but Hauser was glad he regained his balance on the second and third steps.

"Yes, sir," Beck went on. "No telling what life will throw at you from one day to the next, is there, Sheriff?"

Hauser decided he would have to find a way to get Beck to hand over the knife at some point during the course of their meal. Leaving him alone with it just did not make sense. He would also find a way to get his pistol out of his room and keep it locked up in the office of the hotel, along with Beck's rifles.

Beck surprised Hauser by cutting loose with a

clipped laugh. "Listen to me, Sheriff. Guess my time in the desert has made me something of a philosopher. Ought to be wearing sackcloth and ashes instead of new clothes like these."

It was these sparks of lucidity that made Hauser believe that Beck would be just fine with a little time and rest. "Let it all out, John. It doesn't bother me any."

WHEN THEY GOT to the Amenia Hotel, George Hauser was disturbed to hear a loud ruckus coming from the saloon in the back. Someone was abusing the piano something awful while voices thick with drink were raised in some manner of song. A fair amount of hooting and yelling was sprinkled in among the occasional sounds of a glass breaking.

Ma Stanton, at her post at the front desk, did not seem to like it, either. "I'm sure glad you're here, Sheriff. We've got ourselves some ruffians in the back causing all kinds of bother."

Hauser forgot all about Beck for a moment and concentrated on the order he was paid to keep. "What seems to be the trouble, Ma?"

"A group of no-good miners is the trouble, Sheriff," she told him. "About ten of them came in the saloon the back way just after you left with that scruffy Beck fellow. If they had tried to come in the front like civilized folks, I never would have let them in, I assure you."

Hauser had no doubt that Ma Stanton would have tried to stop them. But he had learned the hard way that the most dangerous place in the world was between a mining man and his whiskey, especially after a long time spent deep underground hitting rocks.

The sound of more glass breaking told him things were already rowdy and well on their way to getting dangerous. "Sounds like they didn't waste much time getting drunk."

"I usually don't mind them kicking up their heels on account of them not being tight with their money," Ma admitted, "but I can't have them starting to break things that take a long time to replace. Glassware ain't cheap, Sheriff, and it takes time to come out here from all the way back east. I don't run that kind of place and I don't want people thinking I do, either. Word like that can ruin my hotel's reputation and then where would I be? Why, at my age, what—"

Hauser held up a hand to silence her. "Do you hear that?"

She squinted at the sheriff. "Hear what? I don't hear a thing."

"That's what I mean," Hauser said. "It got awfully quiet all of a sudden."

Ma's eyes widened. "Nothing good can happen when miners and toddlers get quiet."

Then Hauser remembered John Beck and looked around the lobby for him. The brown paper bundle of clothing Beck had been carrying was now on the stairs. And although Beck was nowhere in sight, he had a pretty good idea of where to find him.

Hauser pulled the Colt from the holster on his hip and ran down the hallway toward the sudden eerie silence of the saloon.

CHAPTER ELEVEN

L
ET HER GO," Hauser heard Beck say as he ran down the hall to the saloon. "Let her go right now."

Hauser slid to a stop just short of running into one of the men by the door to the saloon. But he had to push the man out of the way in order to see what was happening inside.

Hauser's blood went cold when he saw one of Ma Stanton's Chinese maids—the one who called herself Lilly—squirming on the lap of a miner who had a Bowie knife at his throat.

Hauser did not recognize the miner, but the man holding the knife was John Beck.

The rest of the men in the saloon had cleared a jagged circle around Beck and the man in the chair and Lilly.

The hat and skin and clothes of the man being held at knifepoint still bore the alkaline dust of the copper mines nearby. And from the look of them, every other man in the saloon was also a miner.

Hauser took that as a stroke of good luck for Beck, as miners were less apt to go around heeled. But they were a rougher bunch than cowboys. They were slower to anger, but more likely to stick together in a fight. He imagined that working all those long hours together down in the dark danger of a copper mine tended to make men loyal to one another.

But just because most of the men were not toting pistols did not mean they were any less dangerous. These men fought with their fists and they fought hard. And the only thing keeping them from rushing Beck right now was the knife blade he was holding to their friend's throat. The Bowie knife was sharp enough to slice him wide open if Beck so much as twitched.

Hauser saw only one way to make sure no one got hurt in any of this, least of all poor Lilly. Beck had probably gotten himself into this mess to save her. She was the only one who'd had no say in this whatsoever.

"John," Hauser called out as he eased his way through the crowd of miners so Beck could see it was him.

Lilly squirmed on the lap of the miner in the chair as he held her arm behind her back. He glared up at Beck, who pressed the tip of the knife against his throat.

"John," Hauser said again. "It's George Hauser. Put the knife down right now before somebody gets hurt."

But Beck did not move a muscle. "Not until he turns Lilly loose."

"And I ain't doing that," the miner said, "until this sorry son of a bitch sets that knife down like I told him to. This bastard's a crazy man, Sheriff."

"I've heard just about enough talk from both of you," Hauser said. "I'm here now. I'm the law, so that means I'm in charge. Both of you do as I tell you before someone gets themselves hurt."

The miner did not let go of Lilly. "Who are you kidding, Sheriff? This boy's in no shape to fight. Hell, he looks nearer to death than to living. I think a good wind might knock him flat."

"You might be right about that, mister." Beck pressed the tip of the blade harder against the miner's neck, drawing a thin line of blood. "Good thing my knife's plenty sharp."

The sight of blood on the miner's neck sent a grumble through the miners watching the spectacle unfold.

Hauser knew if he did not act fast, someone would die, though at that moment he would not lay odds on who that might be.

He decided his best shot at breaking the stalemate would be appealing to Beck. "If you don't set down the knife, I can't be sure either of us will make it out of here alive, John."

"I don't need you or anyone else to guarantee a damned thing to me." Hauser noticed Beck now had that same faraway look he'd seen on the way over to the hotel. "He lets her go, I'll lower the knife. Let them come if they want to come. I got used to the idea of dying a while ago."

Hauser could feel the situation was beginning to slip even further away from him than it already had. He was starting to feel desperate, for he knew he would not be able to hold the rest of the miners at bay for much longer. "Damn it, Beck. You've been through too much to die like this. Let him go and let's be done with it. I'll shoot him if he doesn't let Lilly go."

"Like hell you will," said one of the miners behind him.

"He'll let go of her now," Beck insisted. "Lilly's no dance hall girl and she doesn't need anyone pawing her, especially this dusty son of a bitch right here."

The miners grumbled again and Hauser could feel their resolve to stay out of it was a dam about to give way.

He knew if he didn't get Beck out of there soon, they would both be dead.

Hauser spoke to the miner. "Looks like you'll have to go first, mister. Same rules apply for you. Let the girl go. I'll guarantee your safety. I'll shoot Beck if he doesn't set the knife down."

"This man," the miner repeated. "What was it you called him? Beck?"

Hauser could almost see the name being burned into the miner's mind before he said, "Easy name to remember. And one I'm not likely to forget."

The miner released Lilly's arm with a shove and let her scramble off his lap. She bolted through the group and ran from the saloon.

The miners gathered around the scene made no effort to stop her. They were too busy looking at Beck to care much about her.

Because Beck's knife had remained at the throat of their friend.

"He did his part," Hauser said. "Now you do yours, John. Put that knife away and let's get out of here."

The sheriff began to breathe again as Beck slowly stepped away but did not lower his knife. He held it as if it had still been against the man's throat, only now he turned on the group of men who had begun to close in around him.

He slashed out wildly with the knife, sending the men backward. It was a sudden, vicious movement that reminded Hauser of a rattlesnake snapping at prey.

Beck had spent so much time surviving among the creatures of the desert that he had become one himself.

The men moved back from the knife blade, but not enough for Hauser's taste. He stepped in between them and Beck, keeping his hand on his pistol without drawing it.

"The show is over, boys," he told them. "You'd all best get back to your fun and let us be on our way."

"We've got no quarrel with you, Sheriff," said a redheaded miner as he took a step toward Beck. "You can leave in peace if you're of a mind to. But as for this fella here, that's another story entirely."

Hauser stopped moving backward and stepped in front of the young man. "I wasn't asking you, boy. I'm telling you to let us go."

The miner froze, as did every other man in the saloon.

"That goes for everyone." Hauser held his ground as he looked each man in the eye. "Everyone had just better clear out of our way or I'll start clearing you out personally."

The miner who'd had Beck's knife at his throat was still sitting when he called out, "Let 'em go, men." He pointed at Beck. "Don't worry. This one isn't going far. I'll take care of him in my own time and in my own way." Hauser saw the trickle of blood from the nick in his neck had stained his shirt, but he had made no effort to stop it. "Yes, sir. You and I are going to be seeing each other again real soon."

Hauser wanted to brain the fool for risking starting this up all over again, but he was glad to see Beck kept moving toward the door, where the men had separated enough to let him pass.

Beck did not stop walking backward until he had

reached the hallway that led into the hotel. Hauser moved in front of him and backed out with him.

Over Hauser's shoulder, Beck yelled at the miners. "Anyone wants to hurt me knows where they can find me. Anyone hurts Lilly, I'll find them. And they won't like it when I do."

When they had first entered the hotel a few minutes before, Hauser thought he would have to practically carry Beck up the stairs to his room. Now, as he watched him move under his own steam, this stranger appeared to be a completely different man. Frail men did not pull knives or face down bullies. Crazy men did not speak the way Beck had just spoken to the miners.

When they had reached the hotel lobby, Hauser watched Beck tuck the Bowie knife back into the scabbard on his belt, pick up his parcel of clothing, and ascend the stairs. His parcel of clothes and ammunition was tucked under his left arm.

He did not move like an insane man. He looked like someone who knew exactly what he was doing.

And when Hauser heard Beck's hotel room door close, it was with the finality of a judge's gavel.

Hauser turned when he realized a couple of miners were standing in the lobby with him.

"Your friend's a dead man, Sheriff," one of the strangers said. "I see it only fair to warn you about it right here and now."

The other one added, "No one does that to one of ours. Michael's got his faults, just like any of us, but we don't take kindly to letting one of our own get stuck like that. Hell, his neck's still bleeding."

"Your friend's a dead man, Sheriff," repeated the first one as he glared up the stairs.

But Sheriff Hauser was not so sure. "You keep saying that enough times, mister, you're liable to start believing it. That's a mighty dangerous thought to have."

Hauser left the men as he walked upstairs to Beck's room. He had no intention of bothering the man after all he had been through. He was probably already sound asleep.

But he would make sure people let Beck sleep by keeping an eye on his room from a chair Ma Stanton kept in the hallway. He had no doubt one of the miners would want to try something to avenge their friend, especially once the whiskey started to take hold. He intended on stopping it for their sake. Beck could clearly take care of himself. It was the miners Hauser was worried about.

CHAPTER TWELVE

By the time Beck got up to his room, it was already late afternoon and going toward dark. The window shades had been pulled down, causing a sickly brown light to filter inside. Yet despite how dark it was, he was still able to make out the form of a small young woman crouched in the far corner of his room.

"Lilly?" he asked as he set his parcel on the bed. "Is that you?"

"Please don't make me leave, Mr. Beck," she cried. "I promise I won't bother you. Ma Stanton told me she did not want to see me after all of the trouble I caused and I have nowhere else to go. I just don't want to be out there right now. Not while those men are still here."

"You don't have to leave." Beck shut the door and found some matches next to the candle holder on his nightstand. He struck a match off his belt, bringing the match head to life, and lit the candle. It did not provide much light, but it was better than being in near darkness. "In fact, I'm glad you're here. I was worried about where you had run off to."

He sat on the edge of the bed and watched her wipe away her tears with the sleeve of her shirt. He wanted to comfort her, but she seemed so brittle that he dared not touch her.

"I don't know what happened down there," she said through the tears. "I was walking through the lobby with some clean sheets, and the next thing I know, I'm scooped up and carried back into the saloon by one of those men. They gave me to that man who was holding me as if I was nothing more than some kind of toy doll."

The thought of it was enough to make Beck's neck turn red. He had never liked bullies. He supposed that might have been one of the reasons why he had quit trying to study the law and started enforcing it. He had always believed that everyone was equal under the law, or at least they were supposed to be. He had seen enough of the world to know that was not always the case. But it had not helped him accept it any easier.

"I know what it's like to be manhandled like that," he heard himself say. "To feel like you're nothing."

"You?" she said. "Who could make you feel like that? You're so brave. No one could do that to you."

He smiled weakly. "I wish that were true. It happened back where I'm from. In Mother Lode. I guess that's why I'm here now with you. I was the law there until some bad men came to town and caught me while my guard was down. No, that's not true. My guard wasn't down. I decided to set it down because I was too busy feeling sorry for myself."

"Was it . . ." Lilly began to ask. "Was it because of a woman?"

"No one woman," he told her. "Many women and children and men. The memory of them crying as they begged me not to do what I had been paid to do. Crying after I did what I had to do to earn my daily bread. The memory of the looks in their eyes as they cradled the men I had just killed in their arms. It wasn't hatred. It was just a profound sadness that struck me even though I couldn't understand what they were saying. They all had that same hollow look as they realized life had gotten just that much harsher because of me. A new terror had been stamped on their minds because of what I had done."

He looked across the room at the mirror. He saw his reflection and hated what he saw. Whether he had wild hair and the beard he had acquired in the desert or the clean look he had now, the man he saw was still the same.

Beck forced himself to look away from his own reflection. "Maybe the law doesn't really make us all as equal as it is supposed to, but I'd like to think that justice has a way of winning in the end."

He saw that Lilly was no longer crying. She was still sitting on the floor but had drawn her knees up to her chest and crossed her arms over her legs. "You used to work for the railroad, didn't you?"

"Railroads," Beck said, "mine owners, stockyards, cattle barons. Anyone who could pay the Pinkerton's going rate."

"You shot Chinese?" she asked.

Beck nodded. "Chinese, Irish, Germans, Negroes, Poles, Indians. Teamsters of all sorts. I don't think there's a member of a race in all the world I haven't shot. I'm not proud of that. Guess that's why I left it all behind. That's why I was at Mother Lode. I went there in search of some kind of redemption. Thought I had found it, too, until I gave in to self-pity. Paid the price for it. Paid dearly." He felt the harsh memories of his time in the desert wash over him and he fought to hold them at bay. He would not allow himself to show emotion in front of her. Not after what she had been through that night. "Yes, I suppose justice has a way of finding us after all."

He snapped out of it when he felt Lilly looking at him. Her face bore no hint of what she was thinking and he remembered Allan Pinkerton's amazement at the "inscrutable Chinese." He always encouraged his men, especially those who did undercover work, to study the "Celestials," as he often called them. He encouraged his men to learn how to hide their feelings.

No, Beck might not have been able to see what Lilly was thinking by the look on her face, but he sensed no malice there. "Forgive me for running off at the mouth like that. You've been through enough today without my rambling making it worse."

"You're not rambling," she told him. "You're just hurt and sad. It sounds like you have a reason to be. And you're not that same man anymore. The kind of man you were when you were with the Pinkertons, I mean."

Beck smiled wearily. "That's nice of you to say, but I'm not so sure. I was a coward for letting it all get to me and running away, believing I could be more than that. My cowardice ultimately caught up to me." His backside still stung from the kick Abraham Hogan had given him to send him on his way out of Mother Lode. "I guess I got what I deserved."

"You're no coward, Mr. Beck." Lilly's voice was quiet, but firm. "A coward would not have defended me against those men just now. A coward would not have risked his life to save me. You were very brave down there. I've never seen anything like it."

Although Beck doubted the girl was more than eighteen, he imagined she had seen more than her fair share of life working in this hotel. Arizona had a way of attracting all sorts. Good and bad. Mostly men and women who were a little of both. Men like Beck. "My bravery may have gotten you out of that saloon, but it has probably cost us both our lives. I doubt those miners will let us live after I showed them up like that."

"Maybe," Lilly allowed, "but they would have killed me for sure. Or worse, if it hadn't been for you." She looked down at her arms. "I should know. That's how it has always happened before."

Beck could feel her sadness and it angered him. No one should have to accept treatment like that from anyone. No one at all.

"Ma Stanton let them do that without penalty?"

Lilly shrugged her thin shoulders. "They're paying customers and I'm just a Chinese heathen to her. She didn't believe me when I told her my parents were baptized. Me too."

But Beck had no problem believing her, not that it had made much of a difference to him. He had been baptized, too. A cruel baptism in the Church of the Wilderness.

"Sheriff Hauser didn't do anything about it?" He did not like thinking ill of his new friends.

"When he could," she said. "When he knew about it. But not always. Ma would tan my hide if I complained too much. I need the money from this job, Mr. Beck. My parents are not young anymore. I send them money whenever I can, which is not as often as I would like."

Beck remembered the money he still had from Steve Hogan. It was less than a hundred dollars now, but he would be willing to give all of it and more to Lilly if he could. No one should be so afraid. No one as gentle as she was. "Will Ma Stanton do anything about what happened in the saloon just now?"

"No. In fact, she's probably angry she can't find me." She pushed herself to her feet, a new fear coursing through her. "Now that I'm thinking about it, I should probably go. She'll fire me for sure if she knew I was up here right now. She doesn't like me being too friendly with the guests unless it's in the saloon."

He watched her head for the door but did not have the strength to stop her. But he heard himself say, "Don't go. Please."

She stopped, then slowly turned to face him, but would not look at him. "Mr. Beck, I'm not that kind of girl."

Beck felt himself blush. "No! I didn't mean it that way. I meant it's too dangerous for you to go down there right now and I don't have the energy to go with you. Please stay here for a while. You can have the bed if you want. I'll sleep on the floor."

"I . . . I couldn't ask you to do that."

"I've slept in the wilderness for weeks," he said. "A floor is just fine with me. In fact, it's an improvement."

She looked at the bed. "I suppose it's big enough for both of us because I'm small. We could share it if you wanted. Just until you went to sleep, that is."

He liked the way she thought. Then he remembered the miners downstairs and the threats they had made.

He looked to the table in the center of the room and saw his holster draped across the back of the chair. He decided he should make sure his gun was loaded, though he was pretty sure it was. He would have to sleep with it close that night, probably in his hand. If the miners came for him, he would make sure he took down as many of them as he could before they got him.

"Hand me that holster and slide the chair under the doorknob." He knew the chair would not present much of an obstacle when they came for him, but it might give him enough warning to get off a shot or two before they managed to burst through the door.

Lilly had to use both hands to give the holster to Beck and slide the back of the chair under the doorknob. She wedged it down tight.

He pulled the Colt from the holster and felt a rush of excitement jolt through him. The sound of gunmetal clearing leather had always had a stunning effect on him. He was glad his time in the desert had not taken that much from him.

He opened the cylinder and was glad to find the gun was still fully loaded. He dumped the bullets into his hand and reloaded them. He always liked to have some comfort with any firearm he took in hand. His rifles were still with Good Abraham and he wondered if the liveryman would make good on his promise to bring them over.

He wondered if the miners in the saloon might take the rifles from him when he delivered them to the desk but decided there was nothing he could do about it if they did. His pistol and his knife were all that he had to keep Lilly safe and he would die before he let any further harm come to her.

He snapped the cylinder shut, encouraged by the clean sound of it clicking into place. Steve Hogan might not have been much of a man, but at least he had known how to keep his weapon in fine working order. Beck held the pistol in his hand and found himself wondering how many good men had fallen beneath this gun. *As many as have fallen under yours. Less, even.*

He felt Lilly standing next to him and looked at her. Sitting down, he was almost as tall as she was. And he felt a pang of guilt as he realized how pretty she was.

"I'm sorry." He blushed. "I'm afraid I tend to get lost in my thoughts these days." He looked at the bed. "Which side do you want?"

She rolled into the bed and came into a stop against the wall. She made a pillow out of her arm and placed the bed pillow on the right side of the bed. "Please, put your head down. You need your rest."

Unable to fight the weariness that plagued him any longer, he set the pistol on the bed, pulled off his boots, and lay down. He had not known how small the boots had been until that very moment. The freedom was almost intoxicating.

He realized he had not lain with a woman in his bed for as long as he could remember. Back in Mother Lode, he had taken to sleeping in Dulce's room after a night of drinking. But the liquor had been enough to dull his senses at the time and his memory of it since.

The pillow was soft and clean and he felt the sleep that eluded him for so long come on quickly. "I hope you don't think less of me asking you to stay, Lilly. I'm not up to anything, I promise. I just wanted you to be safe."

But she caressed his face and told him to sleep. She began to sing something to him in Chinese and he could not fight the darkness that quickly enveloped him. Nor did he want to.

CHAPTER THIRTEEN

OWN IN THE saloon, Colm Dunross choked down the whiskey, but its burn did little to soothe the ache in his neck. The boys had wrapped a strip of cloth around his wound—soaked in whiskey to purify the cut—but the ache within him ran much deeper than that.

No amount of bandaging or whiskey could dull the damage in his soul. Or to his pride.

He had been shown up by a skinny fool too weak to stand on his own two feet. If the knife had not been at his throat, he would have beaten the man to death with his bare hands.

But it had not been the knife that had unmanned him. No, he'd had many a knife pulled on him in his day and had the scars on his body to prove it. That had not been what stopped him from taking the knife from the skinny stranger. Nor had it been the squealing Celestial wench he had held on his lap.

No, Dunross admitted. It had been the look in the stranger's eyes that had kept him from doing anything. An unholy, ungodly look that had nothing to do with whiskey or rage. It was the same look he had seen in the eyes of starving beasts like wolves or coyotes circling around a herd of cattle. That look they had where their hunger consumed them and the threat of neither man nor bullets could stop them from attacking. They were already dead, so the fear of consequences no longer mattered.

That was what had kept Dunross pinned to his chair. No man should ever have the look of an animal in his eyes. No man should ever be that inhuman. That base. That dark.

Dunross had not tasted such fear in a long time. Not when he had first left his native Scotland or when he had come to America and worked all those odd jobs that had eventually brought him to the mines. He wondered if so much time spent underground had somehow robbed him of his courage.

The confinement had not frightened him. Nor had the possibility of a cave-in or the endless hours spent choking on dust in encroaching darkness. It was that lack of fear that had led the bosses to name him the foreman of the mines.

But the look in the stranger's eyes had frightened him to his core. It was the look of a man who was already dead, though he did not know it yet. A man who, like those wolves Dunross had seen on the trail, had nothing left to lose, for he was already dead.

Dunross had never taken murder lightly, but he knew there was no harm in killing an unholy thing. And he would have to kill that thing upstairs this very night.

He forced down another shot of whiskey as the men

around him relived what had happened earlier in the saloon. They made no mention of his fear, of course, for he had hidden it well from all but himself.

"Never saw anyone so cool with a knife to his throat," he heard one of the men boast. "Old Ross just looked at that drover like he was something stuck on his boot."

"No fear," said Connelly. He had been working the mine as long as Dunross had. "That's why he's the boss of this crew, my boys. Never been afraid of nothing and never will be."

Connelly patted his shoulder. "You showed remarkable restraint back there. The rest of us wanted to pound that man into fine dust, but you held your ground like a champ. Why, a man could be forgiven for wondering if you've got anything but ice water in your veins."

The comparison was too close to his memory of the stranger for Dunross. He turned on the Irishman and backed him up against the bar. "Aye, 'tis a human man I am, unlike that thing lying asleep upstairs."

"Of course you are," Connelly said, forcing a smile. "We all know that. We were just praising your bravery is all. Most of us would've gone sheet white with a knife to our throats, but not you. You were as calm if you were in church on a Sunday morning."

"Church?" a man named Banner said. "The roof would cave in if Ross went inside one of those."

The men laughed and cheered and once again toasted the bravery of their foreman.

But Connelly did not join them. "What's the matter?" he asked Ross as the men resumed their drinking. "No one meant any offense by it, certainly not me."

Dunross felt the anger leave him as quickly as it had come. "I know you didn't, Barney. It's just that I don't like looking weak in front of the boys is all. The only thing that keeps them working as hard as they do is the respect they have for me. And a man could be forgiven for thinking I was cowed by that man and the toothpick he had pulled on me."

"Not a chance," Connelly assured him. "Me maybe, but not you. You showed remarkable restraint when others would have killed him where he stood."

But Dunross knew his own mind and heart. He knew better. And the longer the stranger breathed living air, the longer his shame would last. "I plan on killing that man, Barney. Killing him dead this very night."

Connelly looked around to make sure none of the other men had heard him. "That's dangerous talk you're speaking now. If this bunch gets wind of that notion, they're liable to charge up there and kill him themselves."

But Dunross had already made up his mind as to what needed to be done. "Not them, Barney. You, me, and Banner will be enough to get the job done right."

"The three of us could take on the world!" Connelly laughed as he reached for his whiskey, but the look on his friend's face made him slowly set the glass back down. "You don't really mean that, Colm."

"I've never meant anything more in all the years you've known me. And that's not the whiskey talking, either. You've seen me drunk enough to know I'm not drunk now. I aim to kill that man and kill him tonight."

"For what? For trying to show you up in front of the others? You've got nothing to prove to the boys and me. Why, they think you're a hero for how you handled yourself. And I hope it's not over ruining your time with that Celestial filly, for if you've an itch that needs to be scratched, there's no shortage of possibilities in this town."

"It's got nothing to do with any of that," Dunross told him. "I've got my reasons. Are you with me or not?"

Connelly pushed the glass of whiskey away from him. "Killing a man in the heat of the moment is one thing. Hell, I think it's even legal in some parts. But what you're talking about is something far different."

"Killing's always killing, Barney, and only a fool believes otherwise. Whether it's in a saloon or on a battlefield or in an alley somewhere, the result is the same." He pointed at the ceiling. "And that man has spent his last night breathing the same air we are. It has to be done and I aim to do it whether you're with me or not."

"We're not killers. We've got jobs. Good jobs at that. If we kill that man, that sheriff will figure we did it and he won't just let that go."

"That sheriff would need witnesses to speak against us first," Dunross said. "Do you think any man in here won't swear on a stack of Bibles that we never left this place?"

"That old woman at the desk . . ."

"Won't say anything that might rob her of our business. Not over a half-dead stranger protecting a Chinese whore."

Dunross finished downing a final shot of courage and slapped the glass flat on the bar. He was resolved to do what needed to be done. "I'm putting an end to that man right now. You coming?"

Connelly drummed his fingers on the bar. "Of course I'm coming with you. Just try to stop me."

Dunross was glad to hear it. Connelly was a good man to have at his side in any situation, be it down in the mine or outside of it. "Fetch Banner and follow me."

* * *

THE TWO MINERS fell in behind their foreman as he walked down the long hallway and into the hotel. Dunross eyed the front desk, but the old woman who was usually perched there was nowhere in sight. The lobby was empty, except for an old man slumped over in an overstuffed chair.

That was good.

Dunross took the stairs two at a time. Banner and Connelly followed. He doubted he would need them to do much of anything more than keep an eye on the hallway while he set about ending the stranger's life. He figured the man would be fast asleep by now and would be no bother at all. And if he happened to get hold of that pigsticker he carried, Dunross would see to it that he regretted it.

The top floor of the hotel was mostly unlit, which Dunross decided would make his job much easier. No one would be able to identify them afterward.

It was not until they got upstairs that Dunross realized his big mistake.

"Damn it," he cursed. "I don't know which room is his."

Banner pointed to a door just to the right of the staircase. "I saw him go in there when I was downstairs with the sheriff earlier."

Banner had always proven himself indispensable in the mines and Dunross was glad he was just as resourceful aboveground. "Good man. Now, the two of you keep watch out here while I go inside and take care of that bastard. Give a short rap on the door if anyone starts heading up here, particularly that pain-in-the-ass sheriff."

Dunross stood in front of the stranger's door and was about to try the doorknob when a voice from the darkness stopped him cold.

"No need to keep an eye out for the sheriff, boys," Hauser said. "He's already here."

Connelly and Banner stood on either side of Dunross as the foreman said, "You didn't strike me as the kind of man who prowls around in the dark, Sheriff."

"I am when a group of backshooting bastards like you is near." The unmistakable sound of a hammer being pulled back cut through the darkness. "So you boys best turn around and head back downstairs to resume your drinking while you still can."

But Dunross had no intention of going anywhere except in that room to do what needed doing. "That pistol won't do you much good in the dark. You're not used to working in such conditions, but we are. You might be lucky enough to get one of us, but you won't manage to get all three of us. Not before we get to you."

"Don't be so sure."

Dunross slightly nodded in the direction of Hauser's voice. That was enough to send Banner and Connelly barreling down the hallway toward the sheriff just as a pistol cracked, lighting up the hallway for a fraction of a second, temporarily blinding Dunross.

Realizing the gunshot had probably woken Beck, Dunross decided he didn't have a moment to lose. Ignoring his flash blindness, he took a step back and was about to burst through the door when he heard a woman scream. He was stopped dead in his tracks as a searing fire punched through his belly. It was quickly followed by another pain, just as hot, through his chest.

Dunross staggered to keep his footing.

He pawed at his belly and looked at his hands. They were covered in blood. His blood.

He managed to look up just in time to see the room door open before a chair crashed down on top of him. A woman screamed again as the blow almost knocked him off his feet, but Dunross did not go down. He was dizzy and winded and tried to steady himself to rush the stranger.

But a sharp blow across his temple staggered Dunross backward and sent him sprawling against the railing.

He scrambled to steady himself when he felt a final push crack the banister and he tumbled over the side. The floor of the hotel lobby rushed up to meet him.

The last thing he remembered was a horrible crunch before the world slipped away.

A FTER HE PUSHED one miner over the railing, John Beck heard the sounds of a scuffle at the far end of the hall, to his left. He plunged into the darkness and heard a man curse and the sound of cartilage snapping.

Beck grabbed hold of the first man he bumped into and tried to pull him out into the light. But he was too weak and the big miner easily broke his grip. A sharp right hand cracked him in the jaw, sending him sprawling backward and flat on his back.

Beck tried to clear his mind as a man leaped out at him from the darkness. Instinct more than skill made him bring his knees up to his chest, catching the man before he fell on him. With all of his failing strength, Beck rolled and shoved the gasping man to his right and through the broken banister. He tumbled out into the same void Beck had just sent the other man falling through.

"John!" Lilly cried as she rushed out of the room and tried to help him to his feet.

"Get back inside!" he told her as he got to his feet and managed to push her into the room.

Another gunshot rang out from the darkness at the end of the hall and Beck heard the unmistakable sounds of a man falling and the rattle of floorboards.

Beck pulled the pistol he had tucked into his pants and aimed it into the darkness as he backed away. "You'd best come out of there nice and slow or I'll start shooting."

"Calm down, son," Hauser said as he stepped into the weak light. His pistol was still smoking. "It's just me. You're safe."

Beck was glad to see the sheriff and he quickly lowered his gun. "What the hell is going on?"

"Your sparring partner from the saloon just tried to kill you, Beck. Luckily, I was already here when he and his friends set about doing it."

The sheriff joined Beck in looking over the ruined banister and down into the lobby. It was not a pretty sight. He recognized one of the men who had fallen as the same man who had been holding Lilly against her will. He was crumpled on the lobby floor at an impossible angle. Beck knew he must be dead.

The other man was sprawled on the floor next to where his friend had fallen. He was banged up something terrible but was moving a little.

"Looks like one of them is still alive," Hauser said as he began heading down the stairs. "Follow me, John. I could stand to have some company."

Beck walked down behind the sheriff, tightly gripping the banister as he went. He had always prided himself on his ability to take a punch, but his brain was still rattled from the blow. He supposed his time in the desert had taken more out of him than he had realized.

They had almost reached the bottom of the stairs when Beck spotted Good Abraham standing by the front desk, holding his Winchester and his Sharps as he looked at the two dead men at his feet.

"Good Lord Almighty!" the liveryman exclaimed. "That fella damned near landed on my head."

"This doesn't look good," Beck heard Hauser say as the first of the miners began to pour into the hotel lobby from the saloon. They stacked up three deep and looked at their fallen comrades. One of the men gagged at the sight of the man who'd had Lilly in his grasp. The sight was even more gruesome now that Beck was closer to it, though he felt no remorse.

But he did feel the gang of miners looking up at him and Sheriff Hauser on the stairs.

And they were not smiling.

"Uh-oh," Beck said.

"Those are the ones that did it," one of the miners called out. "Let's rush 'em, boys!"

"Beck!" Good Abraham cried out as he tossed the Winchester up to him from across the lobby.

Beck stuck the pistol in his pants and snatched the rifle out of the air as he brought it to his shoulder, aiming it down at the miners.

The men stopped as one in midstep.

Beck covered Hauser as the sheriff walked down the rest of the staircase to meet them. His Colt led the way. "It's time for you boys to go home now. That's an order."

"Not a chance," one of the men up front called out. "Not after what you did to Ross and Connelly."

"And Banner," called another.

"No way you get to live after that," yelled another.

Hauser stopped at the bottom of the stairs. "And there's no way any of you get to live unless you back on out of here while you still can."

Beck had seen mobs like this turn in the blink of an eye, which was why he made sure he kept the Winchester aimed at the center of them. All it took was for one man to flinch before the lot of them came streaming after him and Hauser. His Winchester held fifteen rounds, but he realized he might have about ten left after all of the shooting he had done in the desert. Or maybe he had reloaded it. He could not remember.

But he knew there were about twenty men lined up against him and the sheriff. Even if neither he nor Hauser missed a shot, which would be unlikely, it would be impossible to stop all of them.

He figured Hauser must know what they were up against, but if he was afraid, he was doing a hell of a job hiding it.

Hauser shook his head slowly. "Never in all my years have I seen men so anxious to die." He thumbed back the hammer on his Colt. "Have it your way, boys. Who gets it first?"

The group of miners were in a half crouch, waiting for someone to make the first move.

But no one did.

"Come on!" Hauser goaded them. "Who wants to join their friends on the floor over here? Who else wants to die here tonight?"

Beck kept the Winchester on the miners as the second man he had thrown through the banister coughed and stirred on the lobby floor.

As one, the miners looked down at their fallen friend. "Look, fellas," one of them pointed out. "Connelly's still alive."

Hauser shifted his aim down to the wounded man. "But he won't be if you bastards don't start filing out of here right now."

The miners looked at their wounded friend, then at the sheriff. Beck began to wonder if the sheriff might not be as crazy as he was.

"We've already killed two of your friends tonight," Hauser yelled to them. "Might as well make it three out of three before I start in on you boys."

"You can't just leave him like that, Sheriff," one of the miners called out. "Someone get him a doctor quick."

"No one's leaving until all of you leave," Hauser said. "I'll get this boy a doctor as soon as I see the last of you on your way out of town. Now, either you get busy rushing us or you get busy leaving."

The wounded Connelly grabbed for Hauser's leg, but the sheriff sidestepped him and pinned his hand to the floor beneath his boot, causing Connelly to cry out, which sent a shudder through the miners.

"What's it going to be, boys? Or do I have to make up your mind for you?"

Beck might have spent the better part of the day with Hauser, but he did not know the sheriff well enough to know whether or not he was bluffing. And judging by the looks the miners traded with one another, Beck knew neither did they.

The miners had been ready to charge the two men as one. And they seemed to decide against doing so the same way.

One by one, the grumbling men began to file out through the front door of the hotel.

Hauser kept his pistol aimed at the wounded man as they left. "And don't get brave and think you can double back and catch us in a rush. Your friends tried sneaking up on us once and look at what it got them."

The miners walked outside, save for one who hung back. He looked older than the others and his skin was blackened by a lifetime spent underground. He pointed at Hauser and said, "You get him to a doctor quick."

"I told you I would," Hauser said. "Now git!"

Beck kept the Winchester on the last man until he, too, stepped outside with his friends.

Hauser pointed at Good Abraham. "Get over there and lock that door right now."

The liveryman rushed to do as he was told. "Don't see what good it'll do if they decide to rush in here."

"Lock the door to the saloon, too," Hauser told him. "Then go fetch the doctor." He took his foot off the wounded man's hand. "If this boy can be saved, I want him saved. He'll need to stand trial for what he's done. We'll be here when you get back."

Good Abraham locked the door, then started to run off to get the doctor when he realized he was still holding the Sharps. He dashed back to hand the long rifle to Beck before he headed toward the back door.

Beck lowered the rifle and allowed himself to sink down to sit on one of the steps.

Hauser took a knee and began to take a closer look at the injured miner at his feet. "He's busted up pretty good, John. Don't know if he's long for this world."

Beck felt a wave of exhaustion wash over him and he leaned his head against the banister. The coolness of the wood made him feel a bit better and soothed his aching head. "I didn't know if we were long for this world just now."

Hauser waved him off. "Nah. They were more scared than we were." The sheriff grinned up at him. "I've got to say you handled yourself pretty good back there. I thought I was a goner when those two rushed me like they did. I put a round straight through them, but they kept on coming."

Hauser dabbed his bloody nose with the cuff of his sleeve and winced from the pain of it. Beck saw his left eye was already starting to swell shut. "Those boys up there sure kicked like mules."

"I guess I ought to thank you for saving my life." Beck pointed down at the man who had landed crooked on the lobby floor. "I was deep asleep until your shot woke me up. He would've pummeled me dead before I had the chance to do anything about it."

"I doubt that," the sheriff said. "You'd have found a way to get him. If the desert didn't finish you, I doubt a couple of drunken miners could have done the job."

Beck heard a stair behind him creak. He pulled the pistol from his pants and turned, aiming it up at the source of the sound.

It was Lilly, who screamed as she fell backward out of the path of the gun.

Beck immediately tucked the pistol away and held out his hands to her. "I'm sorry, Lilly. I'm so sorry."

She pushed herself to her feet and scrambled down the stairs to be next to him, hugging his arm. "Are you hurt, John?"

"I got my bell rung pretty hard," he told her, "but I'm fine." He looked down at twisted corpse of the miner who had attacked her. "Better than he is, anyway."

Hauser stood up and slid the Colt back into the holster on his hip. "Well, if I didn't know better, John, I'd say you've got yourself a new friend there."

Beck let his head rest on top of Lilly's and found it much more comfortable than the wood banister. "Guess I have at that."

Hauser went on: "And I've gone and found myself a deputy in the bargain."

Beck did not catch the meaning at first until he realized the sheriff might be talking about him. "Who? Me? Your deputy?"

Hauser laughed. "Like you said earlier, son. You owe me. But I'll consider the account paid in full the moment you take your oath and pin the deputy star on your shirt."

Beck felt his head begin to swim, but it was not from the punch he had suffered from the miners.

When he had woken up that morning, Beck had had no idea how many days and nights he had spent in the desert. He had tried to keep track in the cave, but the span of time meant little when life was lived from one meal to the next. He had spent the night on the hard ground of the desert beneath the stars of an open sky. He did not have a friend left in the entire world except for Pokey, and Pokey was a horse.

He had not had a reason to suspect that this day would end any different or any better than those that had come before it.

But it had ended with Beck having a roof over his head, a pretty lady clutching his arm, and a lawman he respected who he could call a friend.

But he did not know if he would ever be good enough to be a lawman again. "I don't know, Sheriff. I don't know if it would work. I don't know if I'm up to it."

Hauser set a foot on the third step from the bottom and bent to look at him. "You got any place you need to be right about now, son?"

Beck had not thought about that. He had not thought about much of anything since he had been turned loose in the wilderness with less than a fighting chance.

Lilly hugged his arm tighter and he rested his cheek on her head. Her hair smelled of rose water and her little body was surprisingly warm against him. He had felt that. He had thought he would never feel anything like that ever again.

He wondered about Mother Lode and about Hogan and the Brickhouse Gang. He wondered if they were still in town or had they moved on by now. He wondered if Dulce was still alive and had already written him off as dead.

Maybe it was better to let the dead stay that way.

But John Beck knew he was not dead. Not really. Not anymore.

"No, Sheriff," Beck told him. "I suppose I don't. Amenia is my home now."

Hauser smiled and slapped his knee. "That's about the best news I've heard all day. Now get yourselves back up there and get some rest. You're going to need it, Deputy."

CHAPTER FOURTEEN

Dulce flinched when Hogan threw the glass against the wall.

"Son of a bitch!" Bram yelled as he vented his frustration to the empty saloon. "What the hell kind of gang am I running here anyway?"

If he was looking for an answer from Pearson or Lem, Dulce knew he would be waiting a long time. Lem simply frowned down at his coffee mug and the giant Pearson looked out the window like a dog waiting for its master to return.

Neither man reacted when Bram brought his heavy hand down on the table, causing it to jump. "I asked you idiots a question."

"Don't know the answer, boss," Lem said. "We don't know any more than you do."

Bram cursed again and wheeled away from them, turning his attention to Dulce behind the bar. "That's what I've surrounded myself with, darlin'. A bunch that aren't even fit to be good yes-men. Just a couple of saddle tramps who spend their days moping around in here like a bunch of old cows."

"What else do you expect us to do?" Pearson said. "You won't let us drink anymore. And no one comes to town on account of them being afraid we'll rob them. At least no one we haven't already milked dry of all their money. You won't let us rob the bank and the store owners aren't making enough for us to take money from." The big man threw up his hands. "No booze. No thieving. No nothing. What's left for us, Bram? Singing hymns in the middle of the street?"

Lem looked up at the leader from his mug of cold coffee. "I told you I thought we should ride out to find Steve and Laredo, but you don't like that idea, either."

"We sent Laredo out after him," Bram yelled, "and look at where it got us. He ain't come back yet, which means that old bandit either got himself killed or rode off back down to Mexico. Either way, going after him doesn't make much sense." Hogan gripped the back of his chair tight enough to make the wood crack. "I don't like what that means for Steve's chances, but there's more than him to be concerned about now."

"Laredo wouldn't just run off like that," Pearson said in defense of his friend. "You know that. If he's not back yet, it's for a good reason."

"And what kind of reason might that be?" Bram prodded. "Think he found himself a nice cave woman out there to cozy up with? Or maybe some squaw of one of them desert tribes caught his fancy? It's not because he's afraid to tell me about Steve. He never liked my brother all that much anyway. What else could it be, Pearson? Or ain't you used to thinking so much?"

Dulce watched Pearson roll his tongue inside his mouth. She could see the big man was becoming awfully tired of getting yelled at by Abraham Hogan. His outbursts were getting worse as more days passed without any sign of Steve or Laredo returning to town. He had all but given up his brother for dead, and with his refusal to allow the men to drink anymore, they had all grown sullen and flat. Time moved slow in Arizona. It moved even slower when you were scared.

Dulce knew it was only a matter of time before Pearson stood up to his boss, but today would not be the day. When the giant had finally had enough of Hogan's insults, she hoped he'd rear up and kill Hogan. She just wanted to live long enough to see it with her own two eyes.

Pearson said, "I don't think Laredo has run off with a woman. And I don't think Steve found one or had an accident, either."

Bram's eyes narrowed. "Then what do you think happened to them?" He let go of the back of the chair and stood to his full height. He was a tall, broad man, and although he was not as big as Pearson, he was still an intimidating sight. "You're not saying Steve got scared and ran away, are you?"

Pearson looked at Lem then down in his coffee mug. "No, I'm not saying that."

Bram waited for him to say more, but when it became clear that Pearson had spoken his mind, he said, "Come on, big man. Spit it out! Tell me what you think happened."

Pearson looked up from his coffee mug. "You know what I think. The same thing you're thinking happened to them, only you don't have the guts to say it."

Bram squared up to the bigger man and balled his fists at his sides. "I've never been afraid of anything in my life. Say it, damn you. Say it now."

Dulce perked up. Maybe this would all end much sooner than she thought.

But Pearson remained seated and would not be hurried. "Do I really have to say it, Bram? Do I have to say I know you're afraid for the same reason me and Lem are afraid."

Dulce watched Pearson wait for Bram to say something, but all he did was glower down at the giant with his fists balled at his sides. Pearson pointed out the window to the thoroughfare. "That town marshal you rode out of here on a rail didn't die, Bram. He's still out there. He found a way to survive somehow and I'd wager Laredo and Steve are dead because of it." He pointed at Bram with a long, crooked finger. "And you know I'm right, too."

Dulce gripped her bar towel tightly. She hoped Pearson was right. She found herself praying for it harder than anything she had ever prayed for in her life.

She saw Lem's mouth open, but no words came out. He was always a stupid-looking man, but looked even dumber with his mouth like that. "You think that's true, Pearson?" He looked over at Bram. "You think that's how it could've happened?"

Bram answered by throwing back his head back and laughing. Dulce thought he had a horrible, ugly laugh that sent ice down her spine whenever she heard it. It was a laugh that had no merriment in it. No joy. It was a flat, mocking sound closer to a crow's caw than anything a man had a right to make. A sound that was usually followed by something painful and cruel.

But Pearson did not laugh. And neither did Lem.

They just sat at the table, looking up at their leader with no small measure of disgust.

Bram turned away from his men and spoke to Dulce. "Did you hear that, darlin'? I'm stuck here trying to figure out what we're going do next and these two are throwing phantoms at me. Ghosts, for God's sake. Of your dead boyfriend, no less!"

"God has got nothing to do with any of this," Lem said. "The big man has a point, boss. We've been talking about it and we can't see our way clear to any other reason why Steve and Laredo haven't come back. None that makes sense."

Bram looked down at his men. "I think this dump must sell spiked booze because it sounds to me like your brains have turned to mush."

Lem shook his head slowly. "No one's talking about ghosts, boss. We're saying that Beck fellow didn't die like you'd figured he would."

Bram waved him off. "Of course he died, Pearson. How could he have lived when we trussed him up the way we did. Hell, you tied his hands, didn't you? I've never known you to make a knot a man could work his way out of."

"You took his pride," Pearson said. "You ran him off and left him to die. You stuck a canteen around his neck and a bullet in his mouth and sent him on his way. You shouldn't have done that, Bram. We should have killed him right here where we wanted to do it. We would've ended it quick and propped him up on Main Street like a scarecrow, just like we've done in all them other towns we've hit. But you didn't want that. You wanted to make a show of it and now we're down to three men because of it."

Bram shook his large head slowly. "I can't believe

what I'm hearing, boys. Steve is my kid brother and I run him down a lot, but he's never been anyone's idea of an easy time. He's the same kind of mad dog killer as the rest of us are. Laredo is, too. Even if Beck managed to live like you say he did, he would've been closer to dead than living when they found him. No way Steve would let a man in that condition get the jump on him like that. No way in the world."

"The desert's a funny place, boss," Lem offered. "You've said so yourself more times than I can count. Lots of things can happen out there to a man who isn't careful. Some good. Some bad. What if Beck is a luckier man than you've allowed for? What if he wasn't as close to death as you thought when Steve came up on him."

"What if Beck put him down?" Pearson continued.

"Put him down with what?" Bram yelled. "A dusty gun and a bullet he probably choked on if he didn't drop the damned thing?"

"A Sharps is a mighty good rifle," Pearson said. "And if he didn't lose the bullet, he could've used it to kill Steve. Or Laredo, if he happened upon them."

Dulce could hear the anger begin to creep into Bram's voice. "I'm hearing a whole lot of 'ifs' coming from you two and not a lot of facts."

"'Ifs' are all we we've got while we're stuck in here," Lem said. "And the facts we've got aren't good. If Beck is dead, how come Steve didn't come back? If Beck is dead, then how come Laredo didn't come back?"

Pearson piled on. "If you had killed that marshal like we wanted to, then Steve and Laredo would still be here and we would've blown this damned flyspeck town a while ago. Instead, we're still here waiting on those boys to show up when we all know they won't."

Dulce's heart jumped when Pearson slowly rose

from his chair and towered over Hogan. Perhaps this would all end right here and now. "So, why don't you quit acting like a man who doesn't know any better and listen to what we're telling you. Steve and Laredo aren't coming back. And we'd better figure out what we're going to do next. Because I'm getting awful tired of sitting here day after day watching the sun crawl across the sky. And I'm getting real tired of hearing your mouth."

Dulce felt her heart quicken as she watched Bram grow very still. She had been wrong after all. Things between the men were worse than she had allowed herself to hope. This was it. This was the end. One way or the other.

"Is that so?" Bram said. "Well, in that case, big man, why don't you step over here and shut it for me?"

Pearson held his ground but did not take that step.

"Come on!" Bram bellowed, causing his men to flinch. "You've got something stuck in your craw. Let's see if we can't shake it loose."

Both men began to step toward each other when Lem shot up from his chair and stood between them. "Hold on, both of you!"

"Out of the way, string bean," Pearson said as he closed on Bram. "This is men's work."

Bram walked toward him. "Best get to work, then."

But Dulce's heart sank as Lem found a way to hold both men back. "I mean it! Hold on a minute. I think I hear someone coming."

Dulce's hopes sagged as both outlaws stopped where they stood and listened.

Bram looked away first, then Pearson.

Dulce closed her eyes as she heard it, too. Someone was approaching the town.

Not just someone, she decided, but horses. A team of horses, by the sound of it. She could hear a whip crack and a bridle jangle as it came closer.

"That sounds like a stagecoach to me," Pearson said.

"Could be a freighter." Bram turned and looked at Dulce. "Any idea who that might be, darlin'? Don't lie."

But Dulce did not know. It could be a wagon full of goods delivering an order one of the shopkeepers had placed before the Brickhouse Gang had come to town two weeks before. It could also be a stagecoach. They were known to come to town every so often, especially if they were short on provisions or had a sick passenger or a storm was coming up. She had hoped the new arrivals might be soldiers, but doubted they were. If she'd had that kind of luck, she would never have found herself in a place like Mother Lode.

"Only one way to know for certain," she told him. "You should go out and see for yourselves."

Bram laughed. "I just bet you'd like that, wouldn't you? Get my head shot off like a prairie dog. No thanks."

He walked over to the bar and motioned for her to pass him one of the whiskey bottles behind it. She handed it to him, along with three glasses.

Bram took them in hand and walked over to the table. "Don't go getting ideas about this, boys. The ban on liquor is still in place. This is just for show so we don't stick out too much if those mule skinners come in here looking for a drink." To Pearson he said, "Get over there and keep an eye on the window and tell us everything you see."

But the big man did not look out the window, only at the whiskey bottle and glasses Bram had set on the table.

Bram gave a heavy sigh as he pulled the cork out of the bottle and filled their three glasses. Dulce watched Pearson and Lem drink deeply, like men dying of thirst.

It made her think of John Beck, something she had refused to allow herself to do since the day Bram and the others had forced him out of town. Could what they had been saying be true? Could he really still be alive? Was it even remotely possible that he could have lived out there all alone for all this time?

She had not allowed herself the luxury of hope since the Brickhouse Gang had ridden into Mother Lode, but she allowed it now. If John Beck was still alive, if even the thought of it was enough to scare Abraham Hogan and the others, then maybe she had a fighting chance to live.

She looked up again when she heard Bram say, "Come on, Pearson. Tell us what you see."

"A team of horses is approaching the town," the big man reported. "Six in all. They're pulling a stagecoach, all right. Looks like a freighter is with them, too. Biggest one I've ever seen. Eight-mule team. The wheels on it are bigger than me."

"Hot damn!" Lem cried out as he slapped the table. "Our luck is finally changing."

Dulce saw that Bram seemed to be taken by the calculations he was doing in his head. "An eight-mule team would put that freighter at damned near eight tons. Hot damn is right, boys. Hot damn."

Pearson continued his reporting. "Three-man team working the freighter, too, boss. No box on the wagon. All freight. That thing is huge."

But even Dulce heard the hitch in his throat and saw the color run from his face.

Unfortunately, Bram seemed to have heard it, too. "What is it, Pearson? Don't just sit there, boy. Tell me what you see."

"Whatever's in that wagon must be awfully important because they've got themselves an escort," Pearson reported from the window. "Cavalry. Four men. All mounted. All of them armed, too. Winchesters and side arms."

Dulce held the bar rag close to her. She might have torn it in half had she been stronger. Maybe her luck was finally beginning to change after all.

"Four soldiers?" Bram asked. "That's all. You're sure?"

"Four's enough," Lem said. "Them cavalry boys ain't easy. Not if they put them out here, they ain't. We could buffalo them freight haulers easy enough, but cavalry's different."

"Not much different," Bram reminded him. "Soldiers are just as human as the rest of us. Everyone's got a price. God knows we did."

"And what if they don't," Lem added. "It'll mean killing. And the army keeps close track of their men. We kill them, we'll be marked men for the rest of our lives, boss. They don't tend to forget those kinds of things."

"Worrying was never your strong suit, Lem," Bram said. "Neither is thinking. Best leave all of that up to me." He poured his men another round whiskey. "Here. Drink up. This'll be the last of it until we know what we're up against. Maybe there won't need to be any killing after all."

Dulce watched Bram and Lem drink up while Pearson remained by the window. He was too busy watching what was happening outside. "They're stopping in front of the general store across the street. They're parking the stagecoach in front of it, too." He looked back at Bram and Lem's table. "I don't like the looks of this, boss. If that storekeeper tells them about us, they'll come looking for a fight."

Dulce shut her eyes and began to pray that would be the case.

But Bram had not wasted any time praying. "Then I guess one of us had better make sure that old buzzard remembers to keep his mouth shut, shouldn't we? Pearson, you'd best get over there and remind him we're still in charge around here. Put any fool notions of heroics right out of his head."

Dulce watched Pearson walk back from the window, take down his whiskey, and lumber out the door. She watched him step into the thoroughfare and walk across the street.

Bram got up and took Pearson's spot at the window. "That's the ticket, by God. One look at the big bastard and that old shopkeeper won't say a word."

"I don't know what you're so happy about, Bram," Lem said. "What are we going to do with all those goods? Hell, the mules will be dead before we can get halfway to Mexico to sell the stuff."

"It's not the goods I care about," Bram said as he continued to look out the window. "It's the money that freighter might be hauling. The stage, too. Don't forget the stage." He glanced back at the whiskey bottle on the table. "Pour yourself another and relax. I've got a feeling today just might be our lucky day."

Dulce kept praying that he was wrong.

CHAPTER FIFTEEN

PEARSON TOOK HIS time as he strode across the street. He knew it would only be a matter of time before the visitors noticed him and would begin to act differently. People always changed whenever they caught sight of him, though he had never understood why. He did not react any differently when he met short people. Why should being tall make any difference?

But for the moment, the teamsters and coachmen and soldiers were too busy securing their respective wagons to notice him. Pearson used their distraction to his advantage.

He breathed a sigh of relief when he saw the stagecoach was not one of the Wells Fargo varieties, but part of the Arizona Overland Company. Wells Fargo men were usually meaner and much harder to kill, having had plenty of experience facing down bandits and the like. Pearson was confident that he and Lem and

Bram could take any stage, of course, but a Wells Fargo stage would require more effort.

He knew the Arizona Overland Company was a relatively new outfit, composed of several smaller coach lines that had run throughout Arizona. He imagined they might have some old Fargo drivers on their payroll, but that was a risk he knew Bram would be willing to take. Besides, a man on foot was a lot easier to buffalo than a man with a six-horse team in front of him.

None of the men tending to the wagons looked familiar. Neither did any of the passengers as he watched them mill around in front of the general store, stretching their legs.

He spotted an old married couple with a little blond-haired girl in tow. He pegged them for the little one's grandparents. Two other men, who appeared to be just a bit younger than the couple, walked into the general store. None of the passengers seemed to be armed.

But the four soldiers riding with them were certainly armed. The youngest of the bunch was a lieutenant who sported waxed mustaches and an impressive set of muttonchops beneath his campaign hat. He looked like a dandy at first glance, but Pearson noticed something in the way he rode the horse that made him think there was more to the young officer than met the eye. The three who rode with him—a sergeant and two enlisted men—showed casual deference to the officer as he gave them an order.

"Sergeant, I want you and the men to break up and scout the town. Nothing formal, just get the lay of the land. Then rally back here to give your report."

The sergeant was a tired sort who looked like he should have been in his sickbed instead of on horseback. But the men obeyed the lieutenant's orders and spread out around town.

Pearson took that as a bad sign. He did not know if the soldiers were there for the Brickhouse Gang or not. Maybe Marshal Beck had lived long enough not just to kill Steve and Laredo, but to ride to the nearest fort or town to tell the army what had happened at Mother Lode. Or maybe a patrol in pursuit of Indians had stumbled upon him right before he died.

But Pearson quickly decided that could not be the case. The army would have sent more men to uproot them from the town. The army never liked a straight-up fight if they could avoid it. They believed in overwhelming an enemy and these odds were entirely too close for comfort.

No, Pearson decided the soldiers were not there because of anything John Beck may have told them. They were there to escort the shipment. Whatever was on that freight wagon must be awfully important.

Or maybe it was the passengers on the stagecoach who were important?

He did not have any answers and imagined he would not get any by watching things from so far away. So he strode across the thoroughfare and stepped up onto the boardwalk in front of the general store. He ignored the remarks the wagonmen made about his size as he ducked his head and walked inside.

"I've never seen a town this size so quiet," Pearson heard the grandfather say to Mr. Welsh, the storekeeper. "Hope your mines haven't played out yet."

Mr. Welsh was about to answer when he saw Pearson had entered his store. Pearson locked eyes on the frail man, which sent a shiver through him.

The customers noticed it, then followed the track of his gaze all the way back up to Pearson.

The shopkeeper offered a brittle smile as he tried to regain his composure. "Well, you know how things go, gentlemen. Towns go through ups and downs, same here as anywhere else. Now, what can I get for you good people while you're here?"

Pearson enjoyed hearing the fear in the Welsh's voice. He reached into one of the jars of licorice on the counter, took out a piece, and bit into it. He gave no indication that he had any intention of paying for it as he smiled at the men who were looking at him.

He nodded to them as he chewed. "Morning."

Two of the men looked away and fumbled requests across the counter to Mr. Welsh.

But the grandfather stood between his wife and the little girl. He was a tallish man and round, but had a hard look in his eyes. "You're mistaken, big fella." He gestured to the clock on the wall behind the counter. "It's actually one o'clock in the afternoon, as anyone can see."

Pearson had not seen the clock and did not look at it now. The iron in this old codger interested him. He was not armed but acted with the confidence of a man who was.

"Morning, afternoon, evening." Pearson shrugged. "Who cares?"

"You should care," the old man said. "A man should know the correct time of day." His eyes moved over the length and breadth of Pearson. "You look to be in fine physical health. Don't you work?"

Pearson laughed and bit off another piece of licorice. "Oh, yes sir. I work. I work very hard all day long.

No regular hours, see. Guess you could say I make my-self available to the good people of this here town."

"Is that so?" The old man's eyes narrowed a bit. "I take it that you must be some kind of lawman, then."

Mr. Welsh dropped something behind the counter and bent to pick it up. The two customers placed their hands flat on the counter and made a great deal of effort not to look his way.

"A lawman, you say?" Pearson smiled as he pondered the notion. "Yeah, I guess you could say me and my friends are a type of law around here. We're all the law Mother Lode needs right now. Guess it just so happens that we're all the law this town's got."

"I see," Grandpa said. "I'd have suspected a town of this size would have itself a proper peace officer. A sheriff, perhaps. Or a town marshal."

Pearson smiled as he enjoyed his bite of licorice. "Oh, they had one when we got here."

The old man cocked an eyebrow. "And what happened to him?"

Pearson's smile held. "He left."

"Did he, now? In what fashion?"

Pearson spat out the licorice on the floor. "On a rail."

"I see," said Grandpa. "I suppose he must've done something to deserve being treated in such a way."

"He did," Pearson told him. "He was a lawman."

With a speed that surprised Pearson, Grandpa pulled a Colt from inside his coat and aimed it at him.

The outlaw recognized the pistol. "Colt Lightning. A gentleman's gun if I ever saw one." He looked at the man holding it. "You're pretty fast for an old man."

"I'm young enough to have gotten the drop on you." Grandpa shook his head slowly. "The bigger the man, the slower the brain, in my experience." He spoke to

Mr. Welsh without taking his eyes off Pearson. "Shop-keeper, you have anything we could use to tie this big fella up?"

"My word," said Mr. Welsh as he ran his hands over his thinning hair. "My word."

"Shopkeeper!" Grandpa yelled. "Snap out of it. A rope, man. Get some rope now."

Pearson's eyes slid over to Mr. Welsh. "Yeah, shop-keeper. Some rope for the gentleman. By all means."

Welsh unfroze himself and ran to the back, where Pearson knew he kept the rope.

"Nellie," Grandpa said to the woman. "You and little Nell go outside. Tell the others what's going on in here. Sit in the coach until I come get you and don't come back in here before I do."

The old woman grabbed the little girl by the hand and quickly took her outside. But she stopped in the doorway. "They're not out there, Jeb."

So Grandpa's name was Jeb, Pearson thought. He would remember that.

"Imagine that?" Pearson smiled at the man who had him covered. "Guess your wagonmen must be in the saloon already. But don't worry, Jeb. My friends are ready to show them a real good time." He repeated the name. "Jeb. Guess that's short for Jebediah."

"Jebediah Standish," the man told him. "Colonel, United States Cavalry."

Pearson cut loose with a long whistle. "Mercy me. A colonel at that. Guess you must rank pretty high."

"Not particularly," Standish said. "But you won't be the first scoundrel I've brought to heel, I assure you." He spoke to his wife without taking his eyes off Pear-son. "Nellie. You two get in the coach like I told you to."

Pearson watched the woman and child walk out of

the store. "You've got a gift, Colonel. I've never been able to get a woman to do what I wanted so easily."

"Can't see why not," Standish answered. "Seeing as how the only women you've ever known are most likely the ones whose company you paid for."

"Now, that's hardly neighborly, boss. I had a mother."

"Bastards always do." Standish called out for Welsh. "Shopkeeper! Where's that rope?"

The two men at the counter flinched and kept their hands on the glass. They would not be any trouble at all.

Pearson laughed. "You've gone and gotten poor old Welsh so worked up, he's liable to cut off his hand before he gets you a length of rope he can use. Why don't you go back and help him. I promise I'll be standing right here when you get back."

"You'd like that, wouldn't you?" Standish sneered.

Pearson held up his right hand. He enjoyed the look of fear in the eyes of the two men at the counter as they saw how big his hand was. "I promise. I wouldn't miss this for the world. I kind of want to see how this all plays out."

Standish's eyes narrowed. "It plays out with you bound and gagged on the floor."

Pearson was getting tired of the old man's tone. "You're awfully confident in Mr. Welsh's rope, aren't you, Jeb?"

"Like I said. You're not the first scoundrel I've brought to heel."

"We'll see, Dad. We certainly will see."

Welsh came out from the back with a good length of rope. His hands were shaking and Pearson thought he might drop it, but he did not.

Standish said, "Mr. Katz, Mr. Davis. I want both of

you to secure that man. Bind his hands behind him good and tight. He won't harm you. I have him covered."

But neither man looked anxious to carry out the colonel's order.

"Now, just wait a minute, Colonel," Mr. Katz said. "Let's think about this for a moment."

Pearson beamed. "Yeah, Colonel. Think about this for a long couple of moments. Because anyone who comes over here is going to get himself killed." He slowly raised his big right hand again. "I swear to that, too."

Standish's gun fired before Pearson could react. A hot poker shot through his right hand and he spun around, cradling his wounded hand against his belly. The pain was strong enough to double him over and make his legs turn weak. He had been shot at dozens of times but had never been hit before.

The pain in his hand was soon matched by a searing pain at the base of his skull that laid him flat on the floor. He did not lose consciousness but he wanted to.

He was powerless to stop the mess of boots and hands that swarmed around him as Standish and the others went to work. He felt his hands being bound behind his back and his legs brought up almost to his backside. He tried to wriggle free, but the effort only seemed to draw the knots even tighter.

"You're hog-tied, mister," Standish said from above him. "No use in trying to get yourself free. You'll only make it that much harder on yourself."

"My hand, you old bastard," Pearson bellowed. "You shot my hand."

"Damned near took it clean off." Standish sounded happy to tell him. "But it looks like I left just enough rope to bind you with. You give me any more trouble, son, the next one goes in your belly. You think you're in pain now, just wait until you feel what a belly wound is like."

"Jeb," Nellie called from outside. "Are you all right?"

"Get in here, woman!" Standish called out to her. "Now!"

Pearson wasn't in a position where he could see anything except the base of the counter in front of him, but he heard the old woman and the girl scramble back into the store.

"So," Standish said to Katz and Davis. "Do you think you two sorry excuses for men can manage to keep an eye on that scoundrel now that I've trussed him up for you?"

"We don't want to be involved." Pearson pegged the new voice as belonging to Mr. Davis, as he had not spoken when Pearson had been standing upright.

"Well, I've got news for you, Mr. Davis," Standish said. "You're already involved. The two of you. And if you think those men in the saloon will see it any differently, you are bigger fools than I already take you for, so you might as well pitch in and do your part."

Pearson heard a new set of boots on the floorboards that came from the back of the store and figured it must be one of the soldier boys coming to see what had caused the gunshot.

"Colonel!" It was a voice of a younger man. "What's happened here?"

"I nabbed me a scoundrel, Lieutenant," Standish announced. "A big one, too. You'll find him hog-tied on the floor right over there next to the counter."

Pearson did not bother to crane his neck to try to look at the young lieutenant. He already knew what he looked like and was content with staring at the officer's boots caked with dust.

"Seems like you hooked yourself quite a prize, Colonel. Good work."

"Says he's got friends over in the saloon," Standish told him. "Don't know how many, but I think the wagonmen are over there right now, so they may be in some danger."

Pearson was hopeful that a few of the lieutenant's men had wandered over to the saloon, too. It would give Bram some leverage that just might get him out of this mess before it lasted too long.

But his hopes were dashed when he heard more boots on the boardwalk outside the store.

"Colonel, Lieutenant," came a gruff voice. "We heard the shot and came running."

"Stand easy, men," the lieutenant told them. "The colonel here was just doing a bit of hunting. He bagged himself a prize buck just over here."

Pearson heard the soldiers walk behind him to get a closer look. "You've done a day's work here, Colonel. He'd look beautiful mounted on your wall."

Their laughter annoyed Pearson. He was not used to being laughed at. "You soldier boys just going to stand around gawking all day or is someone going to patch me up. I'm bleeding pretty bad."

"He is at that," came the gruff voice again that Pearson imagined must belong to the sergeant. "His right hand is mostly gone."

The floorboards creaked as the lieutenant came in for a closer look. Pearson strained to free his mangled right hand to swipe the brat's legs out from under him, but the rope only drew tighter and the pain from the effort almost made him pass out. The old bastard Standish certainly knew how to tie a knot.

"That's a nasty wound, Sergeant. But for a big fellow like him, it's barely a paper cut."

"I don't know about that, Lieutenant. The bulk of his hand is gone. He may bleed to death if we don't cauterize that wound, and fast." The sergeant took a knee and spoke directly into Pearson's ear. "Ever had a wound cauterized, big man? It's awful painful. Only thing worse is the smell."

Pearson lunged and tried to bite the sergeant, but the man easily moved out of the way. "You've hooked yourself a snapper here, Colonel."

"Leave him alone, Sergeant," Standish told him. "We've got bigger troubles than him. Our wagon teams are in the saloon with his friends as we speak. They may be holding them hostage."

Pearson doubted it would come to that. Bram might have gone a bit soft in the head since they had ridden into Mother Lode, but he was still Abraham Hogan, the boss of the Brickhouse Gang. He was still the craftiest man Pearson had ever known and Pearson had known his share. He was probably making those boys a proposition at that very moment. Drinks on the house for the weary travelers and an invitation to join the Brickhouse Gang and split the spoils from here on in.

Bram would be sure to give the new men a choice. Either continue breaking their backs for a meager living or join up with him for a share of the gold they were hauling and live like kings. Nomadic kings without a kingdom, but kings nonetheless. It was the same line he had used on Pearson all those years ago when he asked him to join the gang, and despite his current predicament, Pearson had no complaints.

And when a single pistol shot rang out from across the street, Pearson knew one of the wagonmen must have refused Bram's generous offer of gainful employment. The boss had never been one to take rejection well.

"Sergeant Hastings," the lieutenant called out. "Get over to that window and see what happened."

"Sounds to me like you just lost a man," Pearson said through the pain. "Maybe more than that."

He heard Colonel Standish tell his wife to take the girl behind the safety of the counter next to Mr. Welsh.

"There's a man lying facedown in the middle of the street," the sergeant reported. "Can't tell who it is from here. Might be Holly."

Pearson had no idea who Holly might be, but he figured him for one of the wagonmen. "Didn't I tell you?"

A boot brought down on the rope between Pearson's feet and his hands made him cry out in pain. The lieutenant said, "And I'm telling you to keep your mouth shut until spoken to, big man. You're in no position to be smug with anyone."

Pearson was glad when he heard a familiar voice echo through the deserted main street outside. "Hello to whoever's in the general store. We need to talk. Right now."

The lieutenant took his boot off Pearson's bindings, walked to the front door of the general store, and called out, "Who am I speaking to?"

"I take it you're Lieutenant Samuel Coleman of the United State Cavalry," Bram yelled back. "Or is this Colonel Jebediah Standish doing the talking?"

"He knows your names," Sergeant Hastings said. "How did he know that?"

"Quiet," barked Standish. "I suppose you might as well answer him, Lieutenant. See what he wants."

"This is Coleman," answered the lieutenant. "Now, who in the devil are you?"

"The devil indeed," Bram yelled back. "I'd be Abraham Hogan, leader and founder of the Brickhouse Gang. It's a pleasure to make your acquaintance, Lieutenant."

Pearson could tell by the edge in the young man's voice that he was in no mood for pleasantries. "Tell me what you want or stop talking."

"A direct man," Bram said. "Have it your way. I think you have someone that belongs to me. Maybe you've seen him? Big fella. Well over six feet tall. Closer to seven, by my lights. Ugly and mean as the day is long. Sound familiar?"

Pearson grinned. Bram Hogan certainly had style when it suited him.

"We have him," Coleman admitted. "Got him trussed up on the floor like a Christmas goose. He's hurt pretty bad, though. Got his hand mangled."

"Figured as much when I heard the shot," Bram called back. "Is he still alive?"

"For now," Coleman said. "What happened to Holly?"

"Oh, you mean your friend lying dead out here in the street? His name was Holly?" Bram laughed. "We never had the chance to get properly acquainted. He seemed to have a strong objection to my company, not to mention rejecting a right generous offer I made him, too."

Coleman was about to answer when Pearson heard him stop for some reason. It was the sergeant, who said, "I can see into the saloon from here, Lieutenant. The teamsters are standing right behind him in the doorway, grinning their damned-fool heads off."

Pearson smiled. It seemed as though old Bram had turned the wagonmen, just like Pearson knew he would. Good old Bram had not lost his touch. And had just increased his ranks by a nice number.

"You still have some of our men held hostage in that saloon," Coleman called out. "I guess you want to parlay."

"Parlay?" Bram laughed. "No, I don't need to parlay with you because I don't have any hostages. Your men seem to have had what you might call a change of heart. They asked me to tender their resignations on their behalf."

Pearson could hear a chorus of raspy cackles from the saloon.

"Now, since you're an officer, Lieutenant Coleman," Bram went on, "I guess I'll have to spell that out plainly for you. Your men are now my men. And that puts you at a bit of a disadvantage when it comes to numbers."

"Scoundrels," Colonel Standish cursed. "Low-down, mercenary swine. I'll see to it my boy draws and quarters them for this. They'll hang from the highest flagpole in the territory, I promise you."

But Pearson could tell Lieutenant Coleman had more on his mind just then than military justice. "This doesn't sound like much of a negotiation to me, Hogan. Sounds like all you want to do is have me listen to you brag. Tell me what you want or this conversation is over."

"Fine by me," Bram answered. "I'll state the obvious. You've got yourself maybe five fighting men in there with you, including yourself. I've got your five wagonmen plus my own, which means you're outgunned and outnumbered."

Pearson heard Colonel Standish rush over toward him. "How many in this gang of yours are in there?"

But the outlaw was not in a cooperative mood. "I can't rightly say, Colonel. I never was good with numbers. And I'm feeling a mite sick after what you did to me. Now, if you could loosen these ropes a bit for me, I might be able to think better."

Pearson expected another boot in the back for his insolence, but Standish simply stomped away.

"You might have a slight edge in men," Coleman yelled back. "But you're right about us having five fighting men in here. Those mule skinners have probably told you that much. I assure you we're not parade ground soldiers, Hogan. Each of us has killed more Indians and scavengers than you've ever seen."

"You don't know what I've seen, Coleman," Bram said. "And we've killed our share of men in our time, too. I'd wager that we're probably about even on that score, if not ahead of you. Besides, we don't have innocents to worry about and you do."

Pearson heard Standish rush to the door, but someone hurried to head him off before he got there. Pearson figured it was probably the sergeant who grabbed hold of him. The enlisted men wouldn't dare touch a colonel, even an old fool like Standish.

"We may have innocents," Coleman admitted. "But we also have a store full of supplies. Food. Ammunition. Rifles. We can wait this out long enough to see your bones bleached in the sun if we have to."

"Yes, sir," Bram agreed. "You've certainly got the edge on that score. But we've got ourselves a saloon, see? Plenty of matches, too. Enough to firebomb you bastards out of existence if we're of a mind to. We'll see how much you value all of that ammunition once the flames get to it."

Pearson heard the lieutenant curse. "You, shopkeeper. Where do you keep your gunpowder?"

Mr. Welsh didn't say a word, but Pearson imagined

he pointed to where he kept the ammunition and powder at the back of the store. Pearson knew where it was kept. And he knew Bram knew it, too.

"Now, I know what you're thinking," Bram called out again. "You're thinking the powder's no good to you and you might as well roll it out the back. But anyone who tries to do that will catch a bullet for his trouble. I've already got a man back there waiting for you to try that very thing."

Pearson heard one of the men head toward the back of the store to see for himself. He imagined it was one of the enlisted men. An expendable man. The enlisted men were always expendable to officers.

"Sounds like more bragging to me, Hogan," Coleman said. "You're not too good at this parlay business, are you?"

"Just making sure you understand your situation, soldier boy. Now, seeing as how I'm a reasonable man, I'd like to make you an offer. You let my man go and I'll let you send those women out of there and on their way. I'll give them two horses and let them ride away as free as the day they were born. You can outfit them with all the supplies they can take. They won't be harmed. You've got my word on that."

"His word," the colonel spat. "The word of a no-account brigand means nothing."

But Coleman did not give his answer right away. The delay made Pearson smile. The soldier boy was actually thinking about Bram's offer.

"Coleman," Standish said. "You cannot possibly be considering this man's offer."

Coleman called back to Bram, "And you would allow an old woman and a girl to simply ride away? Unharmed?"

"That's what I said, Lieutenant. Gave you my word, didn't I?"

Standish began to protest again, but something stopped him. Pearson wondered if it might be the sergeant.

"In addition to your man," Coleman said, "what do you get in return?"

"Nothing that's really important to you," Bram answered. "Just the strongbox of the freighter, which I hear has about a thousand dollars in it. And the ten thousand in gold you're hauling on the stagecoach. Army pay, I believe."

Coleman swore and the outlaw heard him move away from the door.

The sergeant said, "Those mule skinners certainly told him everything, didn't they, sir?"

"Will," Coleman said to the other enlisted man, "I want you to start gathering up rifles. Winchesters if he has them. Load them and pass them out among us. Give one to Joe back there and tell him to keep an eye on the back door."

Pearson heard the enlisted man break off and carry out his orders. He knew Mr. Welsh had more than enough rifles and pistols and ammunition in the place to hold out for a month if he had to. Maybe longer if it came to that. But if he knew Bram, it wouldn't last that long.

"Well," Bram prodded from the saloon. "I'm waiting for your answer, Lieutenant. I've made you a nice offer. There's no reason why anyone has to get hurt. That is, anyone else besides your friend Holly over there."

Pearson laughed. Good old Bram.

"I've got a counteroffer for you, Hogan," the lieutenant called back. "You and your men come out unarmed with your hands up and we'll place you under arrest. We'll allow the skinners to go back to work without charges and the entire incident will be forgotten. They have my word on that. You and your men will be given a fair trial and I'll ask the authorities to show leniency. You might only get ten years, but at least you won't hang. I'll also make sure your friend gets medical attention and doesn't bleed to death."

"That so?" Bram said. "And what if I don't like them terms."

"Then you'll die, Hogan. You and every man who stands with you."

Bram grew quiet, but Pearson knew he was not actually considering Coleman's offer. He was probably just waiting for dramatic effect.

And when he did respond, he said what Pearson had expected him to say. "I don't think we'll take you up on your proposition, soldier boy, but we thank you for it just the same. I think I like my proposition better. But no reason to be hasty about it. We'll give you good folks a while to think about it. Let's say until nightfall. Deal?"

"No deal," Coleman called back. "Not now, not tonight, not tomorrow."

"We'll just have to see about that, Coleman." Hogan laughed. "We'll see. Let's you and me talk again in an hour or so. Give you the chance to thaw out a bit."

"I said no deal, Hogan," the lieutenant called back. "Did you hear me? I said no deal."

Pearson heard the sergeant say, "He's gone back into the saloon, sir. No sign of him or the others anywhere."

Pearson heard Will return from the back of the store and, from his vantage point on the floor, saw he was carrying two Winchesters. "Joe's watching the back for us, sir. Looks like Hogan wasn't lying. He's spotted a man back there crouching behind some crates."

"He doesn't strike me as a man who bluffs," Coleman said. "Will, I need you to keep an eye on things here. If anyone goes near the wagon or the stagecoach, shoot them. You've got a nice clean shot from here. Sergeant, I want a complete inventory of everything we've got in here. Weapons, ammunition, dried goods, water. Anything we can use to defend this place. See if the shopkeeper has an accurate count of everything. I have a feeling this will last quite a while and we need to know what we have in our favor."

"Yes, sir," came the sergeant's reply.

As the rest of the soldiers went about carrying out their orders, Pearson heard the colonel pull the lieutenant over to the side. They either had forgotten they had left him trussed up on the floor or just did not care.

"We're in a bad situation here, Sam. I'd wager the water pump is out back and we'll be getting mighty thirsty before long."

"I'm not worried about that," the lieutenant said. "We can clear that man out of there if we have to. I'm more concerned about him setting fire to this place." He knocked on one of the counters. "The wood in here is awfully dry. The damned place will go up like kindling if he starts throwing firebombs at us. He'll be able to pick us off easily enough if we're forced to run out of here."

Pearson heard the colonel sigh heavily. "Sounds like that back door is our only option."

"And not much of one, either. Our horses are in the

front. If he starts picking them off one by one, we're done for."

"We could send a man to ride down to Fort Buchanan," Standish said. "It's only about a day's ride from here."

"Might as well be a week's ride for all of the difference it will make," the lieutenant said. "Our mounts are played out, Colonel. That's why we pulled off into this godforsaken hellhole in the first place. Those animals need rest and water. The troughs out there will help them a little, but that skirmish cost more than just men. It cost us resources and time."

"I'm willing to take that risk," Standish said. "Come nightfall, I plan on taking one of those animals and heading to Buchanan."

"With your trick knee and an exhausted mount under you?" the lieutenant said. "I doubt if you'd make it out of town, much less all the way down to the fort. No, sir. We're stuck here for the time being. All we can do is dig in and wait this out as best we can."

Pearson had not wanted to let the soldier boys know he had been listening to their conversation. It might make them more guarded around him than they already were. But try as he might, he could not hold on to the laugh that burst from him.

Colonel Standish and Lieutenant Coleman walked closer to him. He expected a boot in his side for the trouble.

"We say something funny, mister?" the lieutenant asked.

"Nothing you'd find funny," Pearson told them. "But it's awfully funny to me. You think Bram Hogan is going to give you soldier boys enough time to cook up a plan? Then you don't know what you're up against. Bram Hogan is not a patient man. He ain't a fool, either."

Pearson did not get a boot in the ribs. He caught one in the side of the head instead. And this time, he could not escape the darkness that came for him.

At least his hand no longer hurt him.

CHAPTER SIXTEEN

WHILE THEIR NEW partners enjoyed their whiskey at the bar, Bram and Lem were huddled at the back table of the saloon across the street. One of the men was sitting at the window. He had Pearson's Winchester in his hand. Bram was glad the big man had not bothered to bring the rifle with him. It would have been a waste of a good firearm just when they would need it most.

Lem looked at the five wagonmen and teamsters at the bar. "You sure this is a good idea, Bram?"

"They're not the bunch I want, but they're what we've got." Bram looked at the last member of the Brickhouse Gang he had left. "You've picked a hell of a time to grow a brain, Lem."

"I think pretty good," Lem told him, "especially when it's my backside that might stop a bullet on account of one of them."

Bram was not interested in Lem's thoughts on any

subject, much less on who he brought into the gang. He was in charge for a reason. Lem was a vicious, mean man whose gaunt appearance flat-out rattled some folks. Bram kept him around because he didn't think much and was apt to simply do whatever he was told without question.

Pearson's size was enough to make him an asset in any gang. The fact he could shoot and ride better than most men had not hurt his value any.

Steve had been his brother and had won his spot on that basis alone. Bram knew that he was largely a mimic of him, but he could have picked worse people to imitate in this line of work. He did not want to think about his brother dead out in the desert but had no choice but to believe that was the case. Death would have been the only reason why he had not returned.

Laredo was, well, Laredo. He did just about everything well. Bram had been surprised the Mexican bandit had not formed his own gang. He had half expected Laredo to challenge him for control of the Brickhouse Gang one day, but he had not done so. Now he had ridden off somewhere, leaving Bram in one hell of a lurch.

Bram looked over at his new recruits and did not see much. They were drawn to the whiskey bottle like bees to honey. He did not begrudge a man a drink, especially after a long stretch of time spent out on the trail. But these men were hitting it pretty hard, especially considering Bram had just shot their friend Holly in front of the saloon.

"They're not much," Bram allowed. "I'll give you that." He normally did not confide in anyone but Steve, but as he wasn't around for him to speak to, he decided to break his own rule. "I don't figure they'll stand when the lead flies. I don't think they'll be much use except to absorb some bullets. But we need them, Lem. We don't have a choice, especially since Pearson went and got himself killed."

Lem looked at him. "Pearson ain't dead, boss."

"He might as well be. Even if those soldier boys manage to patch him up, it sounds like he's done for. Got no call for a one-handed giant in this outfit. I don't care how big he is."

"Those boys over there getting killed doesn't help us much at all," Lem observed. "Not enough to make a difference. They've got a store full of supplies and more bullets than we do. They could be in there for a long time if they're of a mind to."

Bram did not like problems. He was not used to dealing with them. He had never had to in the past. If anyone or anything stood in their way, he had always had enough gang members to shoot it until it was not there any longer.

But with Pearson shot up and being held across the street, Lem was his only ally. He did not think the new men could hold a candle to Lem and Lem had always been the weakest member of the gang. But Bram did not need them to ride much or rob a bank. He only needed them long enough to hand over the gold in the freighter and on the stagecoach. Once they helped him do that, they would have served their purpose. Until then, he had to keep them alive and relatively sober.

He only hoped he would not have to do either for long.

Bram decided it would be better if he tried to distract himself with other thoughts. "That man you left to watch the back door any good?"

Lem shrugged. "Good enough to get shot at if it comes to that. He'll keep them pinned down well

enough. I'll go take his place in a little while." He nodded toward the men at the bar. "You might want to
think about making them stop before they get too drunk
to be much good to us."

Bram felt his temper spike. "You telling me how to
run my outfit now?"

"Nope. Just reminding you of the obvious." Lem
touched his glass of whiskey but did not drink it. Bram
watched him turn it slowly. "You believe in things like
luck, boss?"

The outlaw looked at the last member of his gang.
Lem had never struck him as a big thinker. But he saw
no reason why he should not answer the question.

"Guess I'd have to in this line of work," Bram said.
"Been shot at more times than I care to count. Been
hit a few times, but nothing serious. I've had people try
to kill me all my life, both before during and after the
army. Red men, too. I don't know if it's luck or something else, but whatever it is, I believe in it. Why?"

Lem turned the glass between his thumb and fore-
finger. "Because if you believe in luck, it stands to reason that there's the opposite of luck. A curse, maybe. I
know I believe in luck and I know this damned town is
cursed."

Now Bram needed a drink and poured one for himself. He had enough problems facing him without the
gang idiot talking that kind of nonsense like an old
washerwoman. "Knock off that talk."

"I'm serious, boss," Lem persisted. "Think about
everything that's happened to us since we rode into
this miserable town. Nothing's gone right since we
rode that marshal out of town on a rail. The money
dried up. Steve's . . . gone. Laredo, too. And now Pearson's shot up. All those scrapes we were in and none of

us got so much as a scratch. We come here and we're picked apart."

"You forgot about Bennet," Bram reminded him, "and Grimes. They got themselves killed along the way, remember? And I lost others in the gang before you joined up, too."

"I didn't forget them, but we lost them over time. Not all at once like this. This town has cost us too much, boss. And I think it'll kill us if we let it."

Bram had never had patience for weakness, even in the best of times. He did not have patience now that their backs were to the wall. He grabbed hold of Lem by the shirt and pulled him halfway off his chair. "You listen to me. This town has taken a lot from us, but when that wagon train rolled in here, it paid what it owes us and then some. We're going to get that gold and ride out of here with the biggest score of our lives." He looked at the men at the bar, who had not noticed what was happening behind them. But Dulce did. The Mexican woman was always watching and she was watching them now. Bram allowed her to keep on looking.

"That's all this is about. It's what all of this has always been about. So you're going to quit this talk of luck and curses and dead men and remember what we came here to do. Drain this place dry and move on to the next town. With a score this big, we never have to do this kind of work again. Maybe Steve is dead. Maybe Laredo is dead, too. Maybe Beck killed them both. I don't know. But I do know we've got about ten thousand in gold sitting in wagons across the street, and by God, I'm not going to give that up because you're listening to the snakes in your head. Everything we've lost will have been for nothing if we walk away now. I don't know about you, but I plan on getting paid."

He released Lem with a shove and returned to his brooding.

Lem straightened himself out and drank down his whiskey. He cleared his throat and wiped his mouth with the back of his sleeve after he set the glass on the table. "I know I ain't much, boss, but I ain't a quitter. You can count on me for whatever you decide. I'd just like to know what you're planning is all."

Bram was still pulling all of that together in his mind. The wagon train had not been in town an hour yet. It had all happened so fast that he had not had the chance to think much, just react to the good fortune that had parked itself across the street.

But he would need a plan if he had any hope of getting that gold, much less live long enough to spend it.

He decided it was time to break one of his cardinal rules. He spoke his mind before he had it all figured out. "We've got ourselves a siege here. We might not like it, but that's what we've got. We can't just grab the gold out of the stage and take off. Not yet. Those soldiers have a clear shot at us if we try. And I'd wager they'll probably step outside after it's dark and guard the wagons. I know that's what I'd do."

"But we're not pinned down in here," Lem said. "We can go out the back door whenever we want."

"And we're going to do just that," Bram explained. "But we're in a better position than they are. They've got enough food to hold out for a while, but they don't have water. That's why we need to keep an eye on the store's back door. To keep them from getting any and to keep them from escaping. We give them a couple of days and let the thirst get to them. They've got an old woman and a girl with them. They'll be wanting to use the privy. We can use that to our advantage. Use it to negotiate and keep them busy while we angle for the gold."

"Why don't we just burn the place like you told them you would?"

Bram had threatened that, but it was an empty threat. "That place will burn hot and fast. The flames would jump to the freighter and the wagons in no time. I aim on salvaging as much of that as possible." He nudged Lem to take the sting out of his earlier rebuke. "No sense in only settling for ten thousand when we've got a couple of tons of goods to trade in Texas or Mexico."

Lem did not seem like he bought the plan, but he did not argue. He looked at the wagonmen at the bar. "You still plan on cutting them in for a share like you promised?"

Bram shrugged. "Maybe, though I think splitting the money two ways is easier math. Three if we can get Pearson out of there." He poured a drink for Lem and one for himself. "Besides, you and me are used to taking money off dead men, aren't we?"

That got Lem to smile. "Yes, boss. I guess you could say we are at that."

The two men clinked glasses and sealed the deal with a drink.

Bram looked over at the bar and saw the men begin to sway. They were awash in glory and talking about all of the things they were going to buy with their money. He imagined he would not have to kill many of them. They would probably get themselves killed in the course of things. He caught Dulce's eye and waved his hand under his chin, signaling her to cut them off.

She did not acknowledge him and she did not look away. Her eyes bored into him with the same hatred she'd felt that first night in her room and in all of the nights since. Yes, she was quite a woman. Maybe the strongest woman he had ever known. It would be a shame to kill her, but he could not risk bringing her with them. She would cut his throat while he slept the first chance she got. He knew the only reason why she had not done it yet was hope. Hope that they would leave town and leave her behind. He would enjoy taking that hope from her when the time came. He would enjoy seeing that vacant look in her eyes. He would need the memory of it to keep him warm on the cold nights to come.

But for now there was business to attend to.

Bram stood up and Lem stood with him. "Dulce's cutting them off. I want one man watching the front door here and one man on the back door of the store at all times, even at night. Everyone stands a watch, including me. The men who aren't watching should be sleeping. No more whiskey until we're over. I need them ready to shoot, not passed out and hungover. See to it they're ready."

Lem rubbed his hand across the stubble on his chin. "Sure, boss, but what'll you be doing?"

Bram started for the front door of the saloon. "Moving things along."

CHAPTER SEVENTEEN

"LIEUTENANT!" SERGEANT HASTINGS called out when he saw Hogan in the doorway of the saloon. "I think they're looking to talk again."

Coleman and Standish drew closer to the door and waited.

"What the devil does he want now?" Standish asked aloud.

"Probably looking to toy with us some more," Coleman said. "Do me a favor and speak to the women, Colonel. I don't want them bothered by what this lunatic says."

But the colonel did not move. "I was handling men like this while you were still in diapers, Lieutenant. I have no intention of playing wet nurse to an old woman and a girl when the enemy is right in front of us. Besides, Nellie is an army wife. She's tougher than all of us put together. She knows the dangers we're facing."

Coleman shut his eyes and held his tongue. He knew

there was nothing more stubborn in the world than a retired senior officer, especially one with the record to back up his self-importance.

Fortunately, Hogan did not wait long to speak. "Hello in the store!"

Coleman held up his hand for the men to be silent. He kept that silence for a good half a minute, allowing the tension to build across the thoroughfare. He would respond in his own time, not at Hogan's command.

When enough time had passed, Coleman said, "We're here, Hogan. What do you want?"

"There you are, Lieutenant. Hope I didn't wake you. I know you officers aren't used to such hard work."

Under different circumstances, Coleman would have admired the outlaw's banter. "You won't catch anyone sleeping in here, Hogan. Step out into the street and we'll be happy to show you just how awake we are."

Hogan's laughter carried across the street. It was not a pleasant sound. It reminded Coleman of a caw. "I bet that would just make your day, wouldn't it, Lieutenant. Though I doubt you'd be the one pulling the trigger. Such work is beneath a man of your stature."

"No one in this outfit will kill you except me, Hogan. You've got my word on that."

"I'll look forward to holding you to it. Have you thought about my offer?"

Colonel Standish spoke to Hastings. "Sergeant, give him our answer by putting a round through the door."

Coleman said, "As you were, Sergeant." He looked at Standish. "I'm in command here, Colonel. Not you. If you can't remember that, you might as well walk back there with the others right now."

The colonel reddened but held his tongue. "Proceed, Lieutenant."

Hogan seemed to enjoy the silence. "So, you are thinking it over?"

"You're in no position to make demands here, Hogan. You're outgunned and outmanned. You're not up against a bunch of cowed townspeople any longer. Make one false move and we'll put a bullet in you."

"How are the ladies holding up, Lieutenant? Any of them ask to use the privy yet? They will, you know. Your men, too. You might be as tough as you say, but even the toughest men need to answer the call of nature sometime. It'll get awfully ripe in there if you don't, especially in this heat."

"Scoundrel," Standish cursed. "Blasted scoundrel."

"Worry about yourselves," Coleman called back. "We'll be fine."

"Oh, come now, Lieutenant. You sound like you're a West Point man to me. I thought you boys were taught to be chivalrous."

Standish was about to say something, but Coleman managed to clasp his hand over the colonel's mouth in time. He pulled him back against a shelf and held him in place. "Not a word, sir. He's trying to get under our skin. He's trying to get us riled up and show our hand. He's more in the dark about us than we are of him. Don't give him the pleasure of thinking he's winning. The more he talks, the more he tells us about what he's planning. Don't cost us the only advantage we've got. Understand?"

The fire in Standish's eyes told him he did, in fact, understand. Coleman slowly took his hand away from the colonel's mouth. "I know what I'm doing, sir. Let me do it."

Hogan called out again. "You got a stammer or something, Lieutenant? The army must be worse off than I thought if they're promoting officers who can't even hold a conversation."

Coleman moved back to the door. "You're the one doing all of the talking here, Hogan, not us. Say what you want to say or quit bothering us."

"Impolite behavior is an unbecoming trait in an officer," Hogan mocked. "But I guess there's no accounting for manners these days. Lucky for you, I'm a civilized man and I'm about to prove it to you. I've decided to show you good people a bit of old-fashioned Mother Lode hospitality. My friend here tells me you've got someone watching the back door of the store. That's good. You ought to do that. That means you know I already have a man with a rifle back there. I'm making a deal with you. Those womenfolk and your men can use the privy out back whenever the urge strikes them, and you have my word that no one will shoot them. Unless someone fires first, of course. But only the privy, mind. Not the water pump."

Coleman did not know what the outlaw hoped to gain by the gesture. "We didn't ask you for any favors, Hogan. And you won't get anything from us."

"Don't worry, Lieutenant. Your line in the sand is still as deep and wide as it was the moment you drew it. It's just my way of being neighborly. After all, you good people are our guests. I just ask you to consider telling me how the big man is doing. His name is Pearson, in case you're wondering. I was hoping you could see your way clear to telling me how he's doing. Is he still alive?"

Coleman gave the high sign to Sergeant Hastings on the other side of the door. Hastings stepped away from his position and took a look at the wounded man in front of the counter. He spoke to Coleman in a hushed tone. "He's still wiggling, sir. Looks like the bleeding has stopped some."

The lieutenant weighed whether or not he should tell Hogan the truth. He decided it would not cost him anything and might even get Hogan to keep talking. "He's still hurt but alive. The bleeding appears to have stopped."

"See that, Lieutenant? That wasn't so hard, was it? I plan on having some of my men remove this poor soul lying in the middle of the street. A dead body is bad for the saloon business, such as it is in Mother Lode these days. I'd like to have some of my men clear him out of here and I'd like your word that no one will shoot them when they do. We won't go any closer to the store or make a play for the wagons. You have my word on that."

Coleman was about to respond when the colonel grabbed his arm. "Consider your answer carefully, Coleman. He's scouting your lines to see how far he can push you."

Coleman was beginning to grow tired of the colonel's interference. He was not some greenhorn fresh out of the Point. He pulled his arm free of Standish's grasp and called back to Hogan, "One man pulls him clear. Any more than that and we shoot. Anyone comes near the wagons and we shoot. You have *my* word on that, Hogan."

The outlaw laughed. "That's the spirit, Lieutenant. Hold firm. Thank you for being a reasonable man. I wish you folks a pleasant evening. I don't think we'll have much cause to talk before then. But if you get lonely, by all means, give a shout. I'll be right here."

Coleman saw no reason to respond, so he did not. Instead, he spoke to Hastings.

"Get ready, Sergeant. If you see more than one man or woman come out of that saloon, put a bullet in them."

He looked back at Will. "Get ready to move on the sergeant's command. Tell Joe to stand ready back there. This may be some kind of diversion while they try something."

Standish pulled the Colt from his shoulder holster. "If they do, we'll be ready."

"*If* they do, Colonel," Coleman said, "and only if they do. I don't want to start anything if we can avoid it. We're still in a strong position here. No sense in forcing the issue with women and civilians to consider."

Coleman moved to look out the shop window and begrudgingly allowed the colonel to join him. One of the teamsters—Townsend, he believed his name was—pushed through the batwing doors of the saloon and toddled down to where Holly had fallen. The teamster looked a bit worse for the wear and Coleman decided he must have been drinking. He imagined all of the wagonmen were in similar or worse condition, save for whoever Hogan had placed to guard the back door of the store.

"I'll remember his face," Standish said. "And I'll see him swing when all of this is done."

But Coleman held his silence as he watched the wagonman grab Holly's corpse by the legs and drag it away down the alley next to the saloon.

Sergeant Hastings kept the man in his rifle sights the entire time. "No one else is moving in the saloon, sir. Looks like Townsend is alone."

It was the first bit of good news Coleman had heard since this whole mess had started. "Keep a sharp eye, Joe. This Hogan is a crafty one."

Coleman shut his eyes as Standish began to sputter.

The inactivity was clearly getting to him. "I know you're in charge, Lieutenant, but now's the time to make our move. Those teamsters are drunk as skunks right now. I think we should rush the saloon now. Clear them out and end this thing before they get a second wind. They won't be expecting that."

But Coleman had no intention of doing any such thing. "We don't know what we're up against, Colonel. We would be exposed the entire time between here and the saloon and I don't know how many men Hogan has in there with him besides the teamsters. And that big fellow on the floor back there won't tell us, not that I'd trust anything he said anyway. We have the high ground, sir. I'm not going to throw that away on a gamble when I don't have to. Not yet, anyway."

Standish clenched his jaw and rattled the pistol against his leg. "Yes, of course. Good thinking, Coleman. It's just so damned hard to sit here doing nothing."

The lieutenant kept his eye on the saloon. Hogan was not just some bloodthirsty outlaw. He was a crafty man indeed. Crafty men tended to overplay their hand after a while. "But we *are* doing something, sir. We're watching. And learning."

CHAPTER EIGHTEEN

L AREDO HELD HIS hand up to his brow to shield his eyes from the intense glare of the sun. He was looking at the outline of a town shimmering on the horizon. The place was called Amenia and he imagined that was where he would find John Beck.

The Mexican bandit had given up following the marshal's meandering trail the previous day. It was the errant, winding roving of a man who had clearly lost his way and, quite possibly, his mind. If he had continued moving west, he was undoubtedly already dead. Steve Hogan's horse must have been played out by the time he happened upon Beck's warren in the cave. The droppings he had found were almost dry. It was closer to death than it had been to life.

But when Laredo decided to make straight for the nearest town, he picked up the horse's trail once again. The mount's gait had grown, meaning that Beck had found water somewhere in all of his wanderings. The chances that that man and horse had made it as far as Amenia were excellent. No buzzards circled between where Laredo now stood and the town.

He imagined the man must have wandered a week or more in the desert before he stumbled upon the town. It had been less than half a day's ride from the cave he had clearly called home for so long. It was a miracle he had found it at all. He just as easily could have missed this place as found it and the idea of it sent a shudder through Laredo's spine. Did Beck have some unseen hand guiding him through the desert? The idea of it seemed foolish to him, but there was no denying Beck had an intense will to live. Any sane man would have given up and died long ago.

His day would come soon.

Laredo dug his heels into the horse and got it moving again. He kept his mount traveling at a slow and steady pace. He had been careful to keep the animal watered but did not want to risk pushing the gelding if he did not have to. He had a notion that he would need all the strength the horse could muster before the day was through.

An hour or so later, as he rode down the main thoroughfare of Amenia, he cursed Abraham Hogan for deciding to set up shop in a flyspeck town like Mother Lode. The place had not been worth a spent bullet, much less all of the men and trouble it had cost him. If they had only kept riding for an extra day, they would have come upon this place, which offered much more for the taking.

The stores and boardwalks were bustling with people and wagons. Miners in from the hills, their faces black with dirt and grime, clamored outside the claim office and the bank as they looked for a safe place to deposit their wages. Sporting ladies adorned the porches above the rooftops, silently peddling the wares that nature had given them.

Laredo saw them looking at him as he rode into town and fought hard not to meet their gaze. He knew the figure he cut on horseback and knew he would draw their attention. It had been a long time since he had known the company of a woman. Perhaps too long, but he dared not allow himself to be distracted by that now. Not until he knew if John Beck had made it to this place and was still alive.

He drew his gelding to a halt in front of the Coffin Nail Saloon and decided this was as good a place as any to begin his quest. Perhaps the best place, as men tended to gossip like old hens once whiskey and beer began to loosen their tongues.

The Coffin Nail was no different from the dozens of other saloons he had seen in this part of the world. The red paint was cracked and peeling beneath the harsh Arizona sun. Its wood dry and brittle. When he pushed his way through the swinging doors, he found the inside was just as familiar. An ornate bar was lined with men standing about, drinking their fill and telling lies to each other. None of the men sitting at the tables were playing cards. They were hunched over their glasses of beer or whiskey, swapping tall tales of their time in the mines or on the cattle trails that crisscrossed the territory.

It was a good place for information. In fact, Laredo decided, it was the best place.

He edged his way to a clear spot at the bar and, as he was in no particular hurry, waited for the barman to notice him.

He was a bald, fat man with a thick black mustache waxed to curls at the end. He obviously took great pride in his appearance, and Laredo wondered if he might, in fact, be the owner of the Coffin Nail.

Eventually, the bartender came to him and did not look happy. "You'd do best to move along, amigo. This here is an American bar and we don't take too kindly to serving your kind."

Laredo had encountered this kind of thing before and quietly placed a ten-dollar piece on the bar.

The barman's eyes brightened. He was, indeed, the owner. "Do you serve this kind here, amigo?"

The fancy man scooped up the coin and produced a filthy rag to wipe the spot on the bar in front of Laredo. "What'll it be, mister?"

"Tequila, if you've got any."

The man ran his tongue inside his mouth. "Closest we've got to it is cactus wine."

Laredo smiled. The mixture of tequila and peyote tea was a welcome idea. "That'll be just fine."

The bartender rapped his knuckles on the bar. "Coming right up. Got plenty of it, too. You'll be set right in no time."

Laredo stood quietly while he waited for a drink, ignoring the jostling from the men crowded around him. Bram Hogan would have made a scene, insisting on clearing a place for him and his men in the crowded saloon. But Laredo was alone and knew the men meant no slight by it. The tall Mexican simply allowed himself to be bumped into by the men engaged in conversation.

And as he had learned in the course of his travels, passiveness often paid the quickest dividends.

"Can't believe old Ross is dead," he heard one of the men who had just bumped into him say. "Cut down in the prime of his life by a half-crazed drover."

"He couldn't have been too crazy if he got the jump on old Ross," another man said. "That man was a bull if I ever saw one. Why, I heard tell of him taking on five strikers with his bare hands down in the mine. When the dust settled, he made those boys pull a full shift, broken noses and all."

"Well, he's got plenty of dust settling over him in his grave," Laredo heard another man say. "I heard he was thrown clear off that top floor and landed on his damned-fool head. Can't say as I'll be shedding any tears for him. Old Ross was a nasty man when he was drunk."

"Must've been drunk to get done in like that by a half-crazed drover."

"Couldn't have been too crazed to have done that to him, though."

The conversation continued in that circular way as the barman served Laredo his cactus wine. The bitter-sweetness of it caused his mouth to water and he carefully took a sip of the potent drink. The mix slammed home quickly and made him feel like he had just soaked in a tub for a week.

Laredo chanced another sip as he listened to the men retell the tale of the men who had died and what had happened since.

"Must've been legal, though," one of the men observed, "seeing as how the sheriff stuck by him before and since."

"Hauser's getting on in years, boys," said another. "Needed himself a deputy. Man couldn't have been all that crazy if he pinned a star on his chest. Hauser is a lot of things, but he ain't hardly a fool."

"The new fella seems personable enough," one of them observed. "Talks kind of fancy for a drover. Fancier than any man I've ever heard, leastways."

"The hell do you know about fancy anyway?" one of his friends said. "You ain't hardly been outside of Amenia since the day you were born."

"I know a lot more about it than you. I've been to Tucson, boys."

Laredo decided to interrupt the conversation for his own purposes. "Forgive me, gentlemen, but I could not avoid overhearing what you said about this new deputy of Sheriff Hauser's. He sounds like he might be a friend of mine. Do you know his name?"

The men regarded the tall Mexican stranger for a moment, first looking at what he was drinking and then back at him.

One of them said, "Tall, rangy fella. About six feet tall or so. Black hair. My wife thinks he's sporting, but she married me, so I wouldn't go by what she says."

"Touched in the head," another man offered. "I heard he talks to his horse down at the stable at least once a day. He's got old Abraham down there pretty frightened of him, but he seems harmless enough."

"I don't think old Ross would call him harmless," another one said.

Laredo's blood ran cold despite the cactus wine. These men could only be describing John Beck. He had not known the marshal at all, but remembered what he had looked like, and their description of this new deputy fit his memory of the man the gang had ridden out of town on a rail.

He took another sip. Suspecting Beck had survived the desert and knowing he was still alive were two different things entirely. It was one of the only times in his life that he had wished he was wrong.

One of the men shook him from his thoughts. "You say this man is a friend of yours?"

"Could be," Laredo allowed. "Any of you gentlemen know his name?"

"Beck," one of the men told him. "John Beck. Sounds
like a phony name to me, but that's what he calls himself."

Laredo finished his drink and set the glass on the
bar. John Beck lives!

"How do you know Beck, mister?"

Laredo grinned. "I'm afraid that is a long story and
my throat is dry. I'll have to buy you men a drink before I tell it."

The men seemed eager to accept but pulled back
just as quickly.

"That's all well and good, mister," one of them said,
"but we ain't the type who usually cotton to your kind."

Laredo caught the barman's attention and beck-
oned him to come over. "No one's asking you to, señor.
All I want is some friendly conversation. As we say in
Mexico, *Entre las bromas la verdad se asoma.*"

The men looked as puzzled as if he had been speaking Latin.

"Sounds pretty," one of them said.

"So pretty I don't know what it means," admitted
another. "I like to know what I'm drinking to."

Laredo smiled. It meant "Between jokes lies the
truth." But they did not need to know that. "Just an old
saying about good friends, amigos. Now, what do you
say to more drinks?"

B Y THE TIME he slipped out of the Coffin Nail Saloon, the men had given Laredo all the truth he
could handle about John Beck. How he had thrown
himself into his new position as Sheriff Hauser's dep-

uty and even got himself a pretty lady friend in the process. A Celestial maid at the Amenia Hotel named Lilly. She had taken up with Beck since he had come to town and the two of them were playing house. Laredo was glad. A man who had suffered as much as John Beck had suffered should know some happiness before the end of his life.

And John Beck's life would end that very night. Laredo had no choice but to see to it personally.

The men had told him the miners were intending to ambush the deputy the following day and Laredo could not take that chance. Although Beck would be just as dead by their hands as by his own, Laredo owed this man a debt and was honor bound to repay it. A debt that men like Abraham Hogan could not understand. Laredo had disgraced this brave man by taking part in turning him out into the wilderness. He owed him a death befitting a man of such honor and strength.

He had to make sure he was dead with his own two eyes. For although Beck seemed content with his new life in Amenia, he was obviously a very proud man. And it would only be a matter of time before that pride began to eat away at him. As his comfort in Amenia grew, so would the memories of the nightmare he had suffered that fateful day in Mother Lode begin to return. He would eventually seek out the men who had treated him like a dog and would not stop until he put them in their graves. Not even the love of this woman Lilly would be enough to hold him here. He would think himself unworthy of her until the last member of the Brickhouse Gang lay dead in the street. He would not stop until his revenge was complete.

Laredo knew this to be true, for he had felt this same way back when he had been a younger man. It had been a burning hatred that scorched his soul until he had his revenge on the man who had taken everything from him.

The fact that the man had also been his father had only made his burden all that more difficult to bear. The day he took his father's life was the day he was born anew.

Yes, Laredo knew all about revenge, which was why he knew he would never rest until John Beck was dead.

Laredo drew the chill of the coming desert night deep into his lungs. He knew he would need all of his wits about him to bring this great man down.

He looked up and down the length of Main Street for the saloon where the gringos had told him the miners planning to ambush Beck could be found. The Homestead was halfway up the street between the Coffin Nail and the jailhouse. That was good. It would bring his quarry closer to him quickly. He could put several miles between himself and Amenia before nightfall.

He climbed into the saddle and rode his gelding across the street to the Homestead and tethered the horse to the hitching rail out front. The water trough was full and his horse eagerly drank from it as Laredo walked into the saloon.

The place was just as dingy as the Coffin Nail but nowhere near as crowded. The bar only had a few men standing at it, and all of the tables were empty save one. Five men who bore the dusty grime of miners sat huddled together over half-drunk beers, undoubtedly working up the courage to take down the man who had killed their friend.

Laredo felt a small amount of pity for the men, who ignored him as he stepped inside. They had no idea they were about to die.

They did not look at him until the bartender noticed the tall Mexican standing alone just inside the door. Laredo's hand rested on his belt buckle, just next to the handle of the Colt holstered above his belt.

"Can I help you, amigo?"

Laredo watched the miners turn to look at him.

"I'm afraid you can't help me, señor. My business isn't with you, but with these five men here."

The miner in the center of the circle slowly pushed himself out of his chair. His four friends stood, too. "Guess that means you're talking to us."

"Maybe," Laredo said. "If you're the men who aim to kill John Beck tonight."

The miner turned to his friends before looking once again at Laredo. "And what if we are?"

"Then you're going to die."

The men broke toward Laredo just as the Mexican drew his Colt and cut loose. He fired five times and each bullet found its mark in the chest of a miner. The men had all fallen back against the table and chairs, clutching their chests as life slowly left them.

The rest of the men were already running out the back, the bartender among them, by the time Laredo broke open the cylinder and dumped out the spent cartridges on the saloon floor. He calmly but quickly fed fresh rounds from his belt into the cylinder before flicking it shut.

He was glad the men had run away. It would allow him to have more rounds to meet John Beck when he came. And he would surely come, just as the men were sure to run down to the jail and fetch the sheriff.

Laredo smiled. Gringos were so predictable.

He stood with his back to the wall, ready to fire at anyone who came in the front door or from the back.

If Sheriff Hauser was the man Laredo had heard he was, he doubted either he or his deputy would charge headlong into a gunfight. They would approach carefully, but they would die just the same.

Laredo's head snapped around to the front of the saloon when he heard a man call to him from outside. "Hello in the saloon! This is Sheriff Hauser. Come out with your hands in the air. We've got you covered, son."

Laredo judged the lawman to be just to the left of the saloon window. He needed to bring him closer if he had any hope of getting a good shot at him.

Laredo answered in Spanish, but only loud enough for the sheriff to hear him. Loud enough to make him curious.

"I know you've probably been drinking, son," the sheriff said. "I know those men most likely had it coming. No reason for anyone else to get hurt."

A plank on the floorboard creaked. The sheriff's shadow fell over the window. "So why don't you just come on out of there before—"

Another creak sounded and Laredo took careful aim at the wall just beside the window. He heard a man cry out and the street filled with the sounds of panicked men and women.

The Mexican knew that he must have hit his mark. He had no idea if he had killed the lawman, but it did not matter. It should be enough to bring Beck running right into his trap. If it did not, he would have to hunt Beck down this very night.

CHAPTER NINETEEN

J OHN BECK BOLTED upright in bed when he heard the shots, forgetting Lilly's head was on his chest. Sheriff Hauser had given him the night off, so he and Lilly had made love and gone to bed early. He had just begun to allow himself to feel normal again when the sounds of gunfire and screams carried into the room through the open window.

"That was a gunshot," Lilly said in the darkness. "A lot of gunshots."

Beck forgot how comfortable he had been and got moving. In one swift movement, he flung his legs out of bed, pulled up his pants, snatched the Colt from the holster, and bolted through the door. He did not even take the time to pull on his boots.

Beck rumbled down the stairs barefoot and ignored questions as he ran past Ma Stanton perched behind the front desk.

"What's happening, Deputy?" she screeched. "What's going on out there?"

Beck did not waste time answering her. She had seen him run down the staircase. How could he know any more than she did?

He slid to a halt out on the boardwalk in front of the hotel and tried to get a sense of where the trouble was. He looked around at the townspeople who had gathered there for some idea of where the shots had come from.

"Where?" he asked a townsman standing by the hotel.

The man pointed down Main Street in the direction of most of the saloons in Amenia. It was not much help, but at least it gave him some sort of direction.

Beck pushed through the crowd that had begun to back away from that part of town. He commanded them to get out of the way as he rushed by. Most did as he told them, some did not, and it took some mighty fancy footwork to avoid stumbling over the odd leg or walking stick.

But when he broke through the crowd, he saw Sheriff Hauser crouched just outside the window of the Homestead Saloon.

"Hello in the saloon!" Beck heard Hauser yell.

Don't do that, Beck thought as he almost slipped on a woman's skirts. *He'll mark you for sure that way.*

He could not hear the rest of what the sheriff might have said as he regained his footing and kept running to back him up. A moment later, six gunshots rang out. He watched George Hauser flinch as he tumbled off the boardwalk and into the thoroughfare. Light from the saloon bled out from the bullet holes in the walls.

The panicked screams of the townspeople swept

over him as Beck now ran as fast as he could. He did not think of his footing or of the people running all around him. He did not even take time to stop and check on the sheriff.

For he knew that those six shots had been pistol shots, not rifle shots. That meant the man's gun was empty.

He would be ready to fire again in a few seconds, seconds that Beck could not afford to lose. That was why he ran as fast as he could toward the Homestead Saloon. He ignored the splinters that dug into his feet as he gained precious seconds he could not afford to lose while the shooter reloaded his gun.

He did not try to slow down as he reached the Homestead Saloon. He jumped to the side and launched himself through the batwing doors.

Instinct caused him to hit the sawdust floor at a roll. Beck came up to a knee and took aim at the man in front of him.

He saw everything at once.

The gunman was a dark-skinned man and looked oddly familiar. Was he a Mexican?

The man's pistol was open and he had just dumped his bullets onto the floor as Beck squeezed off a shot. But Beck had rushed it and the bullet went wide of its mark. It hit the wall instead.

Beck's next five shots traced the fleeing gunman as he broke toward the bar and dove over it. The Mexican hit the back of the bar first before tumbling behind it.

Beck did not know if any of his shots had hit the shooter but knew his last bullet had shattered the mirror behind the bar, showering his target in broken glass.

Beck remained on one knee as he kept the bar between him and his target. He thumbed open the cylinder and shook the spent bullets from his gun. As the bullets hit the floor, a deafening yell filled his ears. He looked up in time to see the Mexican, bloodied from the cuts of shattered glass, spring over the bar at him.

Beck tried to stand to meet him but stepped on one of the spent casings on the floor and lost his footing.

His misstep saved his life.

As he fell backward, he saw the gunman's blade had sliced the air where his neck had been only a split second before. The Mexican hit the floor chest first and gasped as the air escaped his lungs.

It was not until Beck reached down for a fresh bullet from his gun belt that he realized he had left it back in his room.

He was out of bullets, but far from unarmed.

He lunged for the Mexican and brought the pistol butt down on the back of his head.

The Mexican managed to shift his weight and use his shoulder to absorb the next blow as he pushed off his right arm and sent Beck tumbling off him.

Beck and the gunman got to their feet at the same time. The bloodied bandit brandishing a Bowie knife. Beck holding an empty gun.

That was when he recognized the man.

The sharp features. The scar across his right cheek still visible despite the blood from the cuts from the shattered mirror.

"You!" Beck said as he took a step back. "You're one of them." A name swam out of the darkness of his brain. "They called you Laredo."

The Mexican ignored the blood that ran down his face as he sneered at his opponent. "You remember me. That is good, gringo. A man should know the name of the man who is about to kill him."

Laredo slashed at him, snapping Beck out of his stupor as instinct caused him to spring out of the way.

The Mexican stabbed at his stomach and Beck once again managed to jump to the side, planted his feet, and swung the pistol around as hard as he could. The barrel caught Laredo in the temple and caused him to stagger backward into the bar.

Beck lunged for the knife in Laredo's outstretched hand and pinned it to the bar top. He brought the butt of his pistol down on the bandit's hand once, then twice, then a third time before the outlaw lost his grip on the knife and it fell behind the bar.

Beck cried out when Laredo grabbed a handful of his hair with his left hand and yanked his head back. He grabbed hold of Beck's throat with his right hand and squeezed.

Beck could tell that Laredo's hand hurt from the blows of his pistol but the grip was still tight enough to cause Beck to gag. The bandit shifted his weight and pulled Beck down to the floor with him. Laredo struggled to climb on top of him and wrap both hands around his neck.

Beck felt his own strength begin to ebb as his brain and lungs were deprived of oxygen. Fighting unconsciousness with all of his might, he began pummeling the outlaw's sides with lefts and rights. Each blow was weaker than the last as stars began to form before his eyes.

But the punches paid dividends when the Mexican's grip faltered just enough for Beck to swipe Laredo's hands away and bring a right elbow across his assailant's face, breaking his nose.

The bandit rocked back and brought both hands to his ruined nose.

Using strength he did not know he had, Beck jack-knifed up and headbutted Laredo between the eyes. Laredo fell backward to the floor.

His breath slowly coming back to him, Beck fumbled for the pistol he had dropped during the struggle. He snatched it off the floor as he got to a knee and fell on Laredo, bringing the gun down on his face again and again as the fury that had built up inside him for so long finally broke free.

He struck him for the indignity he had suffered back at Mother Lode.

He struck him for turning him out into the desert and leaving him for dead.

He struck him for the fear he had felt every moment he had wondered might be his last all those days under the brutal sun.

He struck him for not killing him outright.

"John!" came a familiar voice from somewhere behind him.

A voice that did not stop him from striking Laredo again and again until someone slid an arm under his chin and pulled him to his feet.

Still in the grip of his own rage, Beck flailed backward with the pistol, trying to brain whoever was keeping him from finishing this bastard for good.

"It's over, John," came George Hauser's soothing voice. "It's over."

The blind violence that had consumed him slowly faded as he realized his friend was still alive.

"George? Is that you?"

He felt the arm around his neck slacken enough for

him to turn around. He saw Hauser leaning against the bar, his left side a bloody mess. Beck managed to catch him as he stumbled and helped ease him down to the floor. He propped him up against the base of the bar. "Sorry, son. I'm just a little light-headed right now."

Beck pulled open the side of the sheriff's vest and saw his entire side was damp with blood. The worst bleeding seemed to be coming from just under his arm and Beck thrust his hand against it to stop the flow.

"Someone get a doctor!" he yelled out to the people who had gathered at the door of the saloon. "Now!"

He heard a commotion outside and, out of the corner of his eye, saw Lilly rush into the saloon with a blanket wrapped around her. She dropped to a knee and began looking at Hauser's wounds.

"Don't worry about it, darlin'," Hauser slurred. He was fighting to stay conscious. "It's just a scratch."

"It's a lot of scratches, then." She got to her feet and ran behind the bar to grab a bottle of whiskey.

Beck felt his own hands begin to shake as he realized the blood kept leaking from his friend. "Just hold on, George. The doctor will be here in a minute."

Hauser laughed, then coughed a wet cough. "That's a nice sentiment, John, but there's not much he can do for me. I'm done for and you know it."

But Beck would not accept that. "Not a chance. No way a slug like Laredo can get the best of you."

"Laredo, is it?" He looked over at the fallen outlaw on the floor. "I've heard of him. Guess you have, too. That explains it." Hauser offered a weak smile. "He's from Mother Lode, ain't he? One of the ones who . . . did that to you."

"Don't worry about him," Beck said, gripping the

wound even tighter. "You just worry about you right now."

"I'm not worried," Hauser said. "Those cards were dealt a long time ago. I'll end up wherever I belong, I guess. But the one I'm worried about is you, John. I was kind of hoping to be around a little longer to help you mend."

Beck looked at his friend's wounds and winced. There seemed to be so many of them and all of them leaking life. "Don't talk, George." He looked at the saloon door. "Where the hell is that doctor?"

But Hauser patted Beck's mouth to silence him. "You've got to take care of yourself, son. You've got to let whatever happened to you out there go. It'll eat you up inside if you don't make peace with it. Bury it deep and leave it alone. You've got a good town here. They need you and they like you. That's more important than wasting your life going after the men who did you wrong."

Lilly came back with a bottle of whiskey, pulled the cork, and was about to pour it on Hauser's wounds when he grabbed the bottle from her. "That'll do more good inside me right now than on top of me, honey."

His hand shook as he brought the whiskey to his lips and drank deeply from it before setting it on the floor beside him. He smiled again at her. "You're a good woman, Lilly. Make sure you take care of our haunted friend for me, will you? I've grown awful fond of him."

Lilly ignored the tears that fell from her eyes. "You'll be keeping an eye on him yourself, Sheriff. The doctor will be here any minute."

"But I won't be." Hauser stifled a cough and took another long pull on the bottle. "Be good to each other, you two. Don't let anyone . . . pull you apart like they did me and Maria. Life . . . is meant to be lived and . . . love is . . ."

Hauser's head dropped to his chest as the whiskey bottle slipped from his grasp and rolled away from him across the crooked floor.

"No," Beck said as Lilly stifled a sob.

He eased the sheriff down until he lay flat on the floor and he tore away the left side of his blood-soaked shirt. He lunged for the whiskey bottle and poured the rest of the contents over the bullet holes. He knew the pain would be excruciating, but necessary to save his friend's life. He had seen how infections could lay even the biggest men low in no time and Hauser would need all the help he could get if he was going to survive.

But Hauser did not flinch from the sting of the liquor on the open wounds. He did not move at all. His eyes were vacant and staring at nothing at all.

Lilly gently lifted Hauser's head and laid it in her lap. Her tears fell on his face, but he no longer seemed to mind.

Beck felt all of the strength go out of him and he fell backward, looking at the lifeless body of his friend. The first real friend he'd had since finding this place at the edge of the wilderness.

Sheriff George Hauser was dead.

The doctor rushed into the saloon, trailing several men behind him. Beck could not see any of them clearly. His own tears fogged his vision.

The doctor, a young, stocky man with a full brown beard brought a hand to his mouth as he took in the carnage on the floor of the Homestead Saloon. "My God," was all he could manage to say. "My God."

But John Beck knew God had played no part in

what had happened there that night. He had played no
part in what had happened to Beck since the day he
had ridden into the Arizona Territory.

Beck looked at the lifeless body of his friend and
knew that a piece of him had died along with him.

Lilly beckoned him to come to her, but he did not
have the strength to move.

CHAPTER TWENTY

AN HOUR LATER, John Beck found himself sitting in a chair he did not remember sitting down in. Lilly was sitting next to him, holding his hand while the doctor placed a sheet over Laredo's body. The men had carried George Hauser away on a makeshift stretcher some time ago, though Beck could not be sure about that. It might have only been five minutes. He was in no condition to be a good judge of time.

"You say this man was called Laredo?" Dr. Reese asked him. That was his name, Beck remembered. John Reese. He had met him the day before. He had been a witness when George had sworn him in and pinned the deputy star to his shirt.

How could such a happy memory get replaced by something so ugly so fast?

"That's what I heard them call him," Beck said. His own voice sounded hollow and strange to him. "Laredo." The name felt foul on his tongue, like a curse.

"And he's one of the men who caused your troubles where you came from?" Reese continued. "Back in Mother Lode."

"He's one of them. I shot one of his friends in the desert." The dead man's name came back to him. "I think his name was Steve Hogan. He's the brother of the leader. Called themselves the Brickhouse Gang. Or at least I think they did."

The doctor grunted as he folded his arms across his chest. His shirtsleeves were rolled up, but not enough to hide the blood on them. Beck noticed he had massive forearms like some blacksmiths he had known. He did not look like a doctor. "I've heard of them. A bad bunch, that lot. You're a lucky man, Mr. Beck. They aren't known for letting men live, especially lawmen."

But Beck did not consider himself lucky. Just the opposite. He knew he was cursed. "Apparently I wasn't enough of a lawman to be worth a bullet. Guess that's why they turned me out into the desert."

Lilly grabbed his hand and kissed it. "Don't say such things, John."

"Well, I don't know if you intended to kill him, but this Laredo fellow won't be bothering you any further. He's as dead as a man can get. Bad way to go, but I'd wager he deserved it after what he did to you. I plan on ruling this a case of lawful killing."

Beck had not thought of that. He had not thought about much of anything since the moment he saw the life run out of George Hauser's eyes. He had not felt anything, either, except for now. His throat began to hurt and his right hand was sore. He guessed he should expect that after pummeling a man to death with his own pistol. "My Colt," he remembered. "Where's my Colt?"

"I have it right here," Lilly said. "Don't worry."

But Beck was not worried. If Lilly said it was all right, then it was.

Doc Reese looked down at his shoes and cleared his throat. "I know you've been through a hell of a time here tonight, Deputy, but now's as good a time as any to tell you that it looks like you're the new sheriff here in Amenia. The town will be expecting one now that poor old George is gone. And we'll be fortunate to have you."

Beck looked at the doctor, remembering how happy he had been after he had been sworn in as deputy. He remembered Lilly had looked so pretty in her blue dress. Now she was sitting beside him in her nightgown in an empty saloon where two men had just died. Her pretty face swollen from tears and worry.

"Sheriff?" Beck said. "How can you think of such a thing at a time like this? George isn't even cold yet."

"Got to be thought about," Reese told him. "And you need to be ready for it. We're a nice, peaceful town, Mr. Beck. We're not used to these kinds of things happening around here. People are apt to get all sorts of worried when they find out what happened tonight. A lot of folks loved George Hauser and he thought awfully high of you. He'll rest easier knowing the town is in your care. It'll be good for the town. And good for you, too. You look like a man who's in dire need of a home and Amenia's an awfully nice place for a man to live. You can keep it that way if you want to."

Beck could not stand the sight of the doctor any longer. He looked at the place on the floor where Hauser had fallen. The place where his friend had died. "Go away. Go away right now."

Reese looked like he had more to say, but when

Lilly shook her head at him, he thought better of it. He simply took his coat from across the bar, slung it over his shoulder, and quietly walked out of the saloon, leaving Lilly and Beck alone inside.

He felt Lilly grip his hand tighter as she stood in front of him, blocking his view of were George had died. "Come on, John. Let's go home."

Home. That word sounded so foreign to him. He was no longer sure if it had any meaning for him. He was not sure if anything would ever have any meaning for him again.

"I did this, Lilly. I killed George. I killed him just as if I'd shot him myself."

She let go of his hand and pulled his head against her belly. He realized she was only wearing her nightgown with nothing underneath. He thought she should grab her blanket and cover herself before someone saw her, but she was too busy hugging him to worry about modesty.

"Don't say that, my love. Don't even think it. You didn't kill anyone except the man who did this. You made George so happy by coming here. I'd never seen him so happy in all the years I've lived here. You've made me happy, too. You've saved me, John. You've saved me more than you'll ever know."

But John Beck did not feel he had saved anyone. He felt like something out of the Bible, a black plague that had come out of the desert and brought nothing but death and destruction to everything in his path.

He could not allow himself to love Lilly or this town or anyone in it, for he knew that if he did, he would hurt them, too. He knew he should get on his horse and ride back into the desert and die like he should have died all those days before. Back to his cave among the tarantulas and the snakes and the lizards, which would not be harmed by the curse that had followed him here from Chicago.

But just then, as he sat on a chair amid the death and pain he had brought to a town that had shown him nothing but kindness, he was too weak to run away. And too weak to hold back the tears that came.

Lilly only held him tighter against her as the pain flowed from him.

CHAPTER TWENTY-ONE

ABRAHAM HOGAN HELD Dulce's arm pinned behind her head as he lay next to her in bed. She had not fought him as fiercely as she once had while he had his way with her. He began to wonder if she was warming to his affections, but one look at her dead eyes, even in the weak candlelight of her room, told him otherwise. She hated him as much now as she had the first night he had spent with her. He took solace in that. There was something to be said for consistency, especially for an outlaw like him.

He breathed in deeply, enjoying the smell of the sweat from her reluctant body. "We're going to be pulling out of this town in a couple of days," he told her, enjoying the way his voice cut through the tension between them. "And I've decided I'm going to take you with me."

He expected her to fight him, to try to break free

from his grip, but she did not. She was perfectly still as she said, "I'll put a knife in you the first chance I get."

Bram laughed. He loved her spirit. "I know you'll try. That'll be half the fun of it. You'll keep me sharp. And warm. It gets awfully cold out in the desert at night. You'll see. Who knows? You might even like it."

"Watching you die?" she said. "Yes, I would like that very much." She surprised him by looking at him. "You're a drunk and a fool. How long do you think it will be before the liquor and the glory take hold of you? How long do you think it will be before you lose control? And when you do, I'll plunge a knife in your belly and laugh while you die."

Bram admitted the idea of it was somewhat exciting. "You won't do that. You're a survivor, Dulce. You like living too much."

She turned her head away from him again and looked at the ceiling. "Life with you isn't living. It's a prison. I left my prison in Juárez and I'd rather be dead than live in another. And if I can't kill you myself, I'll get one of the others to do it for me. Maybe one of your new friends from the wagons. I have seen the way they look at me. Maybe I'll even corrupt one of them before you leave here." She laughed. "Yes, that might be even more fun to watch."

Bram found himself admiring her. Most people were afraid of him, either by reputation or by what they saw him do. But not her. Nothing he had done had broken her and he doubted anything he could do would. Not if they lived for a hundred years. Some women were like that. Women had a strength to them that was different from men, but stronger in some ways. Dulce was stronger than most. She must be, for she had never once tried to kill herself the way so many other women he had taken had done.

Yes, he may have begun to doubt himself since coming to Mother Lode, but a woman like Dulce had a way of bringing out the best in a man like him. Or the worst. Only time and fate would tell him which.

"We'll see, my sweet Dulce. But come tomorrow, we'll know what the future has in store for all of us."

An uneasy silence settled over them in the dim light of her room, but sleep did not come to him. Just the opposite. There was so much to look forward to now.

THAT NEXT MORNING, a rooster crowed somewhere in the dusty distance around Mother Lode. Bram Hogan strode out onto the boardwalk of the saloon, mug of steaming hot coffee in hand, and spat into the thoroughfare. He had always believed it was important to start off a day with a clean set of lungs.

He eyeballed the store, but quickly realized it was no use. The morning sun was at such an angle that the entire front of the building was bathed in shadow. He could not see inside and he wondered if they could see him. He knew they would be looking. He would be had he been in their shoes.

He knew Lem had thought him a fool for not going after the gold in the wagons the previous night. It had been dark and no one would have seen them. Hogan allowed that Lem might have been right about that.

But Bram also knew this was not a smash-and-grab kind of operation. The soldiers in the store were ready for a fight last night, and since they had not gotten one, Bram knew doubt would begin to creep into their minds. Doubt about whether or not this was a good idea. Doubt as to whether or not Bram would seek a fight at all. Doubt about why they shouldn't just ride out of here and leave the civilians to their own devices. Why should they put their lives on the line for gold they would never see or get rewarded for protecting? They probably would not even get medals for their trouble. Just lousy pay when it came and grunt work.

Bram did not forget about the civilians, either. They were his ace in the hole. Men in uniform could be a stubborn lot, but as long as they had duty to bind them together, they could hold out for a lot longer than reason allowed. Civilians, particularly the old woman and the little girl, weren't soldiers. They were used to the comforts of home. Comforts being holed up in a general store full of men with guns could not provide. Bram knew that being frightened every time they had to use the privy could flat-out wear down some folks.

And the men and women in that general store had endured a night of it. Bram wanted to see if the experience had softened them up a bit. He doubted young Lieutenant Coleman's resolve had been weakened, but the day was just beginning. It was time to sow some seeds of doubt in the minds of the people he was protecting. Maybe they would flower by this time tomorrow.

Then the fun would really begin.

"Hello in the store!" he called out. "I bid all of you a very good morning."

He waited for a moment for an answer, but no answer came.

"Coleman," he called out. "You in there?"

"I'm here," came a gruff voice from the shadows across the street. He recognized it as belonging to Colonel Standish.

"Colonel, is that you?" Bram smiled. "Why, this is truly an honor, sir. I know we spoke earlier in the day yesterday, but the young lieutenant there had taken on the negotiating duties. Guess I kind of rank pretty highly now that I'm parlaying with a colonel. The Standish of Blood himself."

Bram felt his body rock from the impact of a bullet, which was followed by the sound of a gunshot a split second later. He dropped his coffee mug as he fell back against the saloon wall, before sliding to the ground.

"Parlay with that, you son of a bitch," Standish called out to him.

Bram's stomach seized up on him as the world began to tilt before his eyes. He knew he had been shot and knew he was in danger of going into shock if he did not act fast. He chanced to look down at where his shoulder burned with pain. The bullet seemed to have gone straight through, but the front of his sleeve was still soaked with blood. His blood.

Lem rushed out onto the boardwalk of the saloon, pistol drawn, and began shooting at the doorway of the general store. Despite the pain beginning to course through his body, Bram noticed none of the bullets seemed to hit the front of the store, but he heard curses and shouts and breaking glass from deep inside the building. The thought comforted him. Lem might not have been a clever man, but Bram Hogan had not often seen his equal when it came to pistol work.

Lem was also surprisingly strong for such a skinny man, which was why he had no trouble helping Bram to his feet and practically dragging him back into the safety of the saloon.

Inside, the new members of the Brickhouse Gang

were armed to the teeth and cleared a space on the bar, where they placed Bram.

The outlaw looked around for Dulce but could not see her. He doubted she would come down from her room, especially after hearing gunshots. He fully expected her to try to finish the job, so perhaps it was best if she was not around at all.

The pain spiked through his body as hands tore open his sleeve and exposed the wound.

Over the roar of pain in his ears, Bram heard Lem yell from the door, "We're going to burn you out of there for what you've done, soldier boy! We're going to burn you out right quick!"

Bram heard rifle rounds begin to pepper the walls of the saloon, but none came close. The freight wagon and the stagecoach were in the way.

Fisk, the oldest of the wagonmen who were now part of Bram's gang, said, "They won't be able to hit us from the store. Not at that angle."

"And we can't hit them, either," Bram said before he quickly bit off the pain from the whiskey that Elder, another of the wagonmen, poured over his wound. The rotgut Dulce carried in this place smelled bad enough when he was drinking it, but when mixed with the stench of his own blood, it almost made him vomit.

"I know that stings, chief," Sear said. He was the youngest of the new men of the Brickhouse Gang. The quietest, too. "But it's the only way I know to clean out that wound. The good news is that I can see clear through to the other side, so we won't have to go digging around in there for the bullet. We'll keep it bandaged and you'll heal up just fine."

But Bram had been shot many times before and

knew it was not as simple as that. "That hole's got to be closed, boys. For now, soak a cloth in whiskey and pack it tight. Then fetch me a doctor. Lem is in charge now. He'll tell you where you can go."

But Lem had been too busy railing against his enemy across the thoroughfare to have heard him. "You all had better get ready, soldier boy, because the first one of you who steps outside is dead. That goes for the outhouse, too. Man or woman ducks their head out, they get a bullet in it!"

"Lem!" Hogan called out. "Get away from there. Come over here."

Lem pointed at the new man named Whalen and told him to take his spot by the swinging doors, then came over to Hogan. "I've still got Townsend over at the store minding the back door. I know he heard me and he'll plug the first one he sees." He winced when he got a good look at the hole in his boss's shoulder. "They're going to pay for what they done to you, Bram. I promise you."

But Bram did not have time to waste on vengeance. He knew he might pass out at any moment and he did not want to wake up dead. Coleman might have been an officer, but he was one of the few smart ones Bram had known. It would not take long for him to realize that the brains of his enemy had been shot and now was the time to strike.

Bram grabbed Lem by the shirt. "You've got to listen to me, boy. I need you to send one of these men to fetch the doctor. The young one, not the fat old drunk who lingers around here. He'll patch me up better than anyone."

"I can do it, boss," Lem said.

"You're gonna be busy with other things because you're in charge," Bram told him. "You need to keep the men sharp. I want two of them on the back door of that shop, not just one. If anyone comes out that way, fill them full of lead like you threatened to, then move inside. Now's the time to start squeezing them before they squeeze us. Now's the time to start demanding things from them before they find out we're weak. Tell them we want them to send out Pearson to us and we want him right now, or else we start setting fires." He grabbed Lem's shirt harder and pulled him closer. "I do not want you to do that, mind. I just want you to threaten it. Burning them out gets us nothing. Not with those wagons so close."

Bram felt himself grow weak and he let go of Lem's shirt. "You do as I tell you, now, and come back to me later after the doc gets through with me."

Lem turned to Sear. "I want you to get Doc Miller. He's down at the end of town right on Main Street here."

"I know where he is," Sear said. "We've passed by his place whenever we've ridden through town."

"Good. Make sure you get the young doctor. Not the old one. He'll probably be drunk, and even if he's not, his hands will be shaking too much to be of much help to Bram."

Sear told him he understood the orders and began to run out the front door.

Bram called out and stopped him. "Not that way, you idiot. You're liable to get shot if you do. Best go out the back way."

Sear quickly reversed course and did as he was told.

Bram set his head down on the bar with a gentle thud.

Lem patted his boss's good shoulder. "Don't worry, Bram. We'll manage."

Bram shut his eyes and tried to ignore the pain. *Manage to get us all killed is more like it.*

CHAPTER TWENTY-TWO

DULCE BOLTED OFF the bed when she heard the gunshot and grabbed the carpetbag she had kept packed since the night the Brickhouse Gang had ridden into town. She kept it in the bottom of her wardrobe and had not feared Bram finding it. His mind had only been on one thing whenever he barged in here at night.

She had heard Bram yelling over to the people in the store, though she had still been too groggy to hear what he said. To say she had slept since the gang had ridden into town would have been an overstatement, but she did have moments of unconsciousness in which the hell she lived in seemed distant for a few blissful moments. She had always hoped that, when she woke, this would have all been a nightmare and John Beck would be next to her, sober and happy, the way he used to be.

But whenever she woke up, the nightmare began anew.

And when she heard that pistol shot, she knew that Bram Hogan had not fired it.

And he had not fired in return.

Perhaps her nightmare was over after all.

That was why she had grabbed her carpetbag from the bottom of her wardrobe, threw open her door, and ran down the back stairs. She shoved the back door open and ran down the length of Second Street, which was parallel to Main. She stopped when she reached the livery and ignored the cries of Joe, the liveryman, who tried to stop her from throwing a saddle across the first horse she saw.

She whirled when he grabbed her by the wrist as she struggled to take a saddle from the rack and place it on a gray gelding.

"See here, Dulce," Joe said. "What the hell do you think you're doing?"

She slipped the Derringer from her boot and placed the barrel under his chin. "Let go of me, Joe. I'm riding out of here and I'd hate to have to kill you before I do. But I will if you don't back off." She thumbed back the hammer of the tiny, one-shot pistol. "Now."

The old liveryman let go of her wrist and backed away slowly, holding up both hands. "I'm sorry, Dulce. Don't shoot. But you won't get that saddle on that gelding without some help from me. That horse is too much for you anyway. Let me give you another animal that'll be easier for you to ride. She's strong and won't falter on the trail."

She did not trust his sudden change of heart and kept the Derringer aimed at his chest. "Go ahead, then."

Joe grabbed a different saddle from the rack and walked to the back of the livery. She did not know much about guns, but knew the Derringer was a close-up weapon, so she trailed Joe to the back stall. She was careful to keep enough distance between them in case he tried to do something.

But all he did was place the saddle on the back of a brown mare who did not seem to mind the burden. Dulce watched him carefully as he tightened the straps under the horse. Again, the animal did not seem to mind.

"Got any idea of where you're going?"

She did not know, and did not care, either. Maybe she would go after Beck? But there was no reason to tell him that. "That's my business, not yours."

"Fair enough," Joe said. "Best you don't tell me as I never could keep my damned mouth shut. Mary left me for it. But I hope you're not thinking of riding out to look for Marshal Beck. That's a fool's errand. I'd suggest you keep riding south of here in a straight line. You'll come upon a town called Amenia. It's a good place for a woman, Dulce, and less than a day's ride. If you don't push the mare too hard, she'll get you there without breaking a sweat."

His work beneath the horse finished, he stood up and looked at her. "I wouldn't give her to you if she wasn't worthy."

They both looked to the front of the livery when they heard a door bang open somewhere on First Street.

Joe seemed to forget she was holding a gun on him as he moved out of the stable and toward the front of the livery.

Dulce stopped him by pressing the Derringer in the small of his back. "Stop right there. This might not be much of a gun, but at this distance, it doesn't have to be."

The two of them stood together in the cool darkness

of the livery as they watched one of the wagonmen from the saloon run past them without stopping.

"That's Sear," Dulce said. "One of Hogan's new men."

"Looks like he's heading for Doc Miller's place," Joe said. "Hope he gets the old man, not the son. Whoever's in the saloon in need of a doctor deserves that old drunk."

But Dulce did not care who was shot or which Dr. Miller Sear brought back to the saloon. She just wanted to put as much distance between her and this town as possible. And the idea of this place called Amenia appealed to her.

She slipped to the back of the livery, grabbed hold of the mare's reins, and pulled her out of the stable. Joe stepped aside and made no move to stop her. "If you'll let me grab your bag, I'll be happy to tie it to the back of the saddle for you."

She had forgotten all about her bag. She had forgotten about everything except getting away.

She motioned for him to do that as she climbed up into the saddle. It had been a few years since she had ridden a horse and she hoped she had not forgotten how to handle one.

Joe picked up her bag and put it on the back of the horse. He held it there while he reached behind his shirt to grab something. She cursed herself for reacting too late as he pulled a long pistol from the back of his pants, then dropped it into her bag before tying it to the saddle.

He smiled as he finished his work. "Had it on me the whole time but didn't go for it. You'll need a pistol with stopping power and that peashooter you've got won't do the job."

He seemed to read the surprised expression on her

face. "Not everyone in this town is out to get you, Dulce. Now, you set that horse to a gallop for a mile or so and ride her straight to Amenia. Keep an eye on the road in front of you and ride a straight line. You'll come up on the town before you know it. There are a few watering holes between here and there, so let the horse lead you to them if she wants, but don't lose sight of where you're going."

Dulce put her heels into the mare's flanks and steered her down First Street at as close to a gallop as she dared.

She tensed as she sped past the doctors' offices, waiting for a bullet to knock her from the horse, but no shot came.

The mare kept running as she cleared the last building in town and continued south. Dulce was out.

She was finally free.

CHAPTER TWENTY-THREE

WHILE THE MEN and women in the general store screamed, Lieutenant Coleman grabbed Standish by the arm and backed him up against the counter. "What the hell do you think you're doing?"

"My duty, sir!" the colonel barked. "Something I'd like to think you would have done had you been given the chance."

Coleman looked out the window but could not see where Hogan had fallen. All he could see was the bullet hole and the blood on the wall of the saloon across Main Street.

"I hope to God you killed him."

"I may have done just that," Standish boasted. "I was aiming for the center of his chest, but the scoundrel moved as I fired. I caught him in the right shoulder instead, put a mighty big hole in him. They're liable to get a doctor to patch him up, but not before he loses a hell of a lot of blood in the process. And a hole that size is awfully easy to get infected in a climate like this. I've seen it happen to better men than Abraham Hogan."

Standish lowered his voice as he said, "When you gain your faculties, Lieutenant, you'll see that I did us all a favor by shooting that man when the opportunity presented itself."

But Coleman was not so sure. Hogan may have been the reason why they were in this mess, but he was a known quantity. He was in charge of his men, which meant their actions were centralized. To know Hogan's mind was to know the mind of his gang. Now the lieutenant was left with nothing by supposition about who was in charge and what their aims might be. If Hogan's replacement was the bloodthirsty type, Standish may have only served to place them all in a far more precarious position.

As if he could read the lieutenant's thoughts, Standish added, "They're disorganized now, Coleman. They're clamoring for leadership while they're tending to Hogan. Now is not the time for inaction, sir. Now is the time to strike and strike hard."

"With what?" Coleman whispered. "They're on their guard now more than ever and we still have that thoroughfare to cross. He's threatened to cut us off from the privy and the water outside. How long do you think we'll be able to hold out with things as they are? Without sanitary conditions? Without water?"

Coleman looked back into the store. Mr. Welsh, the shopkeeper, and Nellie Standish were tending to one of the passengers—Mr. Katz—who fell when bullets began ricocheting around the store. "How is he?"

Mrs. Standish sat on the floor beside Mr. Katz and wept, telling Coleman all he needed to know.

"He's dead," the shopkeeper said. "He was shot in the eye."

From his spot against the counter, the wounded Pearson let out a low, slick laugh. "Well, ain't that something, boss? Guess that lightens the load on all of us. One less mouth to feed."

Coleman forgot about Standish and stormed over to the wounded outlaw in his care, looming over him. "Who would take over for Hogan if he's incapacitated?"

Pearson's eyes grew to a ridiculous size. "Don't go throwing all them big words at me, soldier boy. A man in my condition can't be expected to understand 'em."

Coleman slammed his boot down onto Pearson's chest, causing him to cry out. "Who's in charge now that Hogan's dead?"

Pearson struggled for enough breath to answer. "How am I supposed to know? I'm in here with you, remember?"

Coleman shifted and put a little more weight on his chest. "Guess."

"I'd be able to think a whole lot better if I could breathe, boss."

Coleman reluctantly took his boot off Pearson's chest.

The outlaw gasped and breathed in deeply. "Thank you for your hospitality, Lieutenant."

Coleman drew his pistol and aimed it down at Pearson's legs. "The next word out of your mouth had better be a name and description or you'll end up a cripple."

The outlaw looked first at the pistol, then at the man holding it. Coleman could feel him taking his measure, to gauge if he was bluffing or if he just might actually shoot.

When he had looked at him long enough, Pearson said, "My money would be on Lem. It would be me if I was still in there, but with Steve and Laredo gone and me in here, Lem's the only old hand he's got left. Your wagonmen haven't earned Hogan's trust yet, but Lem has. He was with Hogan longer than anyone, except his brother, Steve, of course."

Coleman did not aim the pistol at his leg, but kept it at his side. "And what sort of man is this Lem?"

"Wild," Pearson told him. "Drunk most of the time and meaner than hell when he's sober, on account of being hungover. A genuine killer, which is what made him such a good fit for our bunch."

Coleman would have expected no less from the kind of man who would follow Abraham Hogan. "Do you think he'll hit us?"

Pearson nodded. "If Hogan's not able to stop him, sure. And if he's out of commission like that Fancy Dan over there says he is, then you boys are in for a lively day because Lem is a man who's out for blood. Unless there's someone there to keep him in line, that is."

Coleman stood a little taller now that he knew what Pearson was driving at. "You think you'll have some sway over him, don't you?"

Pearson shrugged. "Maybe. Wouldn't know for sure unless I was over there. But I do know that I'm no good to anyone sitting down here with my hands tied behind my back. And I won't be much of a threat to you, seeing as how my gun hand is ruined and all."

Coleman shut his eyes when he heard Standish

walking toward him. "Don't you dare let that man go, Coleman. Cripple or no, he'll tell them everything he saw in here. He'll tell them our strengths and our weaknesses. Hogan and this Lem scoundrel will know everything about us and we won't know anything more about them." He grabbed Coleman's arm. "Don't give up our only advantage, son."

Coleman jerked his arm free of the colonel's grasp. He'd had just about as much of the old man's meddling as he was apt to take. "I'm not your son, Colonel. Your son is in charge of the fort we're going to. I'm the senior ranking officer in command here, not you. I suggest you remember that before you say another word to me."

Pearson let out a low whistle. "Looks like junior here put you in your place, Granddad."

"I'll put you in your place right now, you scoundrel!" Standish fumbled for his pistol, but Coleman grabbed hold of his arm before he could reach it. Sergeant Hastings rushed over to help him and took a firm hold of the colonel.

"Hastings," Coleman said. "The colonel is obviously suffering from the strain of the situation. He needs rest. Bring him to the back room and let him rest."

Standish's eyes blazed as the sergeant began to carry out his order.

Coleman enjoyed his rage. "And relieve him of his sidearm. He'll rest easier without it, and so will we."

Hastings pulled the colonel's gun free and led him toward the back room.

Coleman returned his attention to Pearson, who was grinning up at him. He hated providing amusement for this man, but it could not be avoided. He would have liked nothing better than to put a hole right between his eyes, but that would be a waste of a good resource. And he had few enough resources at his disposal to waste one so valuable.

"Here's what is going to happen next, Pearson. I'm going to let you go."

The outlaw's smile faded. "No foolin'?"

"No fooling," Coleman repeated. "You're going to go across the street and you're going to tell them everything you saw in here. I'm not a fool and I know you're going to do that anyway."

"Then why are you letting me go?"

"Because I was beginning to get a handle on the kind of man Hogan was, but this Lem character is unknown to me. I can't risk him doing something rash and I think you're the only person who can buy us some time. I think you're the only one who can end this whole thing without any more bloodshed."

Pearson did not look as enthused about his freedom as he once had. "Don't know if I can promise that."

"I'm not asking you to. I'm only asking you to deliver a message." Coleman had been toying with this idea since this whole mess started and decided now was as good a time as any to put it into practice. "Those horses out there haven't been tended to since we pulled into town yesterday. They need proper rest and grooming and grain. They're just about played out and staying hitched to those wagons isn't doing them any good. We'll allow him to take two men to unhitch them and tend to them. We won't open fire as long as they're unarmed. In return, we get full use of the privy and the water pump in the back. Tomorrow, when the team is rested and ready, you can hitch them up again and ride out of here without incident. But you're to leave the stagecoach behind."

Pearson's eyes narrowed. "What about the gold?"

"If you take it, we won't stop you," Coleman said, "but you'll be marked men for the rest of your days. However, for now, my concern is the safety of the civilians who are still in my care." He looked back at the body of Mr. Katz. The upper half of him was covered by an empty sack. "I've already lost too many people in my care. I won't lose another. No one else has to die here, Pearson. Mine or yours. Do you think you can get Lem to understand that?"

Pearson looked at the people in the store, who all looked back at him. The little girl held on to her grandmother.

"I'll try, Lieutenant. You've got my word on it. I mean that."

Coleman grabbed him under the arm and helped pull the outlaw to his feet. Even though his hands were tied behind his back, it was clear the man was at least half a foot taller than the six-footer from West Point. "You're a big fella, aren't you?"

"No one's ever called me small."

Coleman led Pearson to the front of the store. "Do you think you can make it across the street with your hands tied behind you?"

"I can manage," Pearson said. "Let's just hope I can manage Lem when I get there."

The lieutenant gestured for him to walk outside, which the outlaw did.

"Don't shoot!" Pearson yelled as he began to cross Main Street. "They cut me loose, boys. It's me. Pearson!"

Coleman watched the big man shuffle across the street, step up onto the boardwalk of the saloon in one stride, and move inside. And with him went the only advantage he had over the Brickhouse Gang.

"What have you done, Coleman?" the lieutenant asked himself. "What on God's earth have you done?"

The only thing I could do, came the answer in his mind.

Only time would tell if he was right.

CHAPTER TWENTY-FOUR

LILLY WOKE FROM a fitful sleep to find John sitting at the edge of their bed. He had his head in his hands and she was surprised to see he was already dressed.

She knew why he was dressed, too. She knew her time of happiness with him was at an end. It had been the happiest time of her life, but she had always known it would not last. She had only hoped it would have lasted a little longer.

"You're leaving," she said. Her voice sounded louder in the weak sunlight of the room.

"I'm not sure," he said without raising his head. "I've been sitting here all night trying to work that out."

She was glad his mind had not been made up. His poor tortured mind must be sore from all of the thinking he had been doing since coming to town. She had spent so many nights with him, living the nightmares that plagued his sleep, holding him when he cried out and fought against the ghosts of his dreams. She held him and sang to him as sweetly as she knew how. He always fell back to sleep in her arms and woke the next day peacefully. She was proud that she had been able to comfort him so. Proud that she could give peace to a good man who had lived through so many bad things.

Which was why she was so deeply sad that she could not help him now.

"Maybe you're not sure," she said, "because you don't need to go?"

"I'm a cursed man, honey. I've done nothing except bring death and blood with me from the moment I came to town. I got those miners killed. I got George Hauser killed. And I'll get you killed, too, if I don't get as far away from this place as soon as possible."

"No." She slid across the bed and wrapped her arms around him. "You didn't get those miners killed. You stopped them from hurting me. You're the only man who ever defended me, John Beck. My father didn't even do that. And you didn't get George killed. That Mexican killed him. George knew the kind of work he did. And he died happy, knowing you were here to protect this town after he was gone."

Beck ran his hands through his hair and grabbed a fistful of it. "Laredo was one of the men who ran me out of Mother Lode. He was here to kill me. He wouldn't have killed George if I hadn't been here."

"George knew the risks," she said. She clung to him now, willing his pain away as she had willed away the nightmares that plagued him in his sleep. "If this Laredo hadn't killed him, then it would have been someone else. He was not young anymore, John, and he should have come and gotten you instead of going up against that man alone. I know you loved him. We all did, but he made a mistake and paid horribly for it."

"He made a mistake, all right," Beck said. "He made a mistake by not running me out of town when he had the chance."

She held him as tightly as she could and was glad he did not push her away. She tried with all her might to pour as much love into him as she could. "If he had run you out of town, those miners would have killed me or worse. You saved me, John. Are you sorry for that, too?"

He let go of his hair and wrapped his arms around her. "Don't say that." She felt his tears drop from his cheeks and onto hers, mixing with her own. "Don't ever say that. I never want anything to happen to you. I don't know what I'd do if anyone hurt you."

"Then stay with me," she begged. "Protect me."

"I can't protect you," he said. "Not as long as the men who rode me out of town are still alive. Don't you understand? They want me dead, Lilly. And they won't stop looking for me until I am dead. I killed Bram's brother and his best gun hand. There's no way they can let me live now."

"Then let them find you. Let them come here where people love you and will fight beside you."

He gently eased her back down onto the pillow. "Do you really think people will do that after what I let happen to George?"

"They need you, John." She touched his face and wiped a tear from his eye. "I need you. Hate can't stand up to love. Not for long."

She closed her eyes as he caressed her face. For a

man who had known so much ugliness, so much pain, he was more gentle with her than any man she had ever known. He was the only man who had ever fought for her. The only man who did not treat her like a Chinese girl to be pawed and roughed up and have his way with. He was the only true man she had ever met, for he treated her like a woman.

"Maybe everything you say is true," he said. "But the men who are hunting me won't stop until I make them. And if Laredo could come here and kill a man like George, then the three that remain can do a whole lot worse to this town. I've seen what they can do, Lilly. They're terrible men who live off killing and hurting people, good people, just because they can. That's why I know they'll come here and ruin everything they see, because that's what they do. It's all they know. And I don't want them to do that. Not to this town and not to you."

He stroked her hair and she knew by the look in his eyes and the tenderness of his touch that his mind was made up.

"You have to go, don't you?" Her own words were like a knife in her belly.

"Maybe I wouldn't if I didn't love you so much," he said. "But I have to. I can't live with you knowing those men can hurt us. We'll never be able to live until they're dead. Not really live the way we should."

She took his face in both of her hands and looked into his brown eyes. She could see the pain in them and the love, too. The love that was driving them apart. "Then go, John Beck, but promise me you'll kill them. Kill them all and come back to me, because this is your home now."

He lifted her off the bed and held her tightly, tighter than she thought he could. "You're my home. And I promise I'll come back."

When they kissed, they kissed as deeply as they had ever kissed before. They kissed as though it might be the very last time because it might very well be.

And when they were done, she turned away from him as he stood, buckled his gun belt, grabbed his hat, and left.

She waited until she heard him going down the stairs before she allowed herself to weep.

W HEN HE REACHED the lobby, Beck was surprised to see Dr. Reese sitting in one of the overstuffed chairs. He had a cup and saucer on the table at his elbow. He was still wearing the clothes he'd had on in the saloon the night before.

Beck did not know for certain, but it looked like the doctor had been waiting for him. "Morning, Doctor."

"Morning." Reese rose to greet him at the bottom of the stairs and shook his hand. "I take it you'll be leaving us."

Beck looked back up the stairs to the room he shared with Lilly. He wondered if their voices had carried down to the lobby, but realized they had been speaking too softly for that to have happened. "How did you know?"

"I figured that would be the case after everything that happened last night." Reese stood aside, making no attempt to block his way. "I'd be honored if you'd let me walk with you awhile. Going to the livery, I take it?"

"I am. And I wouldn't mind the company."

The two men ignored the curious looks they drew from Ma Stanton behind the hotel counter and stepped out into the Arizona morning. It was just after sunrise, but it promised to be a hot one. A tinge of heat was already in the air.

Doc Reese said as they began walking to the livery, "You're a complicated man, Mr. Beck."

"I've been called lots of things in my time, Doc, but never that."

"An educated man, too, I'd wager."

Beck looked at him. "What makes you say that?"

"The way you speak," he said. "The way you carry yourself. The way you listen and take things in. You're not just some gunman or lawman who does things out of habit. You're deeper than that. More thoughtful."

Beck saw no reason to argue. He had never tried to hide what he was. "You see a lot for a small-town doctor."

"That's because I wasn't always a small-town doctor," Reese said. "I saw a fair amount of life before I came to this place and I know you have, too. Lawyer, I take it."

Beck was surprised by how perceptive he was. "I read the law for a while. It didn't take, but I liked the concept of it. Decided enforcing it was a better fit."

Reese snapped his fingers. "A Pinkerton man," he said, triumphant. "Chicago. I knew I'd peg your accent if I kept you talking long enough."

"Glad I could make your day, Doc. Don't know what good it does you."

"It's not about doing me any good, John. It's about doing yourself some good."

It was too early in the morning to talk in circles like this and he had too much on his mind. "I haven't studied rhetoric in a long time, Doc, so why don't you do us both a favor and get to the point."

"Fair enough," Reese said. "Then I'll cut to the heart of it. You've got a good town here, Mr. Beck. The people have taken to you awfully quickly, and what's more, they need you. I know what happened to George last night was ugly, but it wasn't your fault. He's gone and you're alive. Nothing you can do will change that. Whether you stay here or ride back to Mother Lode, George will still be just as dead after it's all over as he is now, Beck. Burying you right beside him won't change anything."

Beck felt himself beginning to lose his grip on his temper. Lilly had said the same things to him, but for some reason, hearing it from the doctor stung a bit more. "I've got no intention of dying, Doc."

"A man aboveground can be every bit as dead as man six feet under it."

Beck turned on Reese and snatched him by the collar. The doctor was only a bit shorter than he but was broader and stockier. The size difference did not matter to him at that moment. "I'm damned sick and tired of being told what to do, Doc. People trussing me up and running me out of town. The desert telling me to give up and die. The snakes and the spiders and the lizards telling me I don't belong out there. I'm tired of men trying to kill me and people telling me I don't know my own mind."

He pulled the doctor closer. "Well, I do know my own mind, Doctor. I'm sick and I'm not going to get any better as long as I've got a target on my back. And that's exactly what I'll have until I know they're dead. Maybe one of them will kill me. Maybe I'll kill all of them. Either way, I'm not alive as long as they are. I'm dead right now and this town doesn't deserve that. Lilly doesn't deserve it, either. She deserves to have a whole man, not half of a haunted one."

When Reese looked down at Beck's hand grasping his shirt, Beck realized what he was doing and let him go. He had no call to manhandle the doctor like that. He was a good man and did not deserve that kind of treatment. He looked up at the balcony of the Amenia Hotel, afraid Lilly might have seen what he had done. She would have thought poorly of him if she had. He was glad the balcony was empty and she had not seen his conduct.

He backed away from Reese. "I'm sorry, Doc. Sometimes I do things before thinking about them."

Reese smiled. "No reason to apologize, Mr. Beck. You've got the soldier's sickness. Saw it in many men in blue and gray after the war. During it, too. I'm not telling you not to go. I just wanted to make sure you remembered what you have waiting for you when you come back. There's a reason why Ma Stanton hasn't fired Lilly for neglecting her duties and taking up with you. I told her she's the only thing keeping you sane and this town needs you. I just figured you needed to know that, too. Because this town does need you, Mr. Beck. Broken man or not, you're a good man and I've never met a good man who didn't have a couple of cracks and chips in him. Not a truly good one, anyway."

He reached out and took hold of Beck's arm. "You might not realize it, but you're already beginning to heal. All I want is for you to continue that healing process. For your sake and for ours."

Beck did not think he was getting better but was not inclined to argue with the doctor after treating him so poorly. Besides, he wanted to hit the trail to Mother

Lode sooner rather than later. "Time will tell, Doc. Time will tell."

The two men continued to walk over to the livery, where they found Good Abraham already had Pokey saddled and ready to go.

Good Abraham also had a second horse with him.

"Fine morning for a ride," the liveryman said. "Took the liberty of fetching your rifles from Ma Stanton and loading them on old Pokey here. Got your ammunition, too."

Beck looked at the brown gelding Abraham had saddled. "You're not going."

"Sure I am," Good Abraham said. "Trail's no place for a man to ride alone, especially one who's apt to wander as much as you. You said you were in the desert for almost two weeks, but the ride between here and Mother Lode ain't hardly half a day's ride. I can get you there and back without incident." He patted the stock of an old Henry rifle he had rolled up in his saddle blanket. "I'm pretty handy with this girl, too. Figured I'd pitch in if it came to that. You've got enough ammunition for two men to raise a fair amount of hell."

Beck stroked Pokey's muzzle and was glad the horse responded to him. He was a good horse and Beck was happy he remembered him. "I'm afraid I can't bring you with me, Good Abraham. I don't know what I'll find when I get to Mother Lode, so it's better if I handle this on my own and my own way."

"That's fine by me," Abraham said. "Never considered myself leadership material and I don't aim to start now at my age. You call the tune and I'll fall in line. But I'm going with you whether you like it or not."

Beck looked at this man who had shown him nothing but kindness since he had come to town and shook his head no.

He watched whatever resolve his friend might have had melt away and Beck feared he had that look in his eyes that tended to frighten people when his mind was made up. It was a look he had never seen personally but had seen its effect on other men. He'd had it before the mind sickness had taken hold of him, and judging by Good Abraham's reaction, his tribulations had not softened it any.

Beck realized he had done enough damage for one day and realized as well that it might be best if he got out of town before he alienated everyone who cared for him.

He set one foot in the stirrup and pulled himself up into the saddle. "Keep an eye on things for me until I get back, gentlemen. The town is counting on you."

Reese held his hand up to him. "And we're counting on you, Mr. Beck. To come back alive."

Beck shook his hand and Good Abraham's, too. "Keep an eye on Lilly for me, if you can. She's a good woman."

"That she is," Good Abraham told him. "The kind a man should come back to if he can."

Beck agreed but saw no reason to state the obvious. He tipped the brim of his hat to his friends and put his heels to Pokey. The horse responded and moved away from the livery at a good clip, heading northward to Mother Lode and whatever awaited him there.

CHAPTER TWENTY-FIVE

INSIDE THE SALOON, Pearson sipped his whiskey as Lem hoovered nearby like a hummingbird at a flower. "So? Tell me what they're like, damn it. What are we up against?"

Pearson had already run through the story twice, but Lem had been so giddy with power that he had not been able to pay attention. He had first thought the young lieutenant a fool for letting him go, but now he was beginning to wonder if Coleman was not smarter than he looked.

Pearson glanced over at the bar, where the doctor was tending to Hogan's shoulder. "He gonna make it?"

Lem looked like he had forgotten all about their leader. "The bullet went clean through. There wasn't even all that much blood. He's lived through worse."

Pearson knew he had. He also knew a hole that size could pose trouble for any man, even a man like Abraham Hogan. "Hope he lives." He looked behind the bar and saw no sign of Bram's woman. "Where's the whore?"

"Gone," Lem told him. "We think she slipped out the back when the shooting started. One of the new men thinks he saw her riding past when he went to fetch the doctor, but she was gone before he could get a shot off." He lowered his voice when he added, "Personally, I think this bunch are more a hindrance than a help, but they're what we've got at the moment." He grinned. "Just about all they're good for is stopping bullets."

Pearson sipped his whiskey. "They're going to have to stop about fifty apiece and it still wouldn't put a dent in what they've got over in the store. That shopkeeper Welsh has a small armory in there. And those four soldier boys ain't afraid to shoot. Got a crazy old colonel in there named Standish. He's the one who put that hole in Bram's shoulder."

"And I'll burn him alive for it, too."

Pearson closed his eyes and took another sip of whiskey. It was finally starting to dull the ache in his ruined right hand. Fortunately, he could shoot just as good with his left hand as his right, but he was glad Coleman had not known that. "The lieutenant is offering us a good deal here, Lem. One I think Bram would take if he could. He let your men lead away the horses and mules without firing a shot. That shows me he's a man of his word. He's even allowing us to head out with the gold as long as we leave the stagecoach behind. I'd say that's more than fair."

"Live and let live, eh?" Lem looked his old partner up and down. "This doesn't sound like you, Pearson. You sure you didn't leave more than your fingers back in that store?"

With his bandaged hand, Pearson reached up, took

Lem around the neck, and pulled him down onto the tabletop. He used the edge to choke Lem until he gagged.

"What's that you said? I couldn't hear you."

Lem gurgled as he tried in vain to get air into his lungs, but could not. Just before he passed out, Pearson released him and kicked him away from the table with a boot to the chest, sending Lem sliding across the sawdust floor.

Pearson grabbed the whiskey bottle and poured himself another drink. Choking Lem had caused the fire in his hand to return.

"You big, crazy bastard," Lem gasped as he clutched his throat. "You almost killed me."

"If I'd wanted to kill you, you'd be dead," Pearson said. "You're not in charge here anymore, Lem. I am. If you don't like it, you'd best ride out of here while you can. But if you stay, I'm in charge, not you."

"No way," Lem rasped. "I'm not letting you cut me out of my share of that gold. Besides, Bram put me in charge, not you."

"Only because I wasn't here and you know it." Pearson looked at him. "The matter's settled unless you want to try to fight for your claim."

For a second, Pearson thought Lem might be foolish enough to try it. And for a second, he was just drunk enough to hope he would. That would leave him alone with a wounded boss and wagonmen he did not trust, but it would be better than having to watch his back until all of this was over. Afterward, too. Lem was a proud man and that pride would eat away at him until he took another run at him. It might be better to get it over with now while their blood was up.

But for all of Lem's recklessness, Pearson had never

known him to be a fool. So he wasn't surprised when the hard look in his eyes softened as he realized he was in no position to take Pearson on and live.

He rubbed his sore neck and said, "I never wanted to be in charge of this outfit anyway. You know that."

Pearson did not know that, but was glad to hear it. "It's settled, then. Pass the word to the boys minding the back door of the store to let the folks over there use the privy and the water pump. The more reasonable we seem now, the more apt they are to let us ride out of here with the gold tomorrow. That old colonel is a hawk and he ain't half-wrong. He's persuasive as hell and the other soldier boys in there are itching for a fight. I can see it in their eyes. He pushes them hard enough, they'll obey an old colonel over a young lieutenant if they think there's glory in it for them. His boy runs the fort these men serve out of. A good word in his boy's ear will get them all promoted. I don't aim to be the reason why they get an extra stripe on their sleeves. Taking their gold will be enough."

Lem set his head back against the saloon wall and laughed. "Ten thousand in gold is enough to make anyone happy." He lowered his voice when he added, "Split two or three ways, all the better."

Pearson decided talking to Lem for too long was making his head hurt almost as much as his hand. He got up from his chair and slowly walked over to the bar, where young Dr. Miller was tending to Hogan. "How's the patient, Doc?"

Miller frowned. "I wish I could be as optimistic about his chances as your sparring partner over there."

Pearson did not like the sound of that. "Meaning?"

"Meaning the bullet hole is large and the round fractured your friend's collarbone," the doctor told him. "If this was wartime, they'd probably take his arm, but I'm afraid that wild fellow over there might shoot me if I did."

Pearson set the glass on the bar before he dropped it. "Take his arm?"

"I might have to do it if gangrene sets in," Miller said, "though from the sound of it, I don't think you'll be here that long. He'll need plenty of rest and care if those stitches have any hope of holding. The shoulder will have to be set properly or else it will heal crooked. That means he can't be moved, but as I said, you don't seem to have that kind of time."

Pearson looked at his boss's face and was glad he was unconscious. News like that would have killed him had he been awake to hear it. "I guess he can't ride, then?"

"I'm sure he can sit in a saddle and hold on with his good hand if he wakes up in time," Miller said, "but he'll be in agony every single step of the way. I can give him laudanum for the pain, but he'll hardly be able to stay on horseback in his condition. The stitches will open up and infection will set in."

The doctor glanced at Pearson. "I know that's not the news you wanted to hear, mister, but it's the only kind of news I have. If you leave him here to recuperate, he might be able to ride in a month or so. But if he leaves with you tomorrow morning like you're saying, he'll be dead in a day or two."

Pearson grabbed a bottle of whiskey off the bar and poured himself another drink. News like this was mighty hard to take in any state of mind, much less being sober. He took it down in one gulp, which was not his custom, and quickly refilled his glass. "That man you're working on is the toughest man I've ever known, Doc. If anyone's got a fighting chance, it's him."

Miller laughed as he continued to sew the hole closed. "Yes, I'm sure he is. But no man can escape medical realities, no matter how tough he is. Maybe he can take the pain, but no man can will himself through an infection, just like he can't will a broken bone to heal. Only rest and time can dictate that, and from what you said, neither is in the offing for the Brickhouse Gang."

Pearson's next drink was a sip, but the liquor was beginning to grease the rusty wheels of his mind. "What if we put him in that stagecoach out there?"

Miller shook his head. "Too cramped for a man of his size to lie comfortably."

Pearson looked out the window at the big freighter parked across the street. The big wagon looked broken and ruined without the team of mules tied to it. "What if we took a mattress from upstairs and put it in the back of the wagon over there."

Miller took a quick glance out the window before returning to his sewing. "It would be better than the stagecoach, but not by much. The jostling will still strain the stitches, but it would give him more of a chance." He held up a bloody finger. "That's not a promise, you understand? I don't want you riding back here looking to kill me if he dies. The odds would be against him living if he was in the finest hospital back east, much less any care I could offer him here. His chances would improve tremendously if you let me take his arm like I suggest, but I'm not going to risk getting shot to do it."

Pearson finished his drink and set the glass on the bar. "Thanks, Doc. You're a big help."

He strode over to the door where one of the wagon-men was standing guard. "What's your name?"

"Elder," the man told him. "Why?"

"What are you hauling on that freighter that we can lose?"

Elder squinted his eyes as he thought about it. "Got some furniture pieces that weigh a lot and won't fetch much of a price anywhere. They're at the back of the wagon, too, so we could easily lose them. Why?"

"Because I want you and one of the men to clear out as much junk as you can so as a mattress can be put down in the back of it for Bram. We'll need to make him comfortable when we ride out of here tomorrow."

"We can do better than a mattress, boss," Elder told him. "There's a bed and all the trimmings on there. We can rig it so he'll ride in comfort."

Pearson looked back at Doc Miller, hopeful. "You hear that, Doc? How's that sound to you?"

Miller lifted his bloody palms to the ceiling and shrugged before going back to work.

It was not ideal, Pearson decided, but it was the best they could do for old Bram. "You get one of the boys to help you. I'll square it with the soldier boys across the street so they don't shoot you."

"You do that," Elder said. "I've got no problem making Mr. Hogan comfortable, but I don't want to stop a bullet in the process. I've got plans for my share of that gold, mister, and I aim to live long enough to spend it."

Pearson liked the way the man thought. He did not expect him to have the same loyalty to Hogan as he and Lem did. Still, greed could keep a man alive despite the odds facing him.

T HE BIG MAN pushed his way through the batwing doors and stepped out onto the boardwalk. "Hello in the store. This is Pearson. I'm coming out to talk. Don't go shooting me, now."

He was glad Coleman answered him. "Come ahead, Pearson. No one will shoot you."

Pearson strode over to the post just past where the wagons were parked and leaned against it. The post would not provide much cover for a man his size, but it was better than standing completely exposed. He could always fall back if he caught sight of a gun. The sunlight had shifted and the front of the store was bathed in light.

"How are you faring in there?" Pearson asked.

"The use of the privy is appreciated," Coleman answered back. "How are the animals?"

"Grateful for the tending," Pearson said. "As are we that you didn't shoot us while we got them."

"No need for thanks," Coleman said. "I gave you my word."

"And I gave you mine." Pearson cleared his throat. He was getting dry again and regretted leaving the whiskey back in the saloon. He would be sure to return to it as soon as possible. "I'm afraid I'm going to have to ask you for another favor, but I'm willing to grant one in return."

Coleman paused for a moment before saying, "What is it?"

"The colonel did a better job on Hogan than he knew," Pearson admitted. "He's shot up pretty good. Got a hole in him about half the size of Texas and broke his shoulder in the bargain."

"Good," he heard Standish yell from deep inside the store before the sounds of a scuffle reached him.

Pearson smiled. The old colonel was nothing if not

consistent. He liked that and knew Hogan would appreciate it, too, if he had been awake to hear him.

After the sounds inside the store subsided, the lieutenant said, "What do you need from us?"

"The teamsters tell me there's a bed and all the fixings on that wagon. I want them to set it up for my boss so he can ride out of here in comfort tomorrow. I'd like your word that your men won't shoot at them while they're doing it."

Coleman thought about it for a moment before answering, "As long as they come unarmed."

But Pearson was not a fool. "Afraid I can't ask the men to do that. Not after the colonel shot old Bram in front of them in broad daylight. But they won't stir up anything with your bunch as long as none of you try anything against them. If you'll give your word they won't be shot at, I promise they won't try anything with you. How's that strike you?"

Coleman seemed to consider it before saying, "And our deal about your leaving the stagecoach still stands?"

Pearson took that as an encouraging sign. "Along with a team of mounts well fed and rested. But we'll leave them down at the livery and we'll have to ask you not to go following us when you boys get your horses. You're still outnumbered, remember?"

"I remember," Coleman said. "And you have my word on that, too. I'm glad to see you're a reasonable man, Pearson."

That struck the outlaw as funny. "I'm not reasonable. I'm greedy. Just so happens I've got a soft spot in my heart for old Bram over here. You keep the peace on your side of the street, Coleman, and I'll keep it on mine. Come this time tomorrow, we'll all be a bad memory for each other."

The sounds of a scuffle coming from the store told him Colonel Standish did not approve of the deal and Pearson was glad the old man did not have much say in the matter. His admiration for the officer only went so far.

Pearson pushed through the doors and stepped back into the saloon. He told Elder, "Grab one of your men and get busy with putting that bed together. Bring your rifles with you. They'll be less likely to start something if you're armed."

Elder was heading off to carry out the order when Pearson grabbed his arm. "Don't start anything, but keep a sharp ear out. That colonel's out for blood."

Elder told him he understood and Pearson released him. He took Elder's spot at the door and looked out across the street. *This might work, Pearson. You just might pull this off at that.*

He looked over at Doc Miller, who was wrapping two pieces of wood on either side of Bram's shoulder to form a splint. "When you're done over there, Doc, best take a look at my hand. We've got a big day tomorrow, and I want to look my best."

CHAPTER TWENTY-SIX

J OHN BECK PULLED Pokey to a halt when he saw
something shimmering on the horizon. The sun was
high overhead by then and his shadow was well beneath him. He brought his hands up to shield his eyes
to make sure he was not seeing things. His time roaming the desert had taught him how to know the difference between a mirage and something real.

That was why he knew his eyes were not playing
tricks on him when he saw a horse and rider in the
distance just off the trail from Mother Lode.

And if he could see them, that meant they could
see him.

He pulled the Winchester from the scabbard under
his left leg, leaving the Sharps tucked under his right,
and drove his heels into Pokey's flanks. The horse
jumped into a trot, seeming as eager to close the distance between him and the stranger as Beck had been.

The black speck took more of a form the closer they

drew. Beck could see it was one horse and a rider, which made him feel better about his chances. Even odds were always best, especially in the desert. The fact that the rider and horse had not moved since they had been spotted made him relax that much more.

It was not until he was about a hundred yards or so away that he could see that the rider was on foot and the horse was nosing the ground. Judging by the way Pokey snorted, Beck wondered if it might be one of the water holes that were known to pop up in this part of the desert. It had not been the part where he had been cast out, of course, which he imagined had been the idea behind it.

When he was about fifty yards away, he realized it was a woman crouched by the water hole next to the horse. And at thirty yards, he brought Pokey to a halt. That woman was Dulce.

Beck dropped from the saddle and ran the last few yards to her.

She looked up at him through the long black hair that had fallen in front of her face and made a dash for her saddlebags.

"Don't, Dulce! It's me. John."

She stopped before she reached the horse and flipped the hair from her face. "John? Is that really you?"

When she realized it was, in fact, him, she ran around the horse and into his arms. He held her with his free hand, careful not to drop his rifle. She smothered his face with kisses as he struggled to keep his feet under him.

"My God, John," she said as she buried her face in his chest. "I can't believe you're still alive. I thought you were dead."

Glad she simmered down a bit, he rested his chin on

the top of her head as she held him tightly. "I'm alive, Dulce. Barely, but alive. I'm glad you are, too."

"Barely, my love," she told him. "Barely. God, it was awful, but I never stopped praying for you. Even when they said there was no hope for you, I prayed anyway, and now my prayers are answered."

He felt himself tighten. He did not have to ask who "they" were. He already knew. He could no longer feel how tightly she held him. He could not feel much of anything anymore as his body went cold. "So Bram and his men are still in town."

"Yes, my love, but it is so much worse than when you left. They are holding people hostage in the general store. Soldiers and men and women. Even a little girl. They are refusing to let them leave until they allow Bram and his men to take the gold they are carrying."

By his counting, Beck figured the Brickhouse Gang was down to no more than three men. Not likely odds against soldiers, even if they did have them holed up in Welsh's general store. That old man kept a stocked shop and plenty of ammunition on hand. Trained men could hold out there for a long time if they had a mind to and the cavalry was not known for surrendering without putting up a fight. "How many does Bram have with him?"

"Pearson, the giant, is being held in the store," she told him. "He was shot by one of the passengers on the stagecoach. An old colonel or general or someone. Bram was never much for details."

"So, it's two against all of those people?" That did not make much sense to him. They should have shot Bram and the other one, Lem, to pieces by now. The saloon was not an easy place to defend.

"No, my love. Lem and Bram turned the wagonmen against the soldiers and the civilians; there were five of them at first, but one managed to get himself killed and now they are only four."

Now he understood the army's reason for caution. Six against four were tough odds made even worse when there were civilians that needed to be protected. The fact that two of them were Lem and Bram did not make it any easier on the army.

He gently eased her from him. "How did you get away?"

"There was a gunshot early this morning," she told him. "I don't know who got shot or why and I didn't stick around to find out. All I know is that I heard Bram call out to the men in the store and then there was a shot and I did not hear Bram anymore. Someone else came out of the saloon and began shooting, so I grabbed a bag I had kept hidden in my wardrobe, ran down to the livery, saddled a horse, and rode away as fast as I could."

Beck pushed her behind him and looked up the trail. Going to the livery meant Joe had seen her leave. He had the biggest mouth in five counties and there were bound to be men coming after her. "How long ago was that?"

"An hour, maybe more," she said. "But Joe helped me. I don't think they have even noticed I'm gone. I checked behind me as I rode away and no one followed me."

She pushed his arms away from her and hugged him again. "I can't believe it's really you."

This time, she was the one who broke off the embrace first. "Were you in the town to the south? Amenia?"

"Wandered in there from the desert," he told her. "They're good people, Dulce. They took me in and gave me a place to live. I thought I had a chance there until Laredo showed up last night and tried to kill me."

"Laredo?" she repeated. "You mean you killed Laredo?"

"I'd be dead right now if I hadn't. He didn't give me much choice."

She took his face in her hands and began to kiss him again, but it just did not feel right to him. He could remember a time in the distant past when he had longed for her to kiss him, but now that he had found Lilly, it just did not feel right.

She felt his resistance and said, "What is wrong, my love?"

He began to guide her back to her horse. "I've got business to attend to in Mother Lode, Dulce. You keep on riding in a straight line along this trail and it'll take you right into Main Street. You'll be there well before sunset, and make sure you stop by the Amenia Hotel when you do. Tell Ma Stanton you're a friend of mine and she'll take care of you. Ask for Doc Reese, too. He's a good man and he'll look out for you until I get back."

She embarrassed him by throwing her arms around him again and squeezing him tightly. "I won't let you leave me again. I will go with you. I will tell you which men are good and which men you can kill."

But John knew that was not a good idea. He was liable to get shot before all was said and done. His conscience was already heavy enough after the death of George Hauser. He did not want Dulce's death on his conscience, especially not after all she had already lived through. He did not dare ask her what she had endured at the hands of Bram Hogan. He knew the kind of man he was and it was a miracle she was still alive. She deserved to keep on living, just as he knew he deserved whatever fate awaited him in Mother Lode.

"It's best if you keep on the trail for Amenia," he told her. "Better for you and for me. They'll see to you, just like I promised they would."

Reluctantly, she allowed him to lead her horse and he helped her climb up into the saddle. He only glanced at her face and dared not to look any harder than that. Her eyes were swollen by tears and hollow from all of the trials she had endured in town.

She pulled a few errant strands of hair away from her face and let the desert wind blow through her hair. "All of the good men in town are gone, John. They fled into the hills and who knows where, little by little until there was no one left. After the soldiers were trapped in the store, everyone else fled town. The only men left are those who ride with Bram. Kill them all, my love. Kill them for what they did to us and come back to me. I will be waiting."

He squeezed her hand one last time and swiped at the horse's backside with his hat. The animal took off at a good gallop south toward Amenia. With any luck at all, he knew Dulce would be there just before nightfall.

By then, John Beck imagined that he would either be with her or looking down on her and Lilly from a place where the troubles of this world could no longer reach him.

CHAPTER TWENTY-SEVEN

A T HIS POST by the front door of the store, Sergeant Hastings stifled a yawn. It was not that he found guard duty beneath him, but the monotony of this posting was beginning to get to him.

He had been in the army long enough to know it was pointless to disagree with an officer's decision, but he disagreed with Coleman's decision to not attack the saloon as soon as Hogan went down.

It was not that Hastings was anxious to get shot at. Far from it. But he was anxious to get to the fort with the stagecoach and the army money that was on it. The men needed their pay and Hastings didn't want a dressing-down from Captain Standish. He figured the colonel would get his son worked up over Coleman's refusal to attack and save the gold. As sergeants tended to pay for the mistakes of their officers, he had no doubt the same would be true here.

Hastings was also itching for some action. He was

tired of being stuck in this store with these civilians. Now that Mr. Katz had been killed, the entire mood changed. Welsh, the shopkeeper, was convinced the outlaws would burn his store to the ground. He was also beginning to gripe about all of the food they were eating and about how the army better pay him for his trouble.

Coleman was not used to having to explain himself all the time and was becoming frustrated by second-guessing. Welsh's constant complaining and the colonel's constant criticism did little to help the young lieutenant's mood any.

Hastings felt sorry for Sam Coleman. He was a good young officer who just might have a bright future ahead of him if he did not allow himself to think too much. But thinking had been a common failing in all of the officers Sergeant Joe Hastings had ever served. Some thought too much and their inaction often got lots of men killed. Some did not like to think at all, preferring to charge ahead with banners flying and bugles blaring before they had considered all of their options. That got a lot of men killed, too.

Hastings figured the ideal officer was a man who could weigh the situation before him and make the right decision quickly. He supposed that was the trick of everything in life, but more so when leading men in the field.

That's why he thought Sam Coleman had a bright future in the army. He was a bit unsure of himself, but any junior officer would be with an old legend like Colonel "Red" Jeb Standish looking over his shoulder. He had acquired the name "Red Jeb" on account of his brutal ways of dispatching the outlaws and renegades who crossed his path back when he had still been in uniform. The fact that Standish's son was also Coleman's commanding officer did not help the situation.

But although Hastings might have disagreed with the lieutenant's idea to stand pat and not attack the men who were holding them hostage, he certainly understood his reasons. He had civilians to consider and a building to defend. If they were going to do nothing, it was easier to do it with a store full of ammunition and supplies. It also helped to know Coleman was no coward. He would fight if it came down to it. That was something to hold on to.

Hastings glanced back when he heard Colonel Standish approach him at the door.

"Damned shame, isn't it, Sergeant?"

Hastings had been in the army long enough to know it was dangerous to suppose he could read a superior officer's mind, especially when that officer was retired. "What do you mean, sir?"

"You know what I mean, Hastings. Standing around here, tethered to this damned place like a bunch of hobbled geldings. We have the superior numbers and firepower. We should've hit them as soon as I shot that braggart Hogan. They were scrambling. On the run. We should have made the most of it. Now they've not only caught their second wind, but they've elected themselves a new leader! One we had tied up on our floor and out of the fight until Coleman cut him loose."

Hastings had no intention of getting pulled into a debate with a colonel. "The lieutenant's a good man, Colonel. He always manages to do the right thing. He's a fighter, too. All of us are. If they start something, we'll finish it. Don't you worry about that."

"But I *am* worried, Sergeant," Standish continued. "I've got my wife and granddaughter to worry about.

The civilians, too. We didn't pick this fight, but we're in it now. We've got a duty to enforce the law wherever we are, no matter the danger to ourselves."

Hastings did not buy it and did not like the direction this conversation might take. "I've got a duty to follow orders, sir, and that's what I intend on doing."

"A *lawful* order," Colonel Standish reminded him. "Not an unlawful one. An order to allow a gaggle of thieves to ride off with army payroll and gold is just about as far from the law as I can think."

Hastings could think of worse orders. Like ordering men to get shot over a lousy wagonload of goods. Sure, he did not like the idea of going another month without pay, but he liked the notion of getting shot to pieces a whole lot less. He liked a fight as much as any other man, but only when the time was right for it.

And he did not want Lieutenant Coleman getting any ideas about his loyalty, so he decided to end this discussion now before any foolishness took place. "I've been in the army a long time, Colonel. And if I didn't know any better, I might think you were trying to put me at odds with the lieutenant."

Colonel Standish did not answer him. Instead, something in the street caught his attention. His eyes narrowed and he looked like he was about to spit. "Well, would you just look at that. Of all the abominable gall!"

Hastings looked out and saw two of the former wagonmen exit the saloon. He kept Townsend and Sear in his rifle sights as they walked across the street, rifles held low. They were walking slowly, as if they expected to get shot at any moment. Their fear made him feel better. It meant they knew they were covered and were less apt to do something stupid.

He only wished the same went for Colonel Standish.

The retired officer's voice trembled as he said, "Just look at them, striding around in the broad daylight like peacocks on parade."

Hastings heard the floorboard creak as Standish shifted his weight. Out of the corner of his eye, he saw the colonel reach for the Colt that Hastings had tucked in his tunic. Standish's Colt that Lieutenant Coleman had told him to hold on to for safekeeping.

Instinct and training caused the sergeant to bring down the butt of his rifle across Standish's outstretched arm. The colonel cried out as Hastings used the rifle as a bar to push him away, knocking the retired officer into the shelves.

Standish recovered with surprising speed and launched himself at Hastings, sending the sergeant back against the wall next to the door. He could feel the colonel grasping for the pistol and dropped his rifle to keep him from grabbing it. He heard Coleman and the others rushing to his side when the pistol went off.

CHAPTER TWENTY-EIGHT

WITH POKEY SECURED to a hitching post behind the old hotel at the edge of Main Street, John Beck slung his saddlebags full of ammunition over his shoulder and brought the Winchester and the Sharps up to the back door of the hotel. The door was locked, but constant heavy pressure made the old lock pop easily and with minimal sound. The glass in the door cracked from the effort, but fortunately did not break. A whisper of dry wood cracking was the only sound that betrayed his position. He felt lucky about that.

He stifled a cough as he walked through the hotel's kitchen. The place felt like it had been closed up for a couple of weeks by then and the air was heavy with dust. No one could ever mistake the old hotel for one of the fine Chicago hotels he remembered, but it had always prided itself on being the cleanest place in the desert town.

Although the saloon and the general store were a

good piece up Main Street, he walked gingerly through the old building, hoping to keep any creaking from the floorboards to a minimum. He wanted to conceal his presence in town for as long as possible if he could help it. He did not want to risk a close-quarters gunfight if he could avoid it. Once the shooting started, that would be inevitable, but the longer he went without giving away his position, the better.

The threadbare carpeting in the lobby helped him reach the main staircase without incident and he quickly took the stairs two at a time until he reached the second floor. He knew the rooms that faced Main Street shared a wide balcony that would make for an ideal shooter's perch, but he also knew it was an easy way for Hogan's men to gun him down. He had no intention of making himself a target.

He went to the narrow door at the end of the hall, tucked the lighter Winchester under his right arm, and opened it, revealing a staircase that led up to the hotel's roof. He set his rifles on the stairs and pulled the door behind him, his only light coming from that which poked through the trapdoor above. It was enough for him to see an old broom tucked just inside the door. He approximated its length, and used his knee to break off just enough of it so that he could place it over the doorknob to keep anyone from pulling it open without a significant effort. It would not hold for long, but every second would count when Hogan's men came for him.

After securing the knob as best he could, he turned the key on this side of the door, locking it in place.

He picked up his rifles and used his head to inch open the trapdoor to the roof. When he got his shoulders high enough to be able to place the Winchester and Sharps on either side of the opening, he eased himself up onto the roof and slowly set the trapdoor into place with a quiet thump. He gathered up his rifles and moved at a crouch toward the edge of the flat roof. There were no eaves up there, just a slight incline that allowed rainwater to roll down from the edges.

He had no cover but would not need much. The hotel was the tallest building in town and the angle from the street would make it tough for anyone shooting up at him from the street to hit him. The rooftop offered an unobstructed view of Main Street and the barren desert beyond.

The same desert that had thrown everything it had against him but had failed to kill him.

He took a knee just before the edge and set his saddlebag down before him, opening each flap and pulling out the boxes of ammunition he had brought with him. The rounds for the Sharps were on his right side. The rounds for the rifle were on his left. He dumped out a neat pile of each so he could grab, reload, and fire without looking for them.

His perch set, he drew in a deep breath and observed.

The front of the saloon was bathed in shadow but appeared to be empty. He saw a man standing in the doorway looking at the general store on this side of the street.

Although he could not see the general store, he saw the huge freight wagon and stagecoach parked in front of it. The teams had been removed and he was glad to see the wagons provided good cover for the people holed up inside the store.

He was also glad the teams were elsewhere, as it meant the wagons would still provide cover for them once the shooting started.

Beck tensed when he saw movement from the saloon and watched two men step into the street. The older of the two was stockier and about fifty. The younger one was rangier and looked like a man who earned his living from a saddle.

The faces of his tormentors in the Brickhouse Gang were seared into his memory, so he knew neither of these men was a Hogan regular. These must be the wagonmen Dulce had told him about.

He brought the Sharps up to his shoulder and took careful aim at the older, slower man as he walked across Main Street. Everything in him wanted to squeeze the trigger and put a hole in him. Beck knew he could quickly reload the rifle and hit the younger man before he reached cover. The single-shot rifle was not ideal for combat, but in his practiced hands, it was.

Neither of these men had been responsible for driving him into the desert. Neither of these men had done anything to him, but he hated them just the same. They were part of the men who had tried to kill him. Who had cast him out, who had humiliated him and left him to die.

They had abandoned their jobs and taken up with the man who had wanted him dead. The men who had robbed him of his sanity and self-respect. Now everything in him wanted these men dead, too.

But something in him told him to wait. A quiet voice in his mind told him to hold the shot and wait to see how things played out. He tracked the man instead as he lumbered toward the wagon.

Beck tensed when he thought he heard the muffled

sounds of a struggle come out of the general store. He watched the two wagonmen stop in their tracks and bring up their rifles, and knew he had not been hearing things.

Something was going on in the store.

The younger wagonman brought his rifle up to his shoulder and aimed it at the store. The bastard saw an opening.

Beck shifted his aim and fired.

The .50-caliber round hit before the echo of the big gun filled the vacant town. The young wagonman's head disappeared in a red cloud of dust. His rifle discharged into the air as his body fell to the packed dirt of Main Street.

The older man froze as he watched his partner fall.

In one fluid motion, Beck ejected the spent cartridge, fed in another one, and brought the Sharps back up to his shoulder. The stocky man had just decided to break back toward the saloon when Beck took aim and fired. The slug caught him in the right side and threw him hard to the ground. His rifle skittered away from him and he made no effort to reach it. He rolled over onto his back and never moved again.

Beck ejected the spent round and fed in another without taking his eyes off the saloon. He had no idea if Hogan had other men throughout the town, but knew if trouble came, it would start there.

He brought the Sharps back up to his shoulder and aimed at the front door of the saloon. He saw someone's feet under the batwing doors and fired. The blast punched a hole in the middle of the doors, blowing them apart. The feet disappeared and Beck knew he had missed whoever he had been shooting at. He cursed himself for rushing the shot but knew he had a little time for whoever was still in the general store. That was more important to him now than hitting a target.

Since Hogan and his men knew someone was firing at them and from where, it was only a matter of time before they made a move on his position. There might be a time for the big Sharps to come, but for now, it was best to switch to the more versatile Winchester. The saloon was still well within its range, though he was sacrificing some degree of firepower.

He did not recognize the voice that now echoed through the street. "Looks like we've got a new guest in town. Mind introducing yourself, stranger?"

Despite all that he had endured, Beck was fairly certain he would remember Hogan's voice when he heard it. This did not sound like Hogan. He wondered if the leader had been hit when Dulce heard the gunshot.

"Don't be shy, stranger," the man called out. "Be neighborly and introduce yourself. We don't bite, I promise."

Beck kept his rifle aimed at the saloon. The Brickhouse Gang might not bite, but he imagined they could certainly shoot. He kept his aim and his silence.

"Come on, mister," the man taunted him again. "There's no reason to be scared. So you shot down two of my men in cold blood. Seeing as how I'm a killer myself, I can understand it. Why, you might say I even admire it. Might do the same thing if I was in your shoes. Now, I'm not going to lie to you and tell you we're not going to kill you for it, but that doesn't mean we can't get to know each other first. Who knows? We might even come to something that you might call an understanding. Maybe there won't be call for any more bloodshed. What do you say?"

Beck slowly lowered his rifle. For a man who was pinned down, he was doing an awful lot of talking. Almost as if he was just talking to hear himself talk.

Or to distract Beck while something else went on.

Beck pushed himself away from the edge and took a closer look over Main Street. No one was moving in the alleyways, at least no one that he could see. And if he could not see them, they probably could not see him. But there were more streets in Mother Lode than Main.

He moved at a crouch to the left side of the roof, where he could get a better look at the area behind the shops that lined the thoroughfare.

That was when he spotted one man break from the cover of a building and sprint toward the hotel. The man did not look familiar, so he imagined this must be another new member of the Brickhouse Gang.

Beck aimed the Winchester down at him. The man should have stuck with his previous employer.

Beck fired and struck the man in the center of the chest. He stopped cold, as if he had run into an invisible brick wall, but did not fall. He staggered but kept his feet.

Beck racked in another round and fired. This shot caught him higher in the chest, sending him into a tight spiral before he fell to the ground. He dropped in a twisted heap and did not move again.

Several rounds began to pelt the edge of the roof where Beck had been, sending chips of wood and planking into the air. None of them came close to his position now, but he knew a bunch like Hogan's men did not fire shots blindly. If they were shooting at him, it was to keep him away from that end of the roof.

That meant at least one of them was probably making a play for the hotel.

They were trying to trap him.

CHAPTER TWENTY-NINE

LEM WAS ABOUT to charge out into the street when Pearson snatched him by the collar and shoved him farther back into the saloon. "What the hell do you think you're doing?"

Lem was about to tell him when the batwing doors exploded into a cloud of dust and splinters. He felt himself gawk at the gaping hole the bullet made in the wooden planking of the saloon floor.

Pearson, unfazed by the chaos, pointed down at the hole. "That would've been your belly if it hadn't been for me. What's wrong with you? You can't go charging at a man like that. Not the way he shoots."

Lem quickly recovered from his shock. "That bastard just killed Townsend and Sear, damn it."

"Better them than us," Pearson said. He looked over at Whalen, who was by the bar keeping an eye on Hogan as he recovered from his operation. He pointed at the rifle the man held uneasily at his side. "You still with us, Whalen?"

"Don't see as I have any choice right now."

"That's right, you don't," Pearson said. "But you'll have a better chance of living to see tomorrow if you keep on doing like I tell you, hear?"

Lem had never been one for talking, and he felt less like talking when bullets started flying. "I'd like to hear how you think we're going to get out of this, big man. That fella seems to be shooting down at us from that old hotel at the end of the street. He could pick us apart with that cannon he's using."

"It's hardly a cannon," Pearson sneered. But Lem's stomach sank as the giant's sneer faded just as quickly as it had appeared. "Could be a Sharps, though." He looked once more at the hole in the saloon floor. "Yes, I believe it could."

Lem knew he had never been accused of being a smart man, but he was far from dumb. Despite all of his years of drunken nights and hard living, he could still form a thought when it was necessary. And it did not require much thought for him to remember the significance of a Sharps rifle since they had ridden into Mother Lode.

He looked up at Pearson, mouth agape. "Jesus, Dale. You don't think it could be him, do you?"

The big man covered Lem's mouth. "Maybe it is, maybe it isn't. Doesn't matter either way because any way you look at it, somebody's out there with a damned big gun and knows how to hit whatever he aims at. We've got to do something about that and right quick."

Lem looked through the window at the dead men lying in the street and gagged. One of their heads was completely gone.

"Going out that door is crazy."

"But going out the back is smart," Pearson said.

"Who do you have keeping an eye on the back door of the store again?"

It took Lem a second to remember their names. "Elder and Fisk. Why?"

Lem could see an idea form in Pearson's mind. "Think you can get their attention from the alley next door?"

"I think so. Might be able to throw a rock or something to get them looking. That is if they don't wing off a shot at me first. Why?"

Pearson pushed him toward the back door of the saloon. "Run out there and get their attention. I want them to forget about watching the back door of the store. I want one of them to run down that backstreet there toward the hotel, but the second one needs to hold back. If the first one gets through, then the second one runs down the back while you run down behind the saloon here and cut over while I cover you."

It was even easy enough for Lem to understand. "I'll try."

"You'll do it or we're as good as dead," Pearson told him. "Now move and don't foul up."

L EM HAD JUST reached the mouth of the alley when he heard Pearson begin to call out to the shooter. He did not concentrate on what he was saying because it was all just nonsense anyhow.

He saw Fisk at the far end of the alley across the street and called out to him. He was glad he caught his attention on the first try. He waited until Pearson paused to ask, in an exaggerated whisper that hurt his throat, "Get Elder."

Fisk disappeared from Lem's view for a moment

and Lem was glad to see he reappeared with Elder by his side.

Lem had not thought far enough ahead to plan out how he was going to get the men to do what he wanted and he began gesturing at them wildly. He exaggerated pointing at Elder until the wagonman pointed at himself.

Lem nodded, held up his rifle, and waved his hand in the direction of the old hotel.

By some miracle, Elder seemed to understand what he meant, took up his rifle, and began running in that direction.

Panicked that Fisk might run off, too, Lem quickly stabbed his finger at him and held up his hand. Then he pointed at Fisk and at himself by turn and indicated that they run down toward the hotel.

Lem spat to get some saliva in his throat before he forced a whisper: "Wait for me."

Fisk nodded that he understood and got into position, never taking his eyes off Lem.

Lem eased down to the back of the alley behind the saloon, keeping his hand raised as if it could hold Fisk in place. He had just reached the back of the alley when he heard a single rifle shot ring out from the end of town. Where the old hotel was. It was followed a few seconds later by another shot and he figured that probably meant the end of Elder. The shooter could have missed, but it wasn't likely.

Lem looked across the alley and waved Fisk to run, but he was already gone.

By the time Lem took off at full speed, he heard Pearson cut loose with his rifle at the front of the saloon.

* * *

LEM WAS BREATHING hard by the time he reached the back of the doctor's office but dared not stop. He was afraid he might fall down if he did. Instead he reached out and grabbed the porch post of the doctor's office and swung himself around between the buildings, toward the old hotel across Main Street.

He shut his eyes tight as he ran as fast as he could, afraid he might lose his nerve if he looked up and saw the outline of the gunman on the roof. He kept running until he thought he had finally reached the boardwalk of the hotel when he realized he had misjudged the distance. He hit the boardwalk just below his knees, which sent him tumbling up onto the floorboards. He fell flat on his face but did not lose hold of his rifle.

And he had not been shot, either. He was still very much alive.

Ignoring the fire that shot through his legs, he pulled himself onto his feet and slammed his shoulder into the front door of the hotel. The place might have looked like it was about to fall down, but the front door was thick and well built. When two more pushes against it proved fruitless, panic began to rise within him. He pulled the pistol from his holster and shot at the lock until the door swung inward.

He pushed his way inside and crouched behind an overstuffed chair in the lobby. The dust the effort had kicked up made his eyes water and he had to struggle not to cough.

He caught movement off to his left and raised his pistol. He almost fired, too, until he saw it was Fisk. He must have found a way into the hotel through the back door.

Lem allowed himself to breathe again. "What about Elder?"

Fisk shook his head, but Lem had already figured as much. The two shots he had heard had meant the end of Elder.

But at least he and Fisk had both made it inside without a scratch.

Now it was time to take care of the bastard up on the roof once and for all.

He thought about sending Fisk up the stairs ahead of him but feared he might kill the shooter first. Lem raced up the stairs instead, with Fisk following quickly on his heels.

He had just reached the middle of the staircase when he heard a door slam at the end of the hallway to his right.

He crouched by the post at the top of the stairs and was glad Fisk stopped just behind him. Lem peered down the dark hall and willed his eyes to see better. He could make out three closed doors at the right side of the hallway. It was impossible for him to know which one had been opened.

Until he saw the narrow door in the middle was not quite closed, and creaked.

Lem decided that must be the door that led up to the roof. And the bastard who had wanted to kill him was only a few steps away.

Lem was too excited to bother telling Fisk what he was about to do. He just got busy doing it. He pitched forward and bolted up the remaining stairs, wheeled to his right, and ran down the hall. He threw the door up to the roof open and bounded up the stairs.

Realizing he had lost any element of surprise, he

burst through the trapdoor and spilled out onto the roof, his pistol sweeping the area in front of him.

But it only took him a split second to realize the roof was entirely empty. The sound of spent brass shells slowly being pushed by the wind was the only sound he could hear.

Lem had run straight into a trap, for there was only one way down from here.

But just because he might have run into a trap did not mean all was lost.

"Fisk!" he called down into the stairwell. "Get back. Don't come up here."

But by then, Fisk had followed Lem's lead up the main staircase and into the narrow stairs that led up to the roof. The wagonman had just begun to stop when a .50-caliber bullet tore through his chest.

Lem tumbled backward and landed hard enough to knock the wind out of himself.

He was too busy gasping for air to notice that Fisk had flopped out onto the roof, where he now lay like a dead fish.

He was still trying to draw air back into his lungs when Fisk's corpse slowly slid out of view as it was pulled back down the stairs. In fact, he had only just begun to be able to breathe again when he noticed the tall man with the Winchester was standing over him.

Lem quickly looked around for his pistol on the roof but could not find it.

"Wouldn't do you any good, even if you had it tucked down in your waistband," Beck said. "I'd have taken if off you by now anyway."

Lem squinted up at him, even though the sun was now almost setting. He squinted up at him through the pain. He squinted up at him through a hazy memory.

The tall man had a familiar look. His black hair was a giveaway, but the haunted eyes would stay with Lem for the rest of his life, however long that may be.

"You're him," Lem said, more for his own benefit than the stranger's. "You're the law dog we ran out of town, ain't you? Beck."

"Glad you remembered," Beck said. "A man ought to know the name of the one who kills him."

Lem had not gotten much breath back into his lungs, but enough to begin to pull himself away from Beck along the roof. "I'm unarmed, mister. You've got no call to kill me now."

But Beck kept his Colt on him as he stepped up onto the roof. "What makes you say that?"

Lem's elbows began to get more traction as he pushed himself away even harder as Beck grew ever closer. "I don't have a gun. Or . . . or a rifle. Don't even have a knife on me." He kept inching back and Beck kept coming closer. "What can I do to you now?"

"Don't sell yourself short." Beck took another step closer. "After all you've already done for me, the least I can do is return the favor."

Lem felt his mouth run dry as his left elbow slipped, sending him flat on the roof for a moment. "Please, mister. That wasn't just me, you know? That was more Steve and Bram's doing instead of mine. I barely did anything."

Lem had even managed to almost convince himself of that. He hoped it was good enough to convince Beck, too.

But it did not seem to be, because the haunted man kept coming toward him. "I remember most everything about that day, except for the parts when I got kicked in the head and blacked out for a time. But I remember your cackle. I remember you were right alongside Bram and Steve and that big fella when they trussed me up and rode me out of town."

Lem's heels kept pushing him backward while his elbows began to hurt from banging them against the roof so much. "Like you said, mister. It wasn't just me. Your memory's fine."

"It sure is. Because I remember you didn't do much to stop them, either." He aimed the Colt down at Lem. "You're just as guilty as the rest of the gang. And now you're going to pay for it."

Lem dropped flat on his back and threw up his arms over his face, hoping in vain that it might somehow stop the bullet.

But when the bullet did not come, he was surprised to hear Beck say, "Keep moving."

Lem slowly lowered his arms and looked up at the man. "What did you say?"

"Keep crawling in the direction you were crawling," Beck said. "Keep going until I tell you to stop."

Lem looked behind him and saw he was already dangerously close to the edge. If he moved back much farther, he would fall to the street below.

Lem was about to tell him as much when a bullet hit the roof just next to his left hand. "Either you move, or you get shot in the belly. Your choice."

Realizing the man had clearly lost his mind, Lem began to kick himself away from Beck, scraping his elbows raw in the hope that he could open up enough room to maneuver and get away from the madman.

He allowed his heel to slip a few times just to see how close he could get to striking Beck's leg. But his tormentor was always careful to remain just out of reach. If he tried to sweep Beck off-balance, he would get shot in the belly before he had the chance. And the look in the man's eyes told him he would be all too happy to shoot him dead.

That was why Lem kept moving backward, hoping an opportunity might present itself.

He kept on hoping right up until he felt a warm rush of air against his back and sensed that he had reached the end of the roof. He twisted his head around and saw he was right.

He imagined he might be able to survive a two-story fall, but he had forgotten that the old hotel had been built on top of a hill that fell away from the back of the building. The drop from that part of the roof would be closer to five stories or so. That would be enough to bust him up good, if not kill him outright.

As soon as he stopped moving, Beck stopped, too, and thumbed back the hammer on his pistol. "Keep going like I told you, or you get one in the belly."

Lem could not move, yet he desperately wanted to. He wanted to lunge at Beck and take his chances with a rushed shot missing its mark. He wanted to curse and scream at this man he had ridden out of town on a rail only a few weeks ago. He wanted to threaten him the way he and the gang had threatened and intimidated hundreds of people in dozens of forgettable flyspeck towns throughout the territory.

But he knew Beck was beyond the reach of his words, and threats no longer meant anything to him. He had the look of a man who had already died too many times to fear death.

Lem felt his body go numb as he watched Beck lower the Colt to aim at his stomach. He wanted to cry out for Bram and Pearson. He wanted to curse them for not being there to get him out of this mess as he had helped them countless times over the years. He wanted to tell Beck they would kill him for this. He wanted to do so many things against Beck, but in the end, could do none of them.

He used whatever strength he had left to roll himself off the side of the roof. And as he fell, he was oddly comforted by the sound of the gunshot.

Beck had made good on his promise. He would have killed him anyway.

It was the last thought he had before he crashed into the dirt.

CHAPTER THIRTY

BECK LOOKED OVER the edge of the roof. He had hoped Lem would not throw himself over the side. He had hoped he would stay there like the coward he was and get shot in the belly.

But the outlaw had shown more grit than Beck had given him credit for. Agility, too. He had thought Lem was all played out until that last burst of energy sent him into the air.

And now, as he looked down at Lem's body going through the last throes of death before finally lying still, Beck decided he had died well. Better than he deserved.

He did some math in his mind as he turned around and headed back down the stairs into the hotel. He had killed Steve Hogan, Laredo, and now the one they called Lem. That left him with Bram and the giant called Pearson to deal with.

He remembered Pearson from the periphery of his

memory. A big man, not just a tall one. Not really a giant, Beck supposed, but certainly tall enough for it to not make much of a difference. His role in his banishment into the wilderness was foggy in Beck's mind, all except for the knowledge that Pearson had been there and done nothing to stop it.

Three Brickhouse Gang members down. Two to go. Based on what Dulce had just told him outside of town, he figured they only had about one or two men left from the bunch who had joined them from the wagon team.

He was still outnumbered and outgunned, but not as much as he had been when he had ridden into town. Things had tilted just enough in his favor to give him hope about making it out of this thing alive. Of seeing Lilly again. Of life.

Beck went into the room at the bottom of the stairs where he had left his saddlebag and rifles. He had just grabbed hold of the saddlebag to sling it on his shoulder when a heavy blow to the side of the head knocked him off his feet. He hit the floor at a skid. His stomach turned as the room violently tilted back and forth. He felt a tug at his belt and knew his pistol and been pulled free.

The world was still upended as a single hand grabbed him by the collar and hauled him to his feet as if he were a rag doll. If the strength of the blow or the size of the hand that grabbed was not enough of a giveaway, the bearded face and hawk nose confirmed for Beck that this was Pearson.

"My God, it *is* you," Pearson said as he shook Beck by the collar. "The law dog himself. Something always told me you weren't dead and I hate to be wrong." Beck's neck rocked back as the big man pulled him forward. "Let's see what we can do about that."

Beck was surprised Pearson released him, then reeled from a backhand that lifted him off his feet and out into the hallway. He landed hard on his right shoulder and the pain caused him to cry out despite himself.

"Hurts, don't it?" Pearson mocked as he came for him again. "And that ain't even nearly as far as you dropped old Lem just now."

He snatched Beck by the back of the collar, but this time did not wait for him to get his legs under him before slamming him into the wall and hurling him once more into the air.

Beck landed on his face, just at the top of the stairway. The dust that was kicked up from the carpet got into his eyes and made him gag.

But the jolt brought a sudden clarity to his dulled mind.

Pearson was only using one hand. His left.

What was wrong with his right hand?

Beck felt Pearson's heavy footfalls on the floorboards. More out of instinct than planning, he flipped over on his back and kicked out with his right leg. His boot heel caught the big man in the groin, which doubled him over as he staggered backward.

Ignoring his own dizziness, Beck scrambled to his feet and brought up his knee into Pearson's face with as much force as he could muster. The giant's head snapped back and he tumbled onto his back.

Beck wanted to dive on top of the man and pummel him, but another wave of dizziness struck him instead and he felt himself falling. He propped himself up on the wall and tried to push himself upright.

But his legs were not strong enough to support his weight and he fell forward toward the stair railing. He draped across it belly first and grabbed hold of the spindles out of fear he might fall over. He blinked his eyes hard and willed himself to get back in the fight. It would not take much effort for Pearson to throw him over the side, even in his condition.

Beck took a deep breath and pushed himself away from the banister, only to be tackled head-on by a charging Pearson. How could such a big man be so quiet?

Despite being carried along by the outlaw's momentum, Beck managed to hook his arm under Pearson's chin and rode the man down headfirst onto the floor.

He had hoped the impact would knock Pearson cold, but it had the opposite effect. The bigger man began to pummel Beck's flanks with lefts and rights as Beck held on to his headlock with all of his waning strength. Each flailing blow only served to make him weaker and he shifted his weight as best be could to pin Pearson's throat against his left arm. With his free right hand and knee, he struck him in the sides as well.

Beck knew his blows must have been having an effect because the giant stopped pummeling him and tried to get to his feet. Beck wrapped his right leg around him and held on for dear life. He knew if Pearson got free at this distance, he could easily beat him to death. All he needed to do was pin him to the floor by the neck and put all of his weight on him until he crushed the life from him. Beck could not let that happen, not until he made Bram Hogan pay for what he had done to him. John Beck needed to avenge himself. He needed to make Hogan know the same fear he had known.

The emptiness.

The banishment.

The death that lurked at the edge of the shadows all those days in that damnable cave.

Beck felt the air escape him as a final, desperate blow from Pearson struck home on the right side, just below his rib cage.

A liver shot. He had seen the same blow knock better brawlers than him flat and he knew he was done for.

Whatever strength he still had left evaporated as his breath left him. He lost his grip on Pearson.

Beck remained on the floor, numb, as Pearson rolled back on his heels and staggered backward. Through his fading vision, he saw the big man teeter and hoped he might fall over the banister to the deserted lobby below.

But Pearson did not fall. He stood at his full height, leaning against the wall as he shook off the pain and confusion of the brawl.

Beck felt a tingling go through him as he saw the blood from Pearson's ruined nose. He had left a mark after all. At least that was something. He might kill Beck before all of this was over, but at least he would know he had been in a fight. That would be something Beck could take with him into whatever awaited him beyond.

Beck had just managed his first full breath in what had seemed like an eternity as Pearson regained his senses and closed in for the kill.

He came at him from the left side this time and dove for his neck with large, outstretched hands.

This was the end, his body said.

But his heart refused to believe it.

With all of his might, Beck jackknifed up between Pearson's hands and slammed his forehead into the bigger man's jaw.

The giant collapsed beside him and Beck wasted no time in rolling away from him. He found himself against the base of the stair railing and desperately held on to it as he pulled himself to his feet.

He shook his vision clear and saw Pearson struggling to do the same. He wanted to use his advantage but simply did not have the strength to finish him off. He needed time he did not have. His right side ached as he leaned on the banister to stumble away and he wondered if he had broken a couple of ribs. The pain that shot through him as he breathed told him he probably had. There was nothing he could do about that now. He needed time to recover. Even a few seconds might do the trick. They would have to be enough, because he doubted Pearson would give him more than that.

When he reached the newel post at the edge of the staircase, Beck bit off the pain as he forced a couple of deep breaths into his lungs.

He remembered the Winchester and the Sharps he had left in the room down the hall and decided to get them. That would give him the only advantage he could hope to have.

His legs finally felt strong enough to support his weight and he took a couple of uneasy steps in that direction.

His whole body shook as Pearson put a shoulder into him and sent him flying.

He landed on the next landing down from the top of the stairs and his momentum sent him hard into the balusters, sending several of them clattering to the lobby floor below. They had given way easily but had been enough to prevent Beck from falling over.

Beck was hurt, but not as badly hurt as he had been. If anything, the impact gave him renewed strength he did not know he had.

Without looking back to see where Pearson was, he used the shaky railing to pull himself upright and half stumbled down the remaining stairs to the lobby.

He ducked as a series of wild gunshots rained down on him, biting into the wood and walls. He did not feel as if any of the bullets had struck him, but knew he was in no state to feel them if they had. All he knew was that he was still upright and breathing.

It was not until he heard the rumbling on the stairs just above him that Beck realized Pearson had been firing as he ran down to finish him off.

Beck dove away from the bottom of the stairs and landed on the floor amid the balusters that had given way just a few seconds before. He grabbed one and swung it like a club in the darkening light of the hotel lobby.

Pearson grunted as the baluster connected with his stomach, doubling him over and bringing him to his knees.

Beck bellowed as he saw his chance, raised the makeshift club again, and brought it down with all of his might on the back of the giant's head.

The blow sent Pearson flat on his face, which only made Beck swing again. And again. He kept bringing the club down, renewed each time it found its mark.

He lost track of how many times he had brought the club down before exhaustion overwhelmed him and the weapon slipped from his hands. He collapsed on his side and managed to roll away from his attacker, fearing there might be some life still left in him.

But after catching his breath, a quick glance at Pearson's ruined head told Beck that he was safe. The monster was finally dead.

Beck's strength failed him and he allowed himself

to roll over on his back, panting. He looked up at the cobwebbed chandelier high above his head as sleep tugged at him.

Just close your eyes, his body told him. *Rest now. Your job is done. You have won.*

Every fiber in his being wanted to give in to the voice. To obey and surrender. To let nature take its course and allow himself to heal.

But he recognized that voice. It was the same infernal whisper that had dogged him each of those endless nights he had spent alone in the wilderness. The same voice that told him to allow whatever stalked him in the darkness to crawl out and bite him, if only to end his misery.

The same voice that had almost won more times than John Beck would ever allow himself to admit.

The same voice he had defied each night he survived. The same voice he would defy now.

He opened his eyes and felt as if he had slept for a month.

"Nothing is over," he told the darkness. "Not yet."

He ignored the pain that shot through him now and got to his feet.

He stepped over Pearson's body and slowly walked up the stairs of the old hotel to fetch his saddlebags and his guns from the room where he had left them a lifetime ago.

CHAPTER THIRTY-ONE

JOHN BECK STAGGERED into the street.

The saddlebag he had draped over his shoulder kept him balanced as he carried his Winchester and Sharps in either hand. He looked up Main Street and saw men in blue milling around the thoroughfare between the general store and the saloon. There were four of them and he figured they must be the soldiers Dulce had told him about. He was glad to see they were still alive.

He had intended on walking up to the saloon on his own power, but another wave of nausea told him that would not be a good idea. He had been forced out of town in humiliation once. He would not allow himself such embarrassment again.

He turned around and walked back behind the old hotel, where he had left Pokey hitched to a rail. He was glad to see his old horse was still there and had lived through it all. Beck smiled at his friend, who had been with him through so much. Who had carried him on and saved his life just when he had believed it was beyond saving.

The horse fussed when he caught Beck's scent in the air, no doubt troubled by the stench of violence that still surrounded him. Beck slid his rifles into their scabbards and gently laid the saddlebag over the horse's back.

Beck caressed the horse's muzzle. "There's a good boy. Thank you for waiting for me. I didn't mean to leave you alone for so long." He placed his aching head against the horse's neck and allowed the warmth from the animal to seep into him. It restored him like a forgotten prayer.

He reached out and undid Pokey's reins from the hitching rail before pulling himself up into the saddle. "Come on, boy. We've still got some work to do."

He gently brought the horse around and let him take the short trip up Main Street at his own pace.

The four soldiers on Main Street seemed to notice him immediately. The stockier of the group approached one of the men and spoke to him. Beck figured the man to be a sergeant and the man he was talking to an officer.

The other soldiers grabbed their rifles tightly as Pokey slowly closed the distance between them. Beck hoped they did not shoot him. It would be a shame to have lived through all of this only to be killed by a nervous private.

The man Beck pegged as an officer broke away from the group and began walking toward him. He did not try for the pistol holstered on his right hip and Beck was glad to see the flap was pinned down.

When they got within shouting distance of each

other, the man called out to him: "You the one who did all that shooting just now?"

Beck found he was too tired to speak, so he simply nodded, hoping that would be enough.

"You've got a store full of soldiers and civilians who are in your debt, mister," the officer said. "And you can count me among them."

When Beck rode closer, the man held his right hand up to him. "I'm Lieutenant Sam Coleman, United States Cavalry, and I'd be honored to shake your hand."

Beck winced as he reached down and shook Coleman's hand. "And I'd be honored if you could help me down. Had me a run-in with a mountain back there and I'm afraid I'm feeling a bit poorly from the effort."

Coleman beckoned the sergeant to take hold of Pokey while he helped Beck ease down from the saddle. Beck was glad he could do most of the work on his own.

"Sorry for not returning the greeting back there, Lieutenant, but like I said, I'm feeling poorly."

"You look it." Coleman kept a tight grip on Beck's arm. "You said you took on Pearson? Yourself."

The sheer memory of it tired him all over again. "He took me on. I guess I just got lucky."

Coleman's hard glare softened. "So he's dead? The big fella?"

"I sure as hell hope so," Beck admitted. "If he's not, he's doing a pretty good imitation. Your men can check for themselves if they want. There's another one at the top of the stairs and that mangy friend of theirs is on the ground behind the hotel." Beck decided to add, "He's dead, too, or soon will be."

Coleman's mouth opened. "Shot him, too?"

Beck shook his head. "He had other plans."

Beck flinched when a tall older man with white mutton-chops blustered his way from the general store. "There's the man I want to meet! Yes, sir. A bona fide hero if I've ever laid eyes on one and I've laid eyes on plenty."

He took Beck's hand and pumped it vigorously before Beck could say otherwise. "Colonel Jebediah Standish, my friend, and I am damned proud to make your acquaintance."

Beck was glad Coleman still had a good grip on his arm lest the colonel's enthusiasm pulled him over. "John Beck," was all he could manage to say.

He bristled when Standish slapped him hard on the back. "John Beck," the colonel said as if he was trying it on for size and glad of the fit. "A fine name, sir. Fine. Easy to remember, not that anyone is likely to forget it after what you've done here today. Riding in here just in the nick of time to save innocents from the wrath of the heathen horde that laid siege to us all these long hours. Why, by the time I'm done, the name of John Beck will be on the lips of every schoolboy in this great country of ours. Men will wish to be you and women will clamor to be with you, for you're just the kind of man this growing nation needs right now, Beck. A man who stands for law and order in the face of all adversity."

Standish poked the lieutenant in the chest. "You could take lessons from a man like this, Coleman. Take charge, by God. That's what counts."

Beck felt his head begin to ache, as much from Standish's bluster as it had from Pearson's fists. He was glad the colonel turned his attention to the soldiers in the street as he went on about the hero, John Beck.

Coleman looked at him as if seeing him for the first time. "Beck. I've heard that name. You're the lawman who—" He seemed to catch himself before speaking what was on his mind and Beck was glad for it.

The lieutenant cleared his throat and said, "I mean, I was told you were dead."

"I was told that myself," he said. "By a little voice in the back of my head for a real long time." He allowed himself to smile. "Funny how I can't hear it too well anymore."

Coleman inclined his head toward the colonel. "How could you hear anything with his big mouth moving. Guess all of that hot air is good for something after all."

But Beck's smile faded as he remembered why he had ridden up to the saloon in the first place. The reason why he was still alive. "Where's Hogan? Bram Hogan."

"You don't have to worry about him anymore," Coleman beamed. "He's in no condition to hurt anyone."

Beck could not see his own reflection, but judging by the lieutenant's reaction, his face must have changed something awful. "You mean he's dead?"

Coleman slowly let go of Beck's arm. "No. At least he wasn't a few minutes ago. Coleman took a shot at him yesterday. Took a good chunk out of his shoulder from what I can see. He's trussed out on the bar where the doc worked on him. Said he'll most likely lose the arm if he lives. And I want him to live, Mr. Beck. I intend on seeing him hang for what he did here. Don't you worry about that."

Beck closed his eyes as he felt a warmth rush through him. A warmth that he had never known before. Finally, something in this whole, horrible mess would be easy. And it just happened to be the last step in his arduous journey.

"Don't you worry," Coleman went on. "I'll see to it you get a good seat at his hanging. Maybe I can even talk the major into letting you pull the lever yourself when we hang him."

Beck opened his eyes. "No."

Coleman looked up at him. "What do you mean?"

"I mean he's not going to hang."

The lieutenant took a couple of steps back from him and Beck sensed the soldiers behind him begin to tense. "That man is my prisoner, Mr. Beck, and he's going to hang for what he did to us."

Beck looked at the officer and saw him all at once. He was loose and ready to go for his pistol if he had to.

Beck did not care if he did. He knew what needed to be done and what needed to be said. "Last I checked, I'm still the marshal here in Mother Lode. He broke our laws long before he took you hostage, which means he's my prisoner. My charge. And I aim to take hold of him right now."

Coleman took another step back. "I can't let you do that, Beck. He's my prisoner."

Beck walked toward him. His steps did not falter. He watched the young lieutenant swallow hard as the man he had just thanked for saving his life drew closer in challenge to his authority.

And he glared at him as Beck walked past him and slowly took the steps up into the saloon.

"Beck!" Coleman called out.

But Beck kept walking.

"Damn it, Beck," Coleman yelled. "One more step and I'll shoot."

The sound of gunmetal clearing leather told him he meant it.

Beck stopped just outside the saloon. "You can't kill me, Lieutenant. I'm already dead."

Beck kept walking into the saloon and Coleman did not shoot.

He did not dare.

CHAPTER THIRTY-TWO

B ECK STOOD JUST inside the doorway and took in all
that he saw. Two men were huddled over a third,
who was stretched out across the bar.

That third man was Bram Hogan and his mouth hung
slack as if he was already dead.

He recognized the younger man tending to Hogan
as Dr. Miller. "Evening, Doc. Been a while."

Both men turned and looked at him.

The older of the two was a stranger to him, so Beck
figured he must be one of the wagonmen who had
joined up with Hogan's bunch when they rode into
town.

Doc Miller had a saw in his hand, but dropped it
when he saw who had spoken to him. "Marshal Beck.
My God."

Beck looked at the strange old man, who was slowly
inching away from the bar. He had a pistol on his belt.
"And just who might you be?"

The man threw up his hands as he increased the distance between himself and the doctor. "Please, mister. I don't want any trouble."

Beck drew his Colt and aimed it at him, causing the old man to flinch and fall down. "I asked you a question."

The man still held out his hands in front of him. "I . . . I'm helping the doc here tend to Bram's wounds."

"Never knew the doc to have an assistant before. Guess that makes you a new arrival in town. Like maybe one of those wagonmen that joined up with the Brickhouse Gang. Caused all this fuss."

"John," Doc Miller called out. "There's been enough bloodshed for one day."

But Beck kept looking at the old man on the floor. "Guess you should count yourself lucky. You're the last of a dying breed. The last member of the Brickhouse Gang alive."

"Please, mister," the old man whimpered. "I've been in here the whole time, see? I didn't hurt anyone. Never fired a shot. Ask the doc here. He'll tell you."

Beck took a step closer toward him and the man crawled away in kind.

"You rode in here awful proud, didn't you? All too ready to take hold of whatever Hogan promised you, didn't you? You didn't care who you hurt. Didn't care what you did. All of it over a lousy bag of money. Funny thing about money. Doesn't do the dead much good." Beck grinned. "Just ask your friends lying outside. They'll tell you all about it."

Coleman and his sergeant rushed into the saloon. "Beck, don't do it."

Beck kept the Colt leveled on the old man on the floor. Based on the stain spreading through his lap, Beck could see that he had already made his point.

He said to Coleman, "You wanted a prisoner, Lieutenant. There he is. Take hold of him before I change my mind."

Coleman motioned to the sergeant, who quickly rushed over, pulled the prisoner to his feet, and hauled him outside.

Miller let out the breath he had been holding. "Thank God, John. You always were a good man. Everyone said so. Now, if you'll just let me get on with my operation here, we'll be done in no time. I'll be glad to tend to your wounds. You look just about all in."

Beck's eyes slid to the doctor. "What operation?"

"His arm," Coleman reminded him. "It has to come off or he'll die."

"No," Beck said. "No operation. Wake him up." Beck aimed the gun at Doc Miller. "Wake him up right now."

Doc Miller stepped back toward the bar. "I can't do that, John. His arm is gangrenous. I should have taken it yesterday, but those other men wouldn't let me. If I don't remove it right now, he'll die."

Beck thumbed back the hammer of his Colt. "You'll die if you don't wake him up. Best get to work, Doc. My time in the desert has left me short on patience."

Miller cast a nervous look at the lieutenant, but whatever he found there was not assurance.

"Best do as he says, Doc. Wake him up."

Reluctantly, Doc Miller reached into his bag and pulled out a bottle of smelling salts.

"Leave it on the bar," Beck ordered. "I'll wake him up."

The doctor did as he was told and slowly stepped away from his patient.

Beck stood for a moment, watching the man who

had caused him so much pain lying helpless atop a bar. It was a moment Beck had seen in countless dreams and nightmares he had suffered since being cast out of town all those weeks before. He had not envisioned Hogan to be as helpless as he was now, of course. He had envisioned him mocking him, threatening him, relishing in all of the agony he had caused.

He had not pictured him helpless and clinging to life as he was now.

But maybe it was fitting, Beck thought, just as he had been helpless and clinging to life in the wilderness all that time.

Beck had pulled himself out of that horror. And he would be happy to visit a new horror upon the man that had caused his own.

Beck eased down the hammer on his Colt and tucked it back into his holster. With some degree of solemnity, he unscrewed the top from the brown bottle and held it under Bram Hogan's nose.

It took longer than Beck would have liked for Hogan to come around, but when he did, he was looking directly at Beck.

It took a moment for him to realize who he was looking at, and when he did, his eyes grew huge.

"You!" he whispered.

"Good memory." Beck slowly wrapped his hand around Hogan's collar. "Now get up."

CHAPTER THIRTY-THREE

B ECK PULLED HOGAN off the bar and let him drop to the floor.

Hogan, still under the influence of whatever Doc Miller had given him in preparation for the operation, hardly seemed to notice.

And Beck found himself lacking compassion. He prodded the outlaw with the toe of his boot. "Come on, Hogan. On your feet. Get up."

Hogan sluggishly tried to comply but found it difficult to coordinate with the use of only one arm. Beck grabbed him by the collar again and hauled him to his feet.

When Beck was satisfied he would not fall over, he began to pull him toward the door.

Coleman followed close behind. "What do you plan to do with that man, Beck?"

Beck ignored him and steered Hogan out the door and shoved him down the steps of the boardwalk into the thoroughfare. The outlaw staggered but did not fall down.

Beck walked over to the rail where the sergeant had tethered Pokey, with Coleman trailing close behind. "Damn you, Beck. I demand an answer!"

Beck grabbed hold of the butt of the Sharps and pulled it from the scabbard.

Hogan had regained some of his senses and watched Beck approach him holding the large gun. He looked at the group of soldiers and Standish, who had formed something of a semicircle around them in the street.

"You're not going to just stand there and let him do this to me, are you?" Hogan implored. "At least give me a gun. Give me a chance to defend myself."

Beck grabbed Hogan by the back of the collar and pushed him forward. "Don't worry, Hogan. I'm not going to shoot you. I'm going to give you exactly the same chance you gave me, remember? Seems only fair, don't you think."

But Bram Hogan was in no condition to think. No condition to run. No condition to fight back.

"Lem!" he called out into the approaching night. "Pearson! Somebody! Where are you boys?"

"Don't worry," Beck said as he dragged him up the street. "You'll be seeing them soon enough."

Bram made a clumsy grab for the Sharps with his good arm, but Beck pulled it away before the outlaw got close.

"You remember how this goes, Bram," Beck said as he led him to the same side street where he had run Beck out of town. "Now, seeing as how you're injured and all, I won't truss you up like you did me, but the game is still the same."

He shoved the outlaw into the side street. "Get moving."

Bram Hogan did not turn to face him. He simply stood alone, gazing into the encroaching emptiness of the desert that lay beyond. "No. I can't."

"Sure you can." Beck reared back and gave him a swift boot to the backside, sending him on his way. "Just put one foot in front of the other. It's as simple as that."

Bram stumbled forward, but again did not fall. His mouth was quivering. His eyes wide. Any bravery he might once have had was long gone.

"I won't make it."

"That's what I thought, and just look at me now." Beck brought up the Sharps to his shoulder and thumbed back the hammer. "Move."

Beck heard Coleman and the soldiers move toward him but did not take his eyes off Hogan. He did not think they would fire at him. He did not really care if they did.

He only cared about one thing at that particular moment.

Watching Bram Hogan face the same horror he had once faced.

Hogan looked at the soldiers. At Coleman and at Standish. Beck enjoyed watching the hope fade from his eyes, as the same hope had once faded from his own. Hogan's men were all dead. He was alone. His shirt was soaked through with sweat and he rocked unsteadily on his feet.

It was the desert or a bullet. The same choice Bram Hogan had given to him.

Beck half hoped Hogan would refuse to go. He

hoped he would stand there and let him shoot him like a staked goat. He deserved much worse.

But when Hogan slowly turned and began to trudge toward the void, Beck knew he had gotten all of the vengeance he needed. Hogan was alone. He was defeated and, what's more, he knew it. Beck had won.

And as he watched his tormentor shuffle off into the darkness, John Beck slid his thumb to the hammer of his Sharps and gently rode it down.

He had just lowered the rifle when Bram Hogan dropped to his knees and fell face forward into the dirt.

At Coleman's order, the sergeant ran ahead and went to Hogan's side. He slid a boot under the outlaw's shoulder and flipped him onto his back.

Beck did not need to hear the words but welcomed them just the same.

"He's dead, sir. And good riddance, too." The sergeant spat on the corpse. "The bastard."

Beck began to walk back toward Pokey. Every step sent another spike of pain through him. His head ached. His hands were sore. His arms felt like rubber and his broken rib stabbed him every time he breathed.

But he welcomed the pain. It meant he was alive.

He slid the Sharps back into the scabbard on his saddle and gently patted Pokey's neck. "We did it, my friend. We won."

He began to walk up the steps of the saloon and hoped to find a bed he could use. He would not use the one he had shared with Dulce, though. He would be sure to burn it tomorrow before he went home to Lilly.

He caught himself as he reached the top step of the boardwalk. Lilly. Home. He had never thought of things that way before but was glad he did so now.

"Sleep well, Mr. Beck," Lieutenant Coleman called out to him.

And for the first time in as long as he could remember, John Beck would welcome sleep and the dreams that came with it.